The Executive Liaison

ANNA STONE

HILDRED BILLINGS

© 2022 Anna Stone and Hildred Billings

All rights reserved. No part of this publication may be replicated, reproduced, or redistributed in any form without the prior written consent of the publisher.

This is a work of fiction. Names, characters, places, and incidents either are the products of the author's imagination or are used fictitiously. Any resemblance to actual persons, living or dead, businesses, companies, events, or locales is entirely coincidental.

ISBN: 9798802229743

Chapter One

"Hey, you can't do that anymore. Remember?"

Isabel bit into her lunch, a sandwich she'd bought at the shop across the street long before work started.

Know what I remember? The sandwich bar we used to have in our old office. Those were the days. Nap pods. Unlimited snacks. Friday night happy hour with drinks paid for by the company.

The startup's old offices had been a broke college grad's paradise. Their new offices in the Black Diamond Building?

Not so much.

Isabel swallowed. "Why does it matter where I eat my lunch?"

Her best friend Alexis shrugged. "I'm just saying. You're not allowed to eat at your desk anymore."

"I always eat lunch at my desk. Besides, this isn't even *my* desk. It's *everyone's* desk." Isabel glared around at the open, sterile co-working space she shared with her coworkers. It was bad enough that they'd moved their entire office to a different building in a completely different part of Seattle, one so far from Isabel's studio apartment that she had to wake up almost an hour earlier just to get to work on time. But to not even have her own desk?

And she couldn't spend her workdays commiserating with Alexis since their departments were at opposite ends of the office. In the old office, they had only been a quick kick of a wheeled chair away from one another. The old office was smaller than this one, but that just made it cozier. Everything had been looser there. Less corporate.

All that had changed when Connect was sold to Black Diamond Holdings. The news had come swiftly, albeit with a big smile from the startup's previous CEO and enough applause and streamers dropping from the ceiling that Isabel wondered if they were transferring to Hawaii. Instead, that was where the CEO retired.

On his yacht. With his new girlfriend half his age.

So here they were, one month later, in their brand-new office in the Black Diamond Building.

Isabel should have been excited. After all, she was twenty-three and already working for a successful startup that was going to change the world. Connect was everything Isabel believed in. It was an app that *connected* people to others in their community. *Want to find the best tamales in your neighborhood? We've got you covered. Want to learn how to start a vegetable garden? There are four people on your street wanting to do the same thing.*

The app's mission statement was simple and to the point. In a world where community life was dying and capitalism ruled, how did one go about making meaningful connections and breaking free from their reliance on big corporations, especially in large cities like Seattle? Many people couldn't afford to move away from the city, but the urban areas were pricing them out all the same. Connect wasn't just about helping someone find a guitar tutor. It was about building community, swapping skills, bartering instead of relying on the almighty dollar.

Everything about it appealed to Isabel when she applied for a graphic design position after graduating from college. She'd become the head of the department within six months. *"We want young, forward-thinking minds,"* CEO Evan Albright had said during her interview. *"You guys are the future. Help us build the world you want to grow old in."* His vision had seemed like such a noble one.

Isabel should have known better.

She sighed. "I miss the sandwich bar."

"You can thank our new overlords for that," Alexis said. "Black Diamond isn't going to give you a literal free lunch every day. Let's face it—it was always too good to last. Everything about this startup was. Evan really conned us into thinking he was different from the other Silicon Valley types."

Isabel murmured in agreement. If she had taken Connect's surprise acquisition hard, Alexis had taken it much harder. She believed in the startup's vision even more than Isabel did. Social media engineer Alexis was the cornerstone for getting the word out about Connect. Marketing spent the money and did the dirty work, but Alexis was the one reaching out to the Twittersphere, and convincing the number crunchers that Facebook was dead and Instagram was the future.

It was how Isabel and Alexis had become friends. They often worked together on social media campaigns, with

Alexis telling Isabel what she needed and Isabel injecting her artistic creativity to attract more clicks and engagement.

Alexis continued to rant. "When will I learn to never trust men who wear black turtlenecks to work? They all think they're Steve Jobs and going to change the world."

"They definitely changed *our* worlds."

Alexis snorted. "I'm a little older than you, so let me tell you how this is gonna work. Our new CEO is going to come in here, tell us that everything 'will be the same' but with 'some changes down the pipeline.' First, they take away or seriously downgrade the snack offerings. Then, they tell us we can only nap during our lunch hour. Then they start chopping staff and spreading their work around. You'll be taking work home not because you're inspired, but because your deadline was moved up two weeks. Which is also how long your notice will be, when they eventually give you the chop, too."

Isabel pretended her chips were so delicious that she didn't hear Alexis's words. Isabel liked routine. She liked familiarity. There had been so many changes already. The idea that there would be even more change to come was something she didn't want to think about.

But it was inevitable. The new CEO had big plans to expand Connect. Initially, the app had launched in Seattle, but it had since grown to include every major city on the west coast. And according to the dossier everyone received at the buy-out, Black Diamond was determined to take the app national by the end of the following year. That made Isabel a little more optimistic about the new leadership. But

Alexis was older and had more experience with these things.

Then again, Alexis was cynical about everything.

She stole a chip from Isabel's bag. "Did you hear the new CEO is coming by this afternoon? She starts today, now that we've done all the hard work of moving in."

"From what little I've heard of her, she doesn't seem too bad."

Alexis almost choked on her chip. "Please. We're talking about Scarlett Black. Do you know who she is?"

"Obviously. She's part of the Black family." Everyone in Seattle knew who they were. They practically owned half the city and had for generations.

"She's not just *part* of the family, Izzy. She's the *heir* to her family's corporate empire. Her father Phillip is the head honcho, and he's a ruthless, cutthroat douchebag. She has to be just like him if she's going to inherit the company. We're her testing ground to prove herself to him."

"How do you know?"

"I just do. *Trust me.*"

Isabel, now halfway through her sandwich, rolled back the paper, dropping a piece of lettuce to the floor in the process. Alexis bent down to pick it up. As her long, dark hair popped back into view, another brunette marched into the room.

Isabel nearly dropped the rest of her sandwich.

She had never met Scarlett Black before, but she instantly recognized the woman's striking face. She looked like she'd emerged from the centerfold of a magazine. Silky brown waves washed over her shoulders as she snapped a briefcase open on a nearby table. Black pumps adorned her feet, and her skintight black dress, cinched at the waist with a golden belt, hugged every delicious curve.

What is she doing in an office like this? She should be taking over Hollywood! Did Victoria's Secret need another Angel? Because this one just fell from lingerie heaven.

Oh, good. Isabel was imagining her new boss in lingerie already.

"Ahem." Scarlett tapped a stack of papers on the desk, commanding the attention of everyone in the room.

Isabel shoved her half-eaten sandwich into her bag. But the chips? The bag fell to the floor, spilling crumbs onto the linoleum beneath her chair. Alexis rolled her own chair into place, blocking Scarlett's line of sight from the mess Isabel had caused while doing something that was now expressly forbidden by company policy.

What is wrong with me?

"Could I please have everyone's attention?" Scarlett's voice was as silky as the hair crowning her flawless face.

She has my attention. The pictures of Scarlett Black did not live up to the woman in the flesh. Photos didn't capture the sheer glow of her skin or the elegant mannerisms that brought more attention to her devilishly red lips and the dangling teardrop earrings that accented her jawline.

All that was missing was a silken scarf. One Scarlett would remove from her throat and dangle before Isabel's gasping visage. *Tie me to my chair and tell me you want me...*

Isabel tried in vain to shove the thought aside. *Great. What a perfect way to start a professional relationship.*

"Thank you," Scarlett continued. "I believe everyone is here today, yes? Soon enough, I'll learn your names and recognize all of your faces, but for now, I'll introduce myself. I am Scarlett Black. I am the new CEO of Connect, and it's my job to bring this company to the next stage of development."

She paused for comments. However, her expression suggested she didn't want to entertain a single interruption.

"Undoubtedly, you've heard some rumors about myself and my company." The way her voice projected through the big, bright office space impressed Isabel. She could barely make herself heard by her coworkers at her table on a good day.

Is her voice naturally so magnetic, or did she train it to sound that way? She looked like the kind of woman with enough money to pay for that, to pay for anything she desired. Either way, the effect was clear. Scarlett's voice made Isabel shiver.

"I've already heard whispers that all I intend to do is fire half of you before the end of the first month. Maybe I'll convince you to quit. Or maybe I'll helpfully suggest another company of my family's for you to transfer to, with the same pay and benefits package. There are many, *many* rumors, aren't there?"

She looked directly at Alexis and Isabel when she said that. Isabel's cheeks began to burn, but Alexis squared her shoulders as if to say, *"Come at me."*

"I can't tell you what the future looks like. All I can say with certainty at this moment is that we are impressed with the numbers and projections your previous CEO Evan Albright left us. His legacy and vision will not be forgotten. I've taken a personal interest in Connect because of what I believe it can do for our fellow Americans. The success of the app so far is all due to your hard work. That said—"

"Here it comes," Alexis muttered.

"—there will be some changes happening at Connect in the coming weeks and months. For today, I'll be settling into my office and taking the time to get to know the heads of every department. If there's time, I'll meet more of you. Do feel free to go about your work as usual, and make judicious use of our coffee and juice bar. It's lovely to meet you all."

Without another word, Scarlett turned and marched her briefcase, papers, and stiletto heels into the back corner office that overlooked Capitol Hill.

Murmurs erupted throughout the office. While Isabel reeled from the storm that was Scarlett Black, Alexis sank deep into her seat and let out a mighty groan.

"We are so screwed," she said.

Isabel unearthed her sandwich and nibbled on a piece of turkey. "That woman. She's…"

"Our worst enemy. Mark my words, Izzy. Scarlett Black spells the end times for this grassroots startup of ours. Fuck you, Evan. He ruined everything for us."

"We don't know what's going to happen yet." Isabel's appetite had flown the coop. She wrapped the paper around her sandwich and buried it in the bottom of her bag. *I'll finish it in the break room.* If it stopped raining outside, she might take it to the Black Diamond courtyard, where office workers and custodians alike were known to congregate, gabbing on their phones and doing mid-morning yoga in their work clothes. "She does seem kinda… tough, though. Way stricter than Evan ever was."

"Well, yeah. Evan had us call him by his first name."

"Maybe Ms. Black will as well?"

"So why are you calling her Ms. Black already?"

"I don't want to be on the boss's bad side on the first day," Isabel said. "Remember, this is my first real job. I don't want to blow it."

"Haven't you heard the oldest Millennial adage yet?"

"Unlike you, I'm not a Millennial."

"Then let me impart some wizened Millennial wisdom on you." Alexis crossed her arms. "If you stay at a company for more than two years, you're being underpaid. If you don't get a nice raise soon, I would start looking for a new job. God knows that's what I'll be doing."

"You really think things are going to go downhill?"

Alexis's expression grew more somber than Isabel had ever seen it. "Yep, unfortunately. But I'd love to be proven wrong."

So would Isabel.

Especially when she thought about that soft, wavy hair and the way those hips moved when Scarlett waltzed off to her new office.

Chapter Two

Scarlett crossed another name off her list. *Toby Deen: Head of Customer Service.* Toby and his two team members handled all of Connect's customer inquiries. One of the things he had asked his new CEO was if he could get one more body in his department. As Connect expanded into more cities, there would be more emails and phone calls, often requiring lengthy conversations and back-and-forth exchanges.

But Scarlett saw only one possible outcome for Toby and his crew. At best, his department would be downsized. At worst, they would lose their positions completely to a third party who could do all the customer service for much, much cheaper.

Scarlett let out a heavy sigh that echoed through the vast room. The corner office was furnished exactly how she liked it. She'd picked everything out herself, from the glass desk to the minimalistic modern art on the walls.

But it didn't make her feel any less like she was in hell.

It was a hell assigned to her by her father. From the moment he had invited her to a private dinner and announced that the family holdings had acquired a "promising new startup," one thing had become clear—this was it. Scarlett's time had come to shine, or to fizzle out like a dead star. She was thirty-eight and had been studying the family business for most of her life.

It's time to prove myself.

There was immense pressure on her shoulders. Her father wanted to retire soon. He hadn't said so, but Scarlett knew him better than anyone else. She even knew him better than her mother, who was usually preoccupied with her own life.

Dad is getting older. Slower. He has places he wants to go and old friends he hasn't seen in years. People met Phillip Black and swore they'd encountered one of the most frightening men in Seattle, but Scarlett knew better.

Sure, he could be blunt, and her sister Parker often joked that he had "resting asshole face." But he was only human. The man had worked hard his whole life. Putting in long hours, neglecting family time, giving himself ulcers over business deals that could destroy everything his ancestors had built over the generations. Perhaps other people couldn't relate to that, but Scarlett knew the feeling well.

She was facing her own ulcer over this acquisition. It wasn't the first she'd been involved with. She often played the role of her father's fixer, whipping smaller companies Black Diamond acquired into shape. But none of those companies had been as important and successful as Connect.

Although, 'successful' wasn't how she'd describe the startup right now.

"Five million dollars," she said out loud, setting aside Toby's personnel file and picking up the next one in the pile. "Somehow, I have to save five million dollars over the next few months."

Connect was a local media darling. Dozens of neighborhoods across the west coast had lauded it as a huge success, helping them forge brand-new communities that bartered with each other and helped those who needed it. Scarlett saw it too, the need for people to have the kind of social lives that their ancestors had enjoyed for thousands of years.

Modern life stifled natural social connections. As Evan Albright had pitched in one of his investor videos, *"Modernity has trapped us in our houses, staring at screens and getting everything we need delivered to our doors. What if I told you that we can build communities again? And we can do it without looking up from our screens."*

He was charismatic, yes. He also had a head for people and what they were thinking and feeling.

The one thing Evan failed at, however, was the financial side of the business.

That was why Scarlett had been brought in, chosen by her father to turn Connect around and make it a money-printing machine. The anti-capitalist app was destined to play its role in the opera that was the NASDAQ stock exchange.

At the very least, it needed to break even.

The only person on the surviving staff who knew the

reality of Connect's finances was the sweating CFO, who had apologized profusely to Scarlett earlier that morning. The man had claimed that his hands were tied when things were run by Evan, who often brushed aside the CFO's suggestions and warnings. Between server costs, marketing, and the sheer number of staff a startup of this size had, it was a miracle that Phillip Black thought it worth acquiring.

God knew Evan had the payday of his life. *He's retired at thirty-three. I can't imagine.* Given her family's wealth, Scarlett could "retire" whenever she wanted, but that wasn't what she desired. There was still too much for her to learn and do in her short life.

"If anyone can make this piece of coal shine like a diamond, it's you," Phillip had told her over dinner the night before. *"I know it. You know it. Now prove it."*

Scarlett tapped her stylus against her desk. *What in the world does my father want with this app?* Phillip was far from technophobic. One might argue that part of his success as chairman and CEO of Black Diamond Holdings was embracing technology as it rapidly changed. Anything he didn't immediately understand, he hired someone to research for him. He knew that young people were the future of consumerism. He had even invested in Apple back in the 80s. Phillip claimed it was because of his personal relationship with Steve Jobs. Scarlett didn't know much about that.

What she did know was that the deck was stacked against her. Her new employees would rather see her hair catch fire than have her sit in this office.

That had been made clear from the moment she called in the head of social media, a sniveling young man named

Ned Paige. He'd looked at her over his glasses, saying, "With all due respect, what do you know about TikTok?" As if Evan had been an expert.

There wasn't much "respect" from the other department heads, either. Toby, the head of IT, talked like he knew his number was up. He chewed his gum and stared down at Scarlett, long after she asked him to please spit out the pink wad from his mouth. Once upon a time, Scarlett would assume it was her gender that made them hostile, but they were well into the 21st century now. Nobody cared if the CEO wore pencil skirts and got a blowout on personal time.

They cared that she was corporate. Some prejudices never died.

"Emmy?" She pushed the button on her intercom, alerting her secretary. "Send in Ms. Diaz, please. I'm ready for her."

"Yes, ma'am."

At least Emmy respected her. Then again, she had come to Connect with Scarlett, having worked her way up from the mailroom in the very building they were in now.

Only one department head remained on Scarlett's list. *Isabel Diaz. Head of Graphic Design. 23. Graduated with honors from the University of Washington with a design major.*

Scarlett stared at Isabel's age again. *Twenty-three? You've got to be kidding.* She didn't care how many honors a graduate had. There was no reason for a kid fresh from college to be *leading* the design team.

What had Evan been thinking?

"Hello?" A head poked through the door. "You sent for me?"

"You must be Isabel," Scarlett said, pasting on her most

genial smile as she motioned to the chair before her desk. "Come in. Have a seat. I'm just introducing myself to the department heads. You know, getting to know everyone and exchanging some ideas…"

The door opened fully. In stepped a young woman Scarlett swore she hadn't seen in the office a few hours ago.

She *definitely* would have remembered Isabel Diaz.

No one in Scarlett's life knew of her sapphic predilections. Her attraction to women was something she kept under lock and key. She had an openly lesbian sister, and even *Parker* didn't know that Scarlett often went to sleep thinking about the perfect woman to round out her life.

And here that woman was, having stepped right out of her dreams.

She was feminine and petite, almost dainty. Not in a way that was proper or affected, but in a way that sparked something deep and primal within Scarlett. Her own feminine presentation meant she often had to fight to be taken seriously, to not be seen as weak in a male dominated world. She practically salivated at the thought of being the strong, confident partner of someone looking for a Mistress to serve and belong to.

Were there gender stereotypes at play? She didn't care. She wanted what she wanted.

And it was right in front of her, dressed in a floaty white blouse and a flirtatiously frilly skirt that showed off graceful bronze legs…

Scarlett shook herself. She didn't need this. Not her perfect woman walking into her office on the first day of her new and extremely important job.

"Hi." Isabel almost spilled into the chair as she attempted

to pull it away from the desk. As her long black hair flipped up into her face and her ankles wobbled in her flats, Scarlett was forced to look away. Partly out of politeness, but also because it would look unprofessional to leap up and catch the delicate beauty in her arms.

Isabel collected herself, sitting firmly in the chair. With flushed cheeks, she rearranged her hair and covered the hint of cleavage peeking from her blouse, her short nails the same alluring shade of pink as her lips.

Hadn't Scarlett fantasized about kissing lips just like those before?

Isabel straightened her shoulders and sat up as tall as she could. "I'm Isabel."

"Hello, Ms. Diaz." Luckily for them both, Scarlett knew to rein in any unprofessional feelings and assume a business-like countenance. Once she was "on," she could talk synergy and strategies with a naked Cate Blanchett for hours. "Let me formally introduce myself. My name is Scarlett Black. I'm your new CEO. I'm looking forward to working together, so I'd like to get to know you a little better."

Isabel nodded mutely. Was she shy? Simply nervous? Scarlett knew her reputation was one of a ruthless ice queen to be feared by her employees. It was exaggerated. Somewhat.

"Your file says you graduated from the University of Washington only a couple of years ago. Honors. How long have you been the head of the graphic design department?"

"Coming up on a year. I've been working for Connect for around eighteen months now."

"That was a quick promotion."

A touch of color graced Isabel's high cheekbones. "Evan really loved my designs and believed in my vision. There was someone else who was probably more deserving of the promotion, but they accepted a job at another startup, so here I am. I designed the app's last two layouts, as well as a majority of the social media graphics. I work closely with social media and IT. We get along really well."

I'm sure you do. Scarlett could hardly imagine this young woman working with those surly men, but when it was everyone against the big, bad corporate world? There were allies everywhere.

"Are you from Washington, Ms. Diaz?"

Isabel tilted her head in thought. "No, I just moved here for college. I'm originally from Phoenix. You know, Ariz—"

"Yes, I know where Phoenix is."

Isabel clipped her mouth shut. In Scarlett's mind, her mother told her to mind her manners. She had inherited her father's impatience for idle chatter. It wasn't the best way to get her employees on her side.

"Must be quite the change in climate for you," Scarlett offered. "From the desert to the marine temperatures."

"What can I say? I like the rain."

Scarlett leaned back in her chair, studying Isabel's face. She was a hard woman to read, her expressions cryptic. "Do you like what you do here, Ms. Diaz?"

"I… yes, of course. Graphic design is something I've always been passionate about. My background is in art, and being able to fuse my love for design with something that has a great message like Connect is a dream come true. These past two years have been exactly what I envisioned when Evan brought me on board. I'd love to see all that continue, even with a new office."

Scarlett understood what Isabel hadn't explicitly stated. *She doesn't want things to change.* Like everyone else in Connect, Isabel had no intention of bowing to the new corporate overlords.

I really have my work cut out for me here. It was why her father had given this task to her instead of one of his many other underlings. He had chosen a harsh proving ground for his heir.

After some more back-and-forth about Isabel's work at Connect, Scarlett decided to wrap things up. "Do you have any questions for me? Concerns?"

Her head of graphic design hesitated, a flash of uncertainty in her eyes.

"Isabel, I would like for you to be honest with me."

Scarlett's words came out as firm rather than reassuring. But they seemed to have the desired effect on Isabel.

"Are the rumors true?" she asked. "Do you and Black Diamond plan on downsizing here at Connect?"

The question took Scarlett by surprise, not because she didn't expect it, but because she didn't think anyone would dare ask her such a direct question. And shy, young Isabel was the last person she expected to do so. Perhaps it was her inexperience.

Regardless, Scarlett needed to answer as tactfully as possible. Anything she said would be repeated to everyone else at Connect as soon as Isabel left the room.

"Currently, there are no plans to make changes to staff numbers and positions." She offered another warm smile.

When Isabel didn't respond to that, Scarlett sat back on the laurels of professionalism. "It's my desire to keep the original teams Connect had under Evan Albright. My family believes in Connect's mission, and I believe that's best maintained with the people who made it all happen in the first place. There will be periodic reviews, yes, but that would have happened under Mr. Albright as well. This is a business, after all. Not a charity."

Isabel nodded. "Sure. Connect has to make money, after all."

"Let me say this. One of your jobs, I believe, is to ensure potential users are taken in by the visual branding of the Connect platform? You've been doing an excellent job of that so far, Ms. Diaz. That's plain as day."

"Oh." Isabel seemed surprised by the compliment. "Th... thank you."

"You have a lot of young, raw talent. I can see that in you." *Alongside your pretty face and the fine lines of your body...*

Scarlett averted her eyes. *She's Bianca's age.* What a crazy thing to think. Her youngest sister was almost the same age as this young woman. Did that comfort Scarlett in some way? Absolutely not.

It only served to confuse her more.

"Thank you, Ms. Black," Isabel said.

"If you don't have any other questions for me, I'll let you get back to work. I myself have plenty to do as I get acquainted with the back end of the startup. Although, I suppose it's not really a *startup* anymore."

Isabel smiled but said nothing.

Scarlett stood and extended her hand across her desk. "It's

been a pleasure meeting you, Ms. Diaz. My door is open, even when it's closed. Simply let me or Emmy know if you would like a word. Otherwise, I'll see you and the other department heads at the meeting first thing on Monday morning."

Isabel stood slowly and took Scarlett's hand. While it wasn't the firmest handshake, something about her soft skin and delicate fingers was electrifying. Scarlett could still feel the sparks after she let go of Isabel's hand.

"Duly noted, Ms. Black." She turned around and showed herself to the door. "Nice meeting you. Welcome to Connect."

Was there a passive-aggressive edge to Isabel's words? Or was she simply anxious about meeting her new boss?

Regardless, Scarlett dreaded the day she'd have to fire Ms. Diaz.

It was the most logical course of action, after all. The graphic design department was best served by being folded into Black Diamond's own in-house art and design studio. Two floors down was an entire office of web designers and graphic artists whose sole job was to do whatever tasks the holdings of Black Diamond threw their way. By appointment, of course.

Scarlett shook Isabel's presence from her head. When she sat back down, she noticed a message on her phone. It was from Adrian Holt. Her 'fiancé.'

"Sorry, I have to cancel dinner tonight. My mother isn't feeling well, and I have extra work to do."

Scarlett couldn't express how much relief the message granted her, even if she'd allowed herself to do so. The last thing she wanted to do after her first day of a big job was to play at happy couples with the man who was her fiancé in name only.

Especially with thoughts of the desirous Isabel Diaz playing in her head.

Thank you, Ms. Black, Isabel whispered in Scarlett's mind.

Those words would tease her for the rest of the week.

Chapter Three

Alexis almost didn't let Isabel go home by herself that evening. In fact, she was still texting Isabel about coming out with her as she walked through the door to her studio apartment.

"Another time," Isabel wrote. *"I'm busy tonight."*

"Oh yeah? Doing what?" Alexis sent back.

"Staying home and watching TV."

"That doesn't count. C'mon, you need to get out more. And when are you going to let me hook you up with my friend Candy?"

"Never. Her name is Candy, for God's sake."

Isabel latched her front door and dumped her bag in a rickety chair that separated her entrance from the efficiency kitchen. A shower called to her, but that could wait until just before bed. As she heated up a TV dinner in her microwave, she stripped off her work clothes and changed into some comfortable pajamas, then pulled her hair up into a loose ponytail in preparation for a cozy night in.

She didn't own a TV. There wasn't enough room in her

studio. Instead, her evening entertainment came from her phone and her laptop, mid-range, but good enough for streaming movies and TV shows. A pair of noise-canceling headphones allowed her to binge all the episodes she wanted while drowning out the sounds of her neighbors, who were incapable of doing anything without rattling Isabel's walls. Watching TV. Playing video games.

Having really, *really* loud sex.

Fortunately, that didn't seem to be in the cards for tonight. Isabel could only turn up her headphones so much. Besides, she hated the constant reminder that she was single.

That was the one thing in her adult life Isabel hadn't mastered yet. She had an amazing job, a modest but adequate social life, and her own place. While it wasn't much of a place, it was hers.

But romantic relationships? Well, Isabel had always had a hard enough time making friends, let alone finding love.

Shy. Awkward. Weird. Those were the kind of words people used to use to describe her. Over time, she'd learned to hide those parts of herself, but it was just a mask. And it didn't change how she felt inside. She'd grown up feeling like she was different from everyone else, and that feeling had never really gone away.

As she got older, she found it easier to connect with people, to find places in the world where she belonged. But romance was a whole other ballgame. It had always proved elusive to her. The fact that she was a lesbian only made it harder to find 'the one.' She'd hoped that moving from Phoenix to Seattle for college would be a boon to her love life, but the few dates she'd been on hadn't led to anything long-term. Certainly not to love.

So she'd spent the last year and a half focusing on her burgeoning career and making friends, all while quietly hoping something would happen on its own. What was it that people said? *Love will find you when you're least expecting it...*

Well, Isabel hadn't been expecting it for years now.

The microwave dinged. Isabel shuffled into her efficiency kitchen and pulled back the plastic on her dinner, separating the few limp vegetables from the sauce-covered rice as she waited for it to cool.

Dinner in hand, she settled on her bed with her laptop, an episode of a show she'd seen half a dozen times playing on it. One of the characters reminded her of Scarlett Black, with her slick eyeliner and impossible curves. *I could grab those curves...*

Isabel stuffed her mouth with food and looked away from her laptop screen. She didn't need reminders of her tragic love life.

But as she threw out her trash and settled back down in bed, laptop closed, she continued to yearn. For something. Anything.

For 'it' to happen.

You'll never get a girlfriend if you don't put yourself out there. That was Alexis's voice in her head. But that wasn't Isabel's style. She loved the idea of being courted. Sought out. *Made* into someone else's beautiful plaything.

Back when Isabel used to sketch more, when she had aspirations of becoming an artist, she'd filled a whole sketchbook with sensual images of women seducing their intendeds. From the tamest looks shared across a bar to one sneaking up on the other in the bath, Isabel had imagined it all. And as she did, she'd prayed for the universe to send her someone who would make her theirs.

But the world didn't work like that. Alexis was right. If she wanted to find love, she had to go looking for it. Or at the very least, stop hiding herself away.

And that was what she was doing. Metaphorically speaking, anyway.

Isabel pulled her phone toward herself and opened an app that lurked in the depths of her device.

Welcome to Darkest Desires, the dating app for those with truly adult tastes... Isabel already had an account, but she hadn't done much with it. Nothing besides setting up her profile, which was sparse on information. The red lips in her display photo weren't even hers.

Our focus is on women who want to play, the app announced. Isabel certainly fit that description. At least, in theory. But the truth was, she couldn't imagine trusting someone so much with her body—and her heart.

Isabel was just as inexperienced with kink as she was with relationships. All the dates she'd ever been on had been more chore than romance, whether or not they'd led to sex. And those encounters had been entirely vanilla, not the kind that the women on Darkest Desires were looking for.

However, Isabel didn't actually expect anything would come out of having an account on Darkest Desires. At best, she could browse and fantasize without having to commit to anything, which was what she'd been doing for the past few weeks.

So she was surprised to see a chat request, flickering away in the corner of her screen.

It was far from her first. Bots, scammers, and God knew who else used the app. Isabel had once chatted with a bot for ten minutes before realizing someone on the other side of the world was playing with her. There was no real person on the other side—just someone trying to take her for a financial ride. She had reported the account and moved on.

"Dominique from New York wants to chat with you..."

Dominique, huh? A bit on the nose. It couldn't be her real name.

Isabel navigated to Dominique's profile. She was greeted with an image of a pair of handcuffs draped across two black stiletto heels. It was probably a stock photo, but it did inspire the imagination. Wasn't that why Isabel was here? To pretend she was somebody else? Somebody confident and beautiful? That's why her username was Beautiful-Dreamer.

Dominique was in her thirties. A New Yorker with a taste for the dominant side of life. According to her bio, she "yearned to tame and tease the right woman." A lesbian? Queer, at least. Could she be real? Or was this another bot? Maybe Dominique was a professional dominatrix looking for paying clients.

Then why was she fishing for profiles in Seattle? Was it a totally online thing? Like Isabel could afford to go to New York. Or perhaps Dominique was rich, the kind of rich that allowed her to fly across the country on a whim...

Isabel shook her head. Her imagination was getting away from her. And there was only one way to find out who Dominique was...

She accepted the chat request.

"Hello, Beautiful," the message from Dominique said. *"Tell me a bit about yourself. Why are you here?"*

Isabel sat up in her bed, eyes squared on her phone screen. *What do I say to that?*

"I'm just looking..."

She deleted those words the moment she wrote them. No. Someone like Dominique deserved more.

"Hi. I live in Seattle. I'm in my 20s. An artist."

That was a lie. While art had always been her passion, Isabel hadn't pursued it seriously in years. Art didn't pay the bills. Graphic design did.

Still, she dreamed of one day becoming the artist she'd aspired to be in her younger days.

"I'm here... well, I guess I'm here to meet a woman who will sweep me off my feet," she sent.

"Before tying you up on my bed?" Dominique's reply came so quickly that Isabel barely had time to consider her words. She was too busy imagining a mysterious woman thousands of miles away. One who wore black stilettos and always carried a pair of handcuffs on her person.

Isabel went with honesty. *"I've never done that before."* She didn't want to get caught up in some kinky game she couldn't fake her way through.

"I like that," Dominique replied. *"It's always so exciting to be someone's first."*

"I'm not a virgin." But Isabel wasn't exactly experienced either.

"Did I say you were?"

Isabel flopped back down to her bed. What was

Dominique's game? The woman had her off balance in more ways than one.

"BeautifulDreamer is such a long name. Is there something I can call you for short?"

At least that was an easy question to answer. *"It's just from the song. I'm not married to it or anything."*

Dominique took her time to respond. Had Isabel said the wrong thing?

"I'll call you Beauty, then."

Beauty. No one had ever called her anything like that before.

And no one had ever shown such rapt interest in her before. As Dominique continued to question her, every word laced with suggestion, Isabel found herself getting more and more drawn in.

"Tell me, Beauty, are you looking for something fun? Something serious? Or are you, like me, looking to test the waters with someone before committing?"

"I guess that one, yeah."

"Then let me tell you what I'm about. I like to be in control. At work, at home, in life. I call all the shots, in and outside the bedroom. If I want you, I decide when and where. If I want you naked, you are naked. If I want to be inside of you, I find a way."

Heat flooded Isabel's body. Dominique was so forward. So commanding. So tantalizing to the part of Isabel that craved a woman just like that.

"Those luscious red lips on your profile picture... I know they're probably not yours, but they make me want you all the same. I want to kiss them, Beauty. I want to unlock the parts of you that you didn't even know you kept hidden."

A thousand images raced through Isabel's mind, images

that went far beyond sex. What she saw, as she was whisked away to the corners of her imagination that always called to her?

Heaven. Paradise. That universal afterlife that ignited her senses and suppressed them all the same.

Bind me. Blindfold me. Gag me. Show me sweet serenity and unbridled surrender. Shrouded in shadows, Dominique offered all of that to her. Strong, confident, and in control, she seemed to be everything Isabel had wanted for so long. Would she whisper into Isabel's ear that she wouldn't be gentle? Would her hands roam Isabel's body until they found the perfect places to torment her insatiable desires?

"Are you the woman I've been looking for, Beauty?"

Her heart began to pound. Everything was happening so fast. Could she really do this, and with some stranger online?

She was out of her depth. She didn't have a script for this. Regular relationships were hard enough for her to navigate, let alone whatever it was that Dominique wanted from her. The woman was all high heels and handcuffs. Isabel had almost tripped over her flats in front of her boss that afternoon because she'd been distracted by how sexy Scarlett was.

This? This was so far outside her wheelhouse that it was on another continent.

Her hands trembled as she sent her reply. *"I have to go now."* A pang of regret hit her. She quickly sent another message. *"We can continue this later. I'm sorry."*

Isabel had already turned off the app's notifications, afraid that one might pop up at an awkward moment, like when she was at work. Nevertheless, she closed the app completely and turned her phone over on her bed.

She buried her face in the covers and sighed. She remained safe inside of her comfort zone, free from the threat of spontaneity and the unfamiliar.

But what if she had instead turned away something good? Something *great?*

Which was the bigger regret that would haunt her for the rest of her life?

Chapter Four

I should reach out to her...

Isabel stared at her computer, hand poised over her mouse, noise-canceling headphones over her ears to drown out the sounds of the open office. Yet none of the words in her emails or the images on the social media graphics on her screen registered in her mind. She was too focused on how she'd left things with Dominique a few nights ago, when she was vulnerable in her own bed.

What if she moves on to someone else?

A ball of paper smacked her on the side of her head. She slipped off her headphones as Alexis waltzed by.

"Caught you daydreaming!" she said. "Don't let the boss see you like that."

Isabel sighed and put her headphones back on. She needed to focus. The palpable tension hanging over the office wasn't helping.

I can't let it get to me. There were graphics to design and people to collaborate with. Like Alexis, but she was in a hurry toward the restroom.

But Isabel had plenty of other work to do. She was supposed to chat with Ned about the next month's campaigns and what his team needed from hers. Although, Isabel was mostly a one-person show these days. A woman named Caroline helped her out sometimes, but she also floated to other departments as necessary. She was supposed to be a dedicated graphic designer, but Evan had liked Isabel's work and productivity so much that he'd had her handle almost everything solo. She didn't mind. She liked working alone.

But her solitude was disturbed when Scarlett's secretary appeared at the corner of Isabel's desk.

"Ms. Black would like to speak with you," Emmy said, her clipped voice and expensive dress marking her as out of place among the rest of the employees at the startup.

Legend says she's been Scarlett's secretary for over ten years. Like Scarlett Black, Emmy the secretary went wherever she was needed, doing whatever dirty work the higher-ups required of her. Disbanding a local co-op and selling the pieces to corporate grocery chains? Scarlett and Emmy were there. After they were finished with Connect, they'd undoubtedly head off to destroy a public daycare with claws out and fangs of fire.

"Okay." Isabel logged out of her computer. "Tell her I'll be right there."

Emmy turned on pale blue heels and marched back to her desk. Isabel glanced down at her own feet. Her old but clean tennis shoes had never been a problem in Evan Albright's casual office. At least they didn't squeak like they used to.

What does Scarlett want with me? Isabel had never felt an

overwhelming sense of dread when Evan called her into his office. Even when he was criticizing something she did, it was with a big smile and helpful suggestions that didn't make Isabel feel like an idiot for existing. But Scarlett? Isabel had only met her one-on-one once before, but everything about her seemed cold as hell.

Isabel had heard the stories, after all. Stories about Scarlett raising her voice to Ned, and Alexis being told she couldn't ride the elevator at the same time as her. Isabel was pretty sure the latter wasn't true. But she had seen the coffee and tea brands swapped out for generics and a memo that asked all employees to keep napping and breaks to a minimum. Evan hadn't cared about that. As long as they got their work done, who gave a crap how many breaks they took?

Scarlett, apparently.

Isabel reached Scarlett's office and knocked on the open door.

"Come in." Scarlett's curt voice was as stiff as the bun on the back of her head. "Have a seat."

Isabel entered the room, the door automatically closing behind her. She often wondered if this office always belonged to whatever acquisition Black Diamond Holdings forced upon Scarlett that month. It would make sense, since Scarlett looked mighty comfortable at that desk in the corner of the room.

And mighty fine, but Isabel wouldn't dwell on that. Lusting after her boss made about as much sense as lusting after Evan Albright. Besides, Scarlett Black had an engagement ring on her hand. Whether she was engaged to a man or a woman, she was already taken.

Man. Definitely a man. Isabel had a hunch.

She barely had a chance to sit down before Scarlett got down to business.

"We need to talk about the app's UI design." Scarlett turned her monitor around to display the current layout for the Connect app. "Do you see this bright red banner across the top?"

Brandishing a #2 pencil as a makeshift pointer, Scarlett gestured to the header bar where CONNECT was written in a bold, impactful font. Right beneath it was the handy mobile drop-down menu that took users straight to their profile, groups, or settings.

"It's garish," Scarlett said. "Whether I look at it on my computer or my phone, I feel like someone is gouging out my eyeballs. What do you think?"

"I—"

"And the pink borders around the images, these red links —they're amateurish. While I expect this from startups funded by local enterprises, this is not how I want Black Diamond to be reflected in Connect. We need to polish the whole thing up. I want a brand-new design, and you're the woman who is going to give it to me." Scarlett turned her attention to Isabel, her pencil tapping against the desk. "You *are* the head of graphic design, are you not?"

Isabel nodded. A heavy silence fell between them. *I'm the one who designed that layout.* Isabel didn't say it. Nor did Scarlett, thank God. It had been a collaboration with Evan, but they were mostly Isabel's ideas, and completely her execution. *I didn't take all of those coding classes in college for nothing.* That was her big selling point upon graduation. She'd found a big way to market her artistic talents in the modern age. *Can't pay me in experience or exposure if I'm coding too.*

"Good. Then I look forward to what you'll come up with when you check in with me. I've already emailed you a list of apps I want you to draw inspiration from. We're going cool and sleek. I'm thinking either a cobalt blue or royal purple color palette. This red, it's too Meetup-y. They've cornered that market, Ms. Diaz. All this is? It's a cheap knockoff."

Her words might as well have been spears, for they skewered Isabel straight through the heart.

"I expect better," Scarlett said. "I expect only the best of the best working for me."

Isabel had half a mind to say, *"Then why don't you hire the best?"*

"You will check in with me once a week. Sketches, mood boards. And I want access to the test server so I can check on you in real-time."

Isabel's hands rolled into fists. She kept them hidden beneath the desk, pushing them into her thighs. "I think you need to talk to IT about those permissions, Ms. Black."

"I will." Scarlett glanced between Isabel and the 'garish' design on the screen. "If there's nothing else, I want your thoughts emailed to me by Monday morning."

Isabel's fists unclenched as the rest of her body deflated. "Monday morning? But it's Friday!"

"A little homework for you to do over the weekend."

Seriously? But Isabel kept her mouth shut.

Scarlett turned her monitor back around. "Welcome to the big leagues, Ms. Diaz."

The crowd shoved Isabel closer to Alexis, who was chattering away about something or other. The music was so loud that Isabel couldn't hear a thing she was saying. Or anyone else for that matter.

Noisy, sweaty bars were *not* her idea of a good time. She'd rather be at home curled up with a book or binge-watching old TV shows she'd seen a dozen times. But tonight was the company 'happy hour.' Before Evan sold Connect, he hired a bartender to come into the office one Friday a month to help his employees 'bond.' Which apparently meant getting plastered together.

Well, it worked on me. Isabel had never been the most outgoing of people. And while she wouldn't say she needed the lubrication of alcohol to help her rub elbows, it certainly didn't hurt. She was a one-cocktail woman, but some of her coworkers, like Alexis and her boss Ned, could pound them back and still live to tell the tales the next day.

The open bar was gone now. Scarlett had axed that like a lumberjack sizing up the biggest tree in the forest. This drove everyone in the office to the nearest watering hole on the block, which happened to be the same place most of the other white-collar, middle-management types on the street came to congregate and share their pains with each other.

"At least the booze is better here!" Miguel from IT held up his bottle of local IPA and received a cheer from his entire department. "Miss you, Evan, but that shit was watered down."

"Yeah, but it was free," Ned croaked over his beer. "Just like those sandwiches we used to eat for lunch every day."

"Don't remind me," Isabel said.

"Hey, watch this." Caroline edged her way into the center of the group and popped a cherry into her mouth. Her tongue worked away inside it while every guy—and several of the women, including Isabel—watched with rapt attention. A few seconds later, she pushed the carefully knotted stem out of her mouth and into her hand, to the cheers of Miguel and Ned.

Alexis nudged Isabel with her elbow. "See? That's how you get a girlfriend around here."

While Isabel rolled her eyes, someone asked Caroline how she did it. Small groups soon broke off, and Isabel joined Alexis and the rest of the social media team outside in the bar's small courtyard in an attempt to escape the noise.

But it wasn't long before everyone started loudly venting about the changes that had happened to Connect over the past few weeks.

"What an asshole," Ned said to everyone who would listen. "I knew that Albright kid was too good to be true, but I didn't expect him to just run off as soon as someone sniffed around with an offer."

"Hawaii," said Connor, another member of the social media team. "He's in Hawaii on a fifty-foot yacht with local honeys hanging on his every word."

"Where did you hear they were local?" Alexis asked. "From Evan himself? Please. They're all models he picked up in LA."

"So? Both are hot to me."

"Does it matter? He sold us out to big capitalism. We

should all exchange numbers now before we start getting chopped."

Toby sidled up beside them, beer sloshing out of his glass as he bumped into Ned. "Y'all shit-talking Black Diamond? Because I want *in* on this!"

He swigged his beer while everyone around him cheered. As he finished it off, he belched loudly enough to drown out the music.

"We're so *screwed*," he said. "Did you hear about the plans to take Connect national? We are *not* ready for that."

"Right?" Alexis threw her hands up. "It's like these corporate suits don't understand the app at all! The whole reason Connect works is because it's local. Sure, we're in a few cities now, but everything is self-contained. If users can connect with anyone all over the country, that'll turn the app into a generic online marketplace. It takes away what makes Connect special. It dilutes Connect's vision."

"You think that's bad?" Ned said. "Have you guys heard about the advertising they're bringing in? Saw the job posting for myself. They're hiring an advertising relations specialist to manage accounts. That's where the new money is coming from. *Advertising.* On our app!"

"What the hell?" Alexis said. "Advertising goes against everything Connect stands for! Fuck Black Diamond, and fuck Scarlett Black."

The rabble grew around them. Coworkers high-fived each other for no reason besides getting caught up in the moment.

Am I the only one who sees it? While Isabel wasn't happy with the changes—let alone having to completely redo Connect's UI while keeping Scarlett abreast of every little change—she wasn't as quick to lay the blame at the new CEO's feet.

"You know she's probably just doing her job, right?" The only reason Isabel was brave enough to speak up was because of the drink in her hand, and because she considered the people she worked with at Connect trustworthy. Yet their judgmental gazes as they turned toward her said otherwise. "It can't be easy. She has to look at it from her company's point of view."

Alexis groaned. "Are you *kidding* me? Come on. You can't be that naive. You know who Black Diamond are and what they do, right?"

"I—"

"They're a bunch of rotten bastards who buy up startups like ours and completely ruin them. Then, when they no longer work the way they're supposed to, they either sell off the remains or transform them into whatever shitty corporate shell they want them to be. Remember Deliveree? The food delivery app from like four years ago?"

Isabel shook her head.

"That's probably because Black Diamond bought them out, squished them for all they were worth, and sold everything off to what are now DoorSmash and GetGrub. We're talking the code, the advertisers, the graphics, everything."

Even the graphics?

"And don't get me started on Scarlett herself. Like I told you, she's nothing but a snake like the rest of them. Have you seen that giant sparkly rock on her finger? She's engaged to Adrian Holt. You know, of *the* Holts."

Beside her, Ned scoffed. "They're the worst."

"Who are the Holts?" Isabel asked.

Alexis was more than happy to answer her question. "Big banking family. The kind that exists for the sole purpose of gobbling up as much money as they can from my pockets and yours. Adrian is their only son. The guy was voted Seattle's Most Eligible Bachelor three years in a row before he started going out with Scarlett. He's just as bad as she is, which makes them the perfect match."

The others jumped in with their own opinions, from how they hated that Scarlett talked down to them to what a big "douchefaze" her fiancé Adrian Holt was. *So she really is engaged.* Isabel wasn't surprised. She was disappointed, though. Disappointed that Scarlett wasn't gay.

Not that anything could have possibly come from that.

Alexis finished off her drink. Before heading back inside for another, she offered to buy one for Isabel.

Perhaps against her best interests, Isabel accepted. Her rule of only one drink per gathering was flying out the window, and she didn't know why.

Is it because everything feels so uncertain? Before downing what remained of her drink, Isabel joined a toast to Connect's longevity. Not that any of them believed it.

But she had to believe it. She didn't know what she'd do if she lost her job. Alexis's comment about changing jobs every two years didn't sit right with Isabel, who thrived on routine and familiarity. She hated change. She longed to find one place to settle and be happy forever. Seattle promised to be that place. What if she had to move somewhere else for her next job?

And what about all the friends she'd made here at Connect? They were a close-knit bunch. Like her, many of them had been recruited straight out of college, and some of them had moved to Seattle from other parts of the country, so their coworkers had become their social circle, their family.

After a lifetime spent struggling to find her place in the world, Isabel had finally found somewhere she fit in.

What if she lost that?

Don't think so negatively. Focus on the here and now. Her friends. Her coworkers. The good times of her twenties.

And maybe a certain someone still waiting for a response on a certain app. The more she drank, the more Isabel thought about responding to Dominique's flirtations.

What did she have to lose? Life was about taking chances and seeing where every path led. And a mysterious woman on a dating app was beckoning Isabel onto a path of self-discovery with her.

And if she happened to imagine Scarlett's face on Dominique's as she took her hand and joined her on that path?

Maybe indulging in some fantasy would keep Isabel from getting weak at the knees every time Scarlett called her into her office.

Chapter Five

That night, Scarlett dragged herself into her apartment, tired to the bone. She was getting much too old to be finishing up work so late.

But her work life—which was her whole life—always followed the same pattern. Acquire a new position, courtesy of her father. Assess the situation. Center her entire existence around that disaster for weeks—months—with no time for anything else beyond eating and sleeping.

Why should a Friday night be any different? It wasn't like Scarlett stayed late at the office so that she wouldn't have to work over the weekend. *The work never ends.* If she was lucky, she'd have dinner out on Saturday night and get half the day on Sunday to run errands or read for a few hours.

That sounds absolutely divine. The days were growing shorter and colder. As the usual rains began to fall in Seattle, Scarlett couldn't think of anything better than curling up on her couch in her sweats with a book. But that was a luxury her life didn't often allow her.

She flicked on the light in her entryway and dropped her bag onto the chair by the door, then slipped off her coat to hang up in the closet. Lastly, she removed her engagement ring and placed it in a small decorative bowl on the credenza.

It was all for show, wasn't it? The ring. The nice coat and shoes. The stern demeanor she presented to everyone at Connect. All lies to project an image she never really believed in.

Unburdened, Scarlett emerged from her entry hallway. But a moment later, every hair on her body stood up.

A light was on in one of the back rooms.

Her heart stopped. *I did* not *leave that light on.* She rarely went into the storage room, where she kept seasonal items that only served to clutter up the rest of her apartment for the remainder of the year. For a woman who could afford to live wherever she wanted and do as she pleased, she did not suffer *clutter.*

Nor did she suffer burglars.

Think rationally, Scar. Slowly, she approached the open doorway at the end of the hall. *It probably isn't a burglar.* It might be her mother, a nosy woman who wouldn't think twice about bursting into her daughter's apartment uninvited. But her mother hadn't let herself into her eldest's home in years, not since Scarlett changed the locks.

Perhaps it *was* a burglar.

Scarlett crept along the wall, phone in hand. Her thumb was poised over the ALERT button that would simultaneously call 911 and send texts to her parents and sister Parker. And Adrian, but only because her mother had insisted that 'the love of her life' be one of the first to know if she was being attacked or kidnapped.

As a deep male voice grunted and cursed in the storage room, Scarlett stopped short.

"Adrian?"

A head of light brown hair poked out of the closet. Tropical vacation gear dropped from the top shelf, falling to the ground around Adrian's feet. As Scarlett let out the breath she'd been holding, she approached her 'fiancé' with mild irritation.

"Oh, hi, Scar." Adrian probably wanted to say more, but his attention was on the avalanche of diving and kayaking gear.

Scarlett stayed back. Adrian had it under control. "What are you doing here? Did you have to scare me half to death?"

"To be fair," Adrian said, closing the closet door, "I got here half an hour ago and politely knocked, but you weren't home. I have a key, remember?"

Scarlett rubbed her forehead. "I'm just tired. What's going on?"

Adrian shoved something into a sleek black duffel bag. "Collette and I are going to Grenada tomorrow. Turns out she's never been snorkeling before. Isn't that a travesty?" He laughed, zipping up the duffel bag. "Remember when we went snorkeling off the coast of Australia? I had never seen you so in awe of nature before. Well, Hawaii came close, I guess. Seems like so long ago…"

"You're still with Collette?" It had been a while since Scarlett had paid any attention to Adrian's romantic life. *His real romantic life, that is.*

Adrian nodded. "Why? Have you heard rumors? I should hope not. Nobody's supposed to know."

"I know they're not. Least of all my family." As far as everyone in the Black family knew, Scarlett and Adrian were happily on their way to wedded bliss. Only they themselves knew the truth.

And Collette, I suppose. Adrian's girlfriend of the moment was a swimwear model who seemed nice enough. *You know, for someone who was seduced by another woman's fiancé.* Adrian swore he had been upfront with Collette from the very beginning. And to her credit, the young woman had approached Scarlett-in her office, no less-to confirm that she was fine with their 'open relationship.'

But even that was just a cover for the fact that Adrian and Scarlett were over.

It's been almost a year now. A year since Adrian met Collette. But his relationship with Scarlett had been broken long before that, long before the two of them had separated.

"Grenada?" she said. "You must be taking a long weekend."

Adrian nodded. "Three days in the Caribbean before we fly back here. I'm over all this rain already. Winter will be brutal."

"At least there are tropical paradises to escape to." Scarlett gestured to the duffel bag full of snorkeling gear. "Why don't you keep those things? I have no intention of going snorkeling again. That was more your thing."

"I don't have room in my place. You know me. Downsizing."

"Right. Well, have a wonderful time. And give Collette my best. She still acts so strangely around me."

"Probably because the press keeps running stories about when you and I will get married." Adrian chuckled, as if the notion was inconceivable. Which it was, at this point. "Seriously, Scar. When are we going to end this charade? While I wouldn't exactly call Collette and me serious, at some point I'm going to want to move on with someone else. Publicly. Won't you, too?"

Did they have to do this now? Tonight, after Scarlett had worked three hours overtime because Connect was a mess? *What I would give to go drinking.* With anyone, even her new employees who hated her guts.

Instead, she would be at home on her couch, remembering the days when she and Adrian used to talk seriously about their future. About marriage.

About what they *really* wanted in life.

She had loved him. At some point. *At least, I think I did.* It was difficult to remember the truth, since Adrian had always been a constant in Scarlett's life. They were around the same age, in the same social sphere, and had even attended the same private school and college.

While they didn't officially start dating until after grad school—which they'd also attended together—the press and their families had always paired them with each other. They were *beautiful. Sophisticated. Regal.* Those were the magic words Americans liked to project upon the rich and successful. *We have no royalty. Families like mine are the royalty.*

Scarlett had taken plenty of history classes and knew what often happened to royalty. She liked her head on her neck, where it belonged.

Was that one of the reasons she grew apart from Adrian so quickly? Because they were too expected?

"We'll tell our families when the time is right," she said. "I'm sorry. I know it was supposed to happen this month, but then Connect fell into my lap, and—"

"Yes, yes. When the time is right. I've heard that a few times before."

"I'm sorry, Adrian. You know I mean it."

He offered her a sympathetic look. "I know you mean well. But I don't know how much longer I can keep this up. Even if Collette and I aren't forever, it's rough having people ask me questions about you and *our* future. You know. The nonexistent future."

Adrian's words cut deep into her already vulnerable heart. "You think I enjoy this?"

He sighed. "I've got what I need. I'll show myself out." He hesitated in the storage room doorway. "You know, maybe things really are nearing the end. I don't see that ridiculous portrait of us in your living room anymore."

"Don't remind me." Ever since her sister Parker had commented on how ridiculous they looked in it, Scarlett had become too self-conscious to have it hanging up any longer.

Slowly but surely, she was removing any trace of Adrian from her home. A fine thing, considering she lived one floor below her childhood home, the penthouse. Rarely did her space truly feel like *hers*.

Rarely did her life truly feel like hers.

Adrian gave her one last smile before letting himself out. His silly grin reminded her of why the two of them had stuck together for so long, despite their lack of feelings for each other. She still cared about him, and she always would. But the feeling was entirely platonic. She didn't love him, not in the way she was supposed to.

Would she ever find anyone she loved in that way?

Scarlett tidied up the closet in the storage room, turned off the light, and shut the door behind her. She still had a couple of hours before bed, and she needed to unwind.

She slipped into something more comfortable for the night and poured herself a glass of wine. Dinner had been a sandwich delivered to her office after everyone else had run off to the bar.

Still, Scarlett could use something to eat. She grabbed some crackers out of her cupboard and sat on her couch, where she turned to her phone instead of the book sitting on the side table. She had a voicemail from her mother. She would listen to it later. If it was something important, her mother would already be blowing up her phone.

And she didn't want to talk to her mother right now. It would inevitably lead to her interrogating Scarlett about Adrian.

When are we going to end this charade? They both knew things weren't as simple as "let's tell everyone we've broken up." It wasn't just her parents, either. It was his. The Holts were as invested in their 'relationship' as the Blacks, who had been more than chuffed to discover Scarlett and Adrian might have "feelings" for each other all those years ago.

To be fair, we did. But hers had never been as strong as his. Her lukewarm feelings toward him weren't because he was a bad person, or because he'd done something to break her trust. That would have made it easier, would have given Scarlett an out. But by the time she realized that he wasn't the one for her, she was several years into *"not tonight, honey"* while she yearned for something that her fiancé could never give her.

Yes, Scarlett had a secret. One she had hidden even from herself for far too long.

It wasn't that she was gay. That was a word reserved for her sister Parker, who used to have a new girlfriend every minute and had caused a giant rift in the family with her lack of sexual inhibitions. That had changed now that Parker had a serious girlfriend. But what hadn't changed was that Parker was out and proud. She was true to herself. She made Scarlett jealous.

Scarlett wasn't quite sure where she fell on the spectrum of sexuality. However, she knew she liked women. Loved them. Fantasized about them. Longed to be with them.

But for most of her life, her experiences with women had been few and far in between. Until she and Adrian decided to see other people. While Adrian had been courting swimwear models, Scarlett had been having trysts with other women in secret. They would come to her apartment under the guise of deliveries or work. Nobody, least of all in her family, questioned it when Scarlett had a nice-looking lady adorning her furniture.

What those people, including Parker, didn't know was that those ladies were often escorts or women with whom Scarlett had unofficial financial arrangements. Often, those women only performed the duties listed on their profiles—acting as dinner dates, travel companions, and someone to talk about a damned book with. Because Scarlett had very few friends. And the friends she had lived in opposite corners of the Earth, convening for drinks and laughs once or twice a year. And the years kept speeding by.

But some of those women had done more than keep her company. Those were the ones Scarlett couldn't keep her hands off. They undoubtedly loved that they had been taken by Adrian Holt's fiancée. A secret they would carry with them to the grave.

Adrian knew. He was the first to know. He understood, even supported her. So here they were, performing their roles for the public while living other lives in secret. Adrian had Collette, who gave him the girlfriend experience he desired. And Scarlett?

She had Dominique.

Or rather, she *was* Dominique. Dominique had been born when Scarlett started to want more than what paid encounters could give her. So she'd started seeking out women in the kinds of places where sex and kink flowed freely. Clubs. Bars. Private parties. She spent every night she could at those places, having sordid encounters with women behind a veil of darkness and disguise, finally satisfying the cravings she'd had for years.

Because it wasn't just a woman Scarlett had always craved. It was a woman on her knees, at Scarlett's feet, serving her.

However, with the acquisition of Connect, she didn't have any spare nights. But Dominique had another playground, one that didn't require her to leave the comfort of her home. It was where she went when she was too busy or too consumed by work to make time for the real thing, both physically and mentally.

She opened Darkest Desires now. Perhaps there was someone online who could give her what she craved.

Control. I am always in control.

It was how she kept the house of cards around her from collapsing. Her mother and her sisters, whose constant drama threatened to topple the family. Her father, who was relying on her to step up and take over the family company when he retired. There was no time for Scarlett's selfish hedonism. Her dissatisfaction with her life, her unfulfilled desires, didn't matter.

Scarlett logged in. A message awaited her. She sipped her red wine, preparing herself to be disappointed. The app was full of bots and scammers.

Hm? The message was from Beauty, the little vixen who had slipped through her fingers only a few days ago. Scarlett had assumed she'd never see that sweet, inexperienced princess again. A shame, since she was the exact kind of woman who haunted Scarlett's fantasies.

She opened the message.

"The answer is yes. I am the woman you need. I am the one you've been looking for."

There was that word. *Need.*

Yes, Scarlett had many needs, didn't she?

"Is that so?" Scarlett wrote back. *"Are you certain? I'm not an easy Mistress to serve."*

"I'm certain. I want this. I want to experience what you have to offer."

She didn't expect to receive a reply so quickly. Scarlett mulled over Beauty's response, her wineglass halfway to her lips. Already, the possibilities were endless.

Her reply flowed from her fingers at the speed of light.

"Do you understand what I need? What I expect from you? Beauty, you will be my servant, my willing thrall. You will do anything and everything I tell you to do, no matter where you are or who you are with. This is what I have to offer you. This is the thrill of my hunt. When I catch you—and I will—you will be mine to completely, utterly control. In return, I will make all of your cares disappear. There will only be me and you."

Scarlett half-expected Beauty to disappear. After all, who wouldn't balk at such demands?

But Beauty's reply was almost instantaneous. *"That sounds perfect."*

Scarlett finished off her wine. *"Then get some sleep. We'll get started soon."*

She logged off, then got up to pour herself more wine. Her fantasies soon drove her to the bedroom, where she turned in early—but did not sleep.

Chapter Six

"What are you doing right now?"

Isabel was technically on her break, but she remained seated at her desk, where the new prototype UI design for Connect was still up on her screen. Her phone was hidden on her lap as she exchanged messages with Dominique.

"*I'm at work,*" Isabel sent. "*I'm supposed to be working on a project, but instead, I'm a bad girl who is talking to you.*"

Dominique's reply was swift. "*On company time? You really are a bad girl. If one of my employees did that, I'd take great pleasure in laying into them for it. I'd call them into my office and watch them shudder as I verbally undress them for their insubordination.*"

"*Do you really do that?*" Dominique had been just as vague about her job as Isabel had, but she had gathered that the woman was some kind of executive.

"*Yes. When you're running a company, it's just part of the job.*"

"*That's so... intense.*" *Awful* was what Isabel wanted to say, but she had other things on her mind. Every one of

Dominique's words was laced with sexual innuendo. After all, she'd said 'undressed' for a reason. *"If I were in your office, I'd get into trouble on purpose, just so you'd do that to me."*

"If you did that in my office, I'd lock the door, bend you over my desk, and spank you until your skin turned pink before having my way with you. I bet you're an absolute delight to fuck while your fingers curl around the edge of my desktop."

Isabel jerked back in her chair, her whole body growing hot. *Calm down!* She couldn't have the whole office looking at her and wondering what the hell she was up to. Her real boss was no Dominique. Scarlett Black would just yell at her. Maybe fire her. Or make her start all over on the new UI layout simply out of spite.

Isabel glanced around surreptitiously before replying. *"If that's the only way to make me learn…"*

They had been flirting like this over messages since Friday night, when Isabel had returned from her outing more than a little tipsy. She hadn't expected Dominique to respond to her with such alacrity.

And she hadn't expected to be so into Dominique's games. Yet the more they flirted, with Dominique's provocative comments and the growing suggestion that she expected Isabel to 'serve' her very soon, the more excited Isabel got.

Too bad Dominique lived in New York. When Isabel pressed for more details, her new Mistress only told her not to worry about it. *"I can travel anywhere in the world. The only thing keeping me from getting on a plane right now is my real-life responsibilities. But trust me, Beauty. I'd love to spoil you silly. With gifts. With love. With sex."*

That was certainly fun to hear. And there were advantages to the anonymous nature of their liaison. It was easier for Isabel to embrace the part of her that was Beauty from behind the comfort of a screen.

At least for now. She was definitely interested in meeting Dominique in person, and maybe sooner rather than later. Because right now, her biggest real-life crush was her boss, who had a habit of marching through the office and catching her employees out at the most inopportune of moments.

But this time, it was Alexis who interrupted Isabel's break.

She sidled up beside Isabel's desk. "What's got you smiling like you've just won the lottery?"

Isabel locked her phone before her friend could catch a glimpse of the wicked words on the screen. Had she noticed the blush on Isabel's cheeks?

"Is it a meme?" Alexis asked. "I bet it's a great meme Ned sent you. I don't know what happened, but I'm somehow glitched out of the company Slack. IT is supposed to be working on it—"

Isabel couldn't contain the excitement bubbling through her any longer. "I'm sort of talking to someone. On a dating website. It's... going really well, if you can believe it."

Alexis raised an eyebrow. "Really? Someone from Seattle?"

"New York, actually."

"Huh..."

"I'm fine with long-distance," Isabel said quickly. "You know me. I'm not big on dating in person, anyway. I'm willing to make things work for the right woman somewhere out in the world. We gay girls don't have the biggest dating pool. We sometimes have to go to extremes to find that special someone." *Wow, I'm really babbling here.*

"Kind of like that lady in this article I was reading."

"Hm?"

Alexis grabbed a nearby chair and rolled it over to Isabel, straddling it backward as she sipped her coffee. "There was this story about a woman who was catfished by someone claiming to be another woman. It was a seriously long con. We're talking *years*."

"Years?"

Alexis nodded. "The woman had pictures and everything. They had 'online relations,' which you know is a euphemism for cybersex. Anyway, eventually the requests for money started, but they were three years into the relationship at this point, so this lady was like, *of course I'll help my honey out!* So she starts sending hundreds, then thousands of dollars to help out her 'girlfriend.' Anyway, long story short, it was actually a man who was catfishing a ton of lonely lesbians he scouted online. Go figure. He knew how to play the game."

"Wow…"

Alexis shrugged. "Just saying. You gotta be careful out there. I guess it's a sign of progress, though. Gay people are so accepted now that scammers have figured out how to get to you guys. It's a cold world out there."

"Thank you so much for the vote of confidence as I embark on a brand-new and exciting online relationship."

Alexis gave a half-hearted salute as she stood back up again. "That's what I'm here for, kid. To dash your dreams before they run away from you. That way you can drag them away from certain death, at least." She offered a smile, but Isabel was more than wary of it. "Have fun, just don't be dumb."

"Thanks, Mom."

Alexis chuckled as she walked away. She may have been half-joking, but she had planted a seed in Isabel's mind, and it was beginning to take root.

As she picked up her phone to check for a new message from Dominique, she wondered how much of what the mysterious woman had said was true. Did she really live in New York? Was she really a Domme looking for love?

Or was she too good to be true?

~

As she sat on her bed that night, a granola bar in one hand and her phone in the other, Isabel faced one of the most pressing questions of her day.

Is Dominique real?

She hated how much Alexis's words weighed on her mind. For a woman who was often full of snark and sass, Alexis couldn't always be taken seriously.

Yet she had her moments of profoundness. Isabel had already done some homework, and the "lesbian catfisher" was a real guy who had skimmed tens of thousands of dollars off a number of lonely women. Why should Isabel's experience be any different? How quickly had she fallen for Dominique's charms and promises of something more?

When did fantasy end, and the scam begin?

Isabel polished off her after-work granola bar and brushed crumbs off her fingers. It was time to get out the big guns. Namely, her laptop and her critical thinking skills.

She rarely used Darkest Desires on her laptop. Isabel saw laptops and computers as workstations, and her phone was for personal use. However, she did appreciate the larger screen for streaming movies and TV shows, since she didn't own a TV. Seattle studios weren't known for their square footage, and Isabel had become a master of making every inch count.

Her desk doubled as a dining table when she needed to sit up to eat. Her wardrobe was divided into two seasons, with the current season hanging up in her tiny closet and the other stored in a large plastic bin that sat atop her closet. String lights offered some fun warmth and color to the apartment, and she didn't need long ones.

Besides, she was trying to be a minimalist. Even if she didn't have a small studio and an even smaller bank account balance, being friends with people like Alexis made it easy for Isabel to avoid partaking in consumerist culture more than necessary.

Digitizing everything? That was the future.

Why not relationships, too? So when she plugged in her laptop and popped open the Darkest Desires desktop site, she was only mildly surprised to see a new message from Dominique.

"Are you home from work yet? Have you slipped into something more... comfortable?"

Isabel didn't let herself be seduced by those words. She thought of only practicality as she responded with, *"I'm in my pajamas. Nothing sexy though, Mistress. A baggy shirt and some sweatpants."*

"How is that not sexy? I'm sure I would eat you right up if I saw you."

"I could send you a picture if you'd like."

"In due time, my Beauty. How about we talk a little first?"

Isabel bit her thumbnail in frustration. She had been hoping to trade photos, knowing damn well that Dominique could send her a fake one. But Isabel could work with that. She could look for clues in it, perform a reverse image search to check whether it had been taken from somewhere online.

But for now, she had to try a different approach. *"All right. How was your day, Mistress?"*

"Tiring. Stressful. My job tends to be. That's why I like to spend my downtime with an enchanting woman like you. Even if I can't touch you, I can imagine it. That fills my heart with relieving song."

Isabel stared at that message, her body sinking deeper into her bed. *I want to believe her.* Yet Isabel wouldn't succumb to naivety. She may have been young and desperate for some romance in her life, but she wouldn't let herself be taken advantage of. Even if Dominique really were a woman—and experienced in the kinky side of life— there was no guarantee she had good intentions.

Isabel needed to be cautious. She needed to gather all the information she could.

"How old are you?"

Three dots appeared in the chat window, indicating that Dominique was typing, but that quickly ended. Had Isabel scared her off?

"Like my profile says, I'm in my thirties. What end of that spectrum doesn't matter. I have experience, both professionally and personally. I am old enough to know what I want and am willing to share my experience with a younger woman such as

yourself. In fact, I prefer it. There's something intoxicating about being someone's first."

So, she was in her late 30s. Only a woman on that end of the thirties "spectrum" would dodge the question. Isabel didn't mind. She actually liked the idea of having an experienced woman show her the ropes. She just wanted her to be open about it.

"What do you do?" Isabel asked. *"You can be general, of course."*

This time it took even longer for Dominique to answer. *"Why are you asking me these questions, my Beauty? Don't you believe I'm who I say I am?"*

Isabel cursed. She'd been caught.

She almost slammed her laptop shut. Instead, she breathed in all her courage and answered with the truth. *"Forgive me. There are stories, you know? People like me get taken advantage of by unscrupulous men and women who aren't who they say they are."*

Dominique's response took some time to arrive. *"I see. I'm a little hurt, but it's wise of you to be careful. But I see it from your point of view. I have much to lose, too, should someone wile their way into my heart to steal my money and time. But I assure you, I'm exactly who I say I am. And I have every intention of meeting you in person once we've developed a certain level of trust."*

It was the first time Dominique had explicitly stated a desire to meet her face to face. But when would that be?

Dominique continued. *"For now, how about this? I will get on camera, using the app's video chat. I won't show my face, but I'll prove to you that I'm who I say I am. In return, I expect you to do the same."*

Video chat? Isabel had been wondering if things would escalate to that, but she didn't think it would be so soon.

"Show me what I am fantasizing about all day, my Beauty."

Isabel hesitated, then sent off her reply before she could lose her nerve. *"Okay, Mistress."*

"Good. Give me five minutes to get ready. I believe the app will tell you when I'm live."

Isabel grabbed a glass of water to wet her dried lips. *Why am I so parched?* Could it be the anticipation of seeing her dreams come true? Because this wasn't just about Dominique proving she was real. This was the moment when Isabel would discover if she was as attracted to Dominique physically as she was in every other way.

A green light lit up in the middle of Isabel's laptop screen, followed by a pop-up message that someone on her contact list wanted to video chat.

Isabel kept her own camera and mic off as she accepted the request. Soon, her screen was taken over by live video from Dominique's webcam. Dominique's mic was off too, but the image?

Exquisite.

A woman sat in an armchair, legs crossed and clad in fishnet stockings, wispy black lingerie clinging to a toned body. The video only showed her from the neck down. No face. Yet when Isabel's eyes weren't being drawn to the lace-adorned breasts or the thighs peeking out of delicate panties, she was staring at the long red hair framing Dominique's slender shoulders. That vivid shade of scarlet had to be a wig. But Isabel didn't care.

Dominique was real. And she was stunning.

On screen, she picked up her phone and tapped away at it. Seconds later, a message popped up on Isabel's phone.

"Hello, Beauty. I am very, very real."

Isabel gulped down more of her water. She needed it.

Dominique leaned back in her armchair as she typed on her phone. *"I've shown you mine. Now, show me yours."*

Isabel looked down at her clothes. She hadn't been kidding when she said she was wearing her schlubby PJs. How could she show herself off in *this?*

It was time to be brave. Dominique had put herself out there for her. What was Isabel willing to do?

"I'm waiting," came Dominique's message.

"Just a second, please. I don't want you seeing me in my pajamas when you look like this."

"I would love anything, Beauty."

Isabel drew in a deep breath for luck. *Here goes nothing.*

She stripped off her pajamas, leaving herself in only her cotton underwear. Unfortunately for her—and fortunately for Dominique—Isabel had removed her bra as soon as she'd stepped through her front door. She pulled her long, dark hair over her shoulders and covered her naked breasts as best as she could, then angled her screen down so that her face was out of view of her camera.

Then, she turned it on.

Why am I sweating? It was a cool day, and she was mostly naked. Yet her palms were wet and her chest perspired from the nervousness shaking her core. Isabel had never done anything like this before. The only people to see her naked in a romantic light? Well, the few times she had sex before, it had been in the dark. Had anyone actually seen her in the nude? Like this?

"You are radiant," Dominique messaged. *"I've seen beautiful women before, but you are something truly special."*

Isabel let out a sigh of relief. Dominique approved. But hearing those words only made the butterflies in her chest flutter harder.

But Dominique wasn't done. *"The way you tease me with your hair... I wish you were here in my bedroom, laid out for me on my bed. I would brush aside those silken locks, all so I could flick my tongue against your sweet nipples. Pink or brown? Tell, don't show."*

Isabel wet her lips. *"Brown."*

"Delicious. Just like the rest of you. But I am disappointed that you would doubt me. You should know that I don't like being disappointed." A finger waved before Dominique's camera. *"I should punish you, don't you agree?"*

Isabel hesitated. *"I think so."*

"Good. Every day this upcoming week, I want you to find a private place at your work. You will touch yourself, and you will think of me while doing so. Except, you are not allowed to come, not once. If I were there in person, I would be the one doling out your punishment, pleasuring you while withholding the ultimate release. But since I'm on the other side of the country, you'll have to do it yourself. All. Week. Do you understand?"

Isabel swallowed. *"At work?"*

"You heard me. I want to own your thoughts even when you're being paid to report to someone else."

"You already do, Mistress."

"Then let me own your pussy, too."

Isabel almost dropped her phone. Which also made her hair fall from her chest, almost exposing her bare nipples to the woman who doled out punishment like it was candy.

Sweet, sour candy…

"If you make it through the week, I will have a wonderful surprise for you next weekend," Dominique sent.

Already, Isabel's mind raced with the possibilities. There were myriad places she could steal away on her work break. The bathroom was too obvious, but she would find the perfect place. A place where she could dedicate her mind and body to a woman over three thousand miles away.

Isabel had never felt so alive. She prayed that she could make Dominique feel the same way.

Chapter Seven

Her father's favorite Waldorf salad arrived with minimal fanfare. Scarlett accepted her Cobb salad and garlic breadstick with a smile that unnerved the man in the serving jacket. She was one of the few people in her father's office who treated the staff like humans with emotions. When would she learn?

Not soon enough, according to Phillip Black, who dove right into the business of Connect as he picked up his knife and fork. It was why Scarlett had foregone her usual lunch at her desk to come up to her father's office at Black Diamond headquarters. They sat on either side of a table by the window, a large flatscreen TV at the far side of the room playing a golf tournament. She'd never seen that TV play anything other than golf or news. Her father would be a hilarious stereotype if he wasn't so serious about both.

Scarlett mixed her salad and eyed the breadstick ravenously. She had foregone breakfast in favor of sleeping in on account of staying up late the night before, chatting with someone who made her feel more alive than any of the other people in her life.

What was Beauty doing at this very moment? Perhaps she was carrying out Scarlett's orders, performing the delicious 'punishment' Dominique had bestowed upon her. But she was the last person Scarlett wanted to think about while discussing business matters with her father.

"Connect is still hemorrhaging money. *Our* money." He stopped attacking his Waldorf salad for a moment to take a long drink of mineral water. "Tell me you've come up with some way to stem the flow. Making money from subscriptions and advertisements later on won't mean anything if we have to fold the whole project due to a lack of funds."

Scarlett flipped open the manila folder beside her plate and pulled out a single piece of paper. "After surveying the operation for the past few weeks, I can say with certainty that Connect has a significant number of personnel and departments that are redundant."

She immediately thought of the graphic design department. Sure, that clever young woman Isabel Diaz had been hard at work on the new UI design, but it would all be for nothing if Connect went bankrupt.

"I only hesitate to make cuts so quickly," she continued. "Some of the employees are still finding ways to prove that they're valuable to our bottom line. And I looked at the employee benefits package. It's quite generous." She'd also heard a few things about various employees' health conditions. Cutting them off from their health insurance would make their lives much more difficult.

Phillip didn't waste time telling his daughter what he thought of those concerns. "It's easier to do it now than to continue wasting money and resources on people we don't need. Connect has over twenty-five dedicated employees, not including yourself and your secretary. That's simply not necessary for a company that small. We'll save more money by cutting numbers and paying everyone a decent severance package to tide them over between jobs, but only if we do it soon. Who's making the most money? The head of IT?"

Scarlett didn't want to admit her father was right, but he was. "Yes. One hundred and twenty thousand a year."

"Jesus. I know this is an expensive city, but we can't afford that when we have our own IT department in the building. What else can we consolidate? Customer service? Graphic design?"

"It's looking like we could at least cut one member from each department. We have a floater named Caroline who is technically a part of graphic design, but really, the head of that department does a vast majority of the work. I hesitate to let Isabel Diaz go."

Right now, anyway. Even if they outsourced Connect's graphic design to the in-house crew of Black Diamond Enterprises, it would mean acclimating a team there. That took time. And patience. *It's not like Isabel is making a ton of money for her position.* Honestly, Scarlett wondered how Ms. Diaz lived off forty thousand a year in a city as expensive as Seattle.

"Then cut this Caroline and be done with it."

Scarlett hesitated. "I'm not sure if—"

Her father sighed. "I know it's unpleasant, Scarlett. But you're going to be in my position sooner rather than later. Getting your hands dirty is part of the job. You'll always have to fire people for one reason or another. Acquiring companies like this startup usually means heads on the chopping block, and you're the one holding the axe. That's the world we operate in. You have to set aside your feelings on the matter."

Scarlett didn't need to be told twice. She understood how these things worked. After all, she'd been raised from birth to take over from her father.

But did that mean she had to be nothing other than a clone of him—cold, calculating, and ruthless?

"Besides, if these employees are smart, they're not supremely loyal to us, anyway," her father said. "Times are changing. While unfettered company loyalty in exchange for a fantastic benefits and retirement package used to be the norm, those days are long gone. Consider yourself lucky, Scarlett. Had you been born into any other family, your work life would be very different."

"I'm aware of that," Scarlett said. "You're right. I'll take a closer look at the numbers this week and come up with a truncated list of people and departments we can consolidate or terminate. We need to save money now to swing things into the black later on." But speaking those words made bile rise in her throat.

"Yes, 'the black.' If that wasn't our family name, I'd suggest changing it to just that."

It wasn't the first time Philip had made that 'joke' to his oldest daughter. It was one of the few in his repertoire. He wasn't exactly known for his humor.

Which must have been why he thought it hilarious to move on to an even more awkward topic. "How is Adrian doing? We haven't seen him around lately."

Scarlett held back her growing discomfort, not wanting

her father to sense it. "He's fine. Everything's fine." She assumed, anyway. Adrian had returned from the Caribbean with Collette without anyone noticing.

"That's good. I'm quite looking forward to your wedding. Not only because you're my oldest and it's high time you do something with your personal life." Philip chuckled. "Your marriage will be a great benefit to this company, and to our family. I know I've told you this before, but it's true. Especially in the wake of your sister's... well. We all know how Parker is."

Scarlett hid her real thoughts behind bites of her lunch. *Yes, Parker, the only one of us who has managed to break free of our family's expectations and do her own thing.* Her lingerie business was booming.

But Parker's business wasn't what Phillip had been referring to. Parker was out and proud, and dating a woman who spent most of her time working with abandoned cats. Nobody had much hope that Parker would marry someone of note, but when she'd made her intentions with Julia clear, the pressure only mounted on Scarlett.

Because I'm the oldest. Because I'm the responsible one. She was set to inherit the bulk of the family's fortune.

In return, she had to sell more of her soul than her sisters did.

"Have you set a date for the wedding yet?" her father asked.

Scarlett almost choked on a piece of bacon. "Not yet, no. We haven't had much time to discuss it."

"You need to set a date, even if it's for two years from now. Plans need to be made and invitations sent. I've got quite the list of associates I want to invite. If we give them plenty of advance notice, they'll be more likely to come."

"Of course. I'll talk to Adrian about it the next time we have dinner."

Her father cocked his head. "Everything's all right between you two, yes? Because your mother has been bothering me about it, as if I know anything."

"Everything's fine."

"You keep saying that, don't you?"

Scarlett pretended to hurry to chew her breadstick so she could respond. In truth, she was struggling to think of what to say. *Be honest for once. Tell your parents how it really is. End this whole charade and move on with your life.*

God, Scarlett would give half her fortune for that to be a possibility. Adrian was tired of hiding, and so was she. The prospect of keeping this up for another year filled her with dread.

And how much longer could they get away with it? At some point, Adrian would walk, and she wouldn't blame him. At least if Scarlett broached the subject, she could be in control. It could be done in the most advantageous way.

But how? When?

Tell him.

She almost did. The words were on her lips, much like the vinaigrette that tantalized her tongue.

But like the weak person she was, she hesitated for too long. And her father changed subjects yet again.

Scarlett barely heard a word he was saying. *I can't keep going on like this.* Yet telling her parents the truth seemed even more difficult. Scarlett's father saw the business opportunities that came from joining families with the

Holts, along with the security of knowing that his legacy would be assured long after he was gone in the form of her heirs. Never mind that Scarlett was on the fence about having kids in the first place, and she wasn't getting any younger.

And her mother? Vivianne Black was invested in the social connections the Holts offered and was already close friends with Adrian's aunt. *Not to mention, I'm fulfilling my womanly duty.* The thought alone was enough to make Scarlett gag. While their mother didn't expect her daughters to *only* be housewives and mothers like her, she *did* expect them to marry and have children.

And Scarlett was the only real candidate for that, at least in their mother's eyes. She made no secret of her resentment toward Parker's sexuality and 'lifestyle.' And Bianca would forever be treated as an asexual child, even though she was in her 20s now. Meanwhile, her mother celebrated the thought of her oldest daughter riding Adrian Holt into the sunset.

What the hell was she supposed to do?

"Scarlett."

She straightened up at the sound of her name. On the other side of the table, her father narrowed his eyes in her direction, his fingers steepled.

"Yes?"

"Whatever you decide, it will be fine. As long as you stick to your decisions. That's one of the most important things I've ever taught you."

Was he talking about Connect? Scarlett had lost track of the conversation. Surely he wasn't referring to her relationship with Adrian?

As the conversation moved on, her mind wandered again, this time, not to her responsibilities, or her problems. But to the only person to give her light in her day.

Beauty.

What she wouldn't give to show up to a family dinner with Beauty on her arm. Scarlett hardly knew her. She'd never even seen Beauty's face. While she'd seen her body, knowing what her body looked like wasn't the same as knowing *her*.

But that would change with time. While, for now, Scarlett's life was too complex for anything other than a 'long-distance' liaison, she was already dreaming of the day she would behold her Beauty in person.

Chapter Eight

The supply closet door latched shut behind Isabel. Hand sanitizer drying on her hands, she attempted to look nonchalant as she carried a ruler and compass back to her desk as if they were the reason she'd spent the last five minutes locked in the supply closet.

In truth, she had been a very, very naughty girl.

Five minutes for five days. That had been her punishment, and she had taken to it like it was a new kind of art. *Eat your heart out, graphic design degree.* Smug didn't truly convey how Isabel felt by that Friday afternoon, when she emerged triumphant, but still oh so sexually frustrated, just how Dominique liked her. Nobody in the office had a clue.

It was lucky that, aside from Caroline, there were no other graphic designers around to question why a digital designer needed physical tools of the trade. Alexis had once stopped by the large coworking table to ask her what she was doing, but Isabel had told her that since the redesign was such an important project, she was seeking inspiration in the physical, drafting layouts on paper before attempting them on the computer. Her elaborate excuse had only elicited a shrug and a, *"Well, whatever works..."* from Alexis.

That was the same response Scarlett Black seemed to have the few times she walked by the table and saw her head of graphic design hunched over. *Drawing lines. Moving blocks around. Pretending one side of the table is mobile, and the other is desktop.* IT sometimes joined Ms. Black, scratching their heads and nodding as if this were par for the course in an innovative startup like Connect.

In reality, it was all a front so Isabel could spend five minutes a day imagining Dominique in the supply closet with her.

Although, her Mistress had no way of knowing whether Isabel *really* did as she was told. But perhaps she sensed the excitement through her phone every time Isabel sat back down at her desk and texted, *"Yes, I did it. I couldn't stop thinking about you in there with me. Kissing me, touching me... ravishing me."*

Since Isabel's chances to go into the closet were sporadic, she sometimes didn't hear back from Dominique for hours. But when she did? *"I'd give anything to be there with you. One day soon, I'll hear your sweet cries, my Beauty."*

Those texts always made Isabel smile. And gave her a pressing need to run home to finish the job. But she had promised Dominique that she would be a pressure cooker of desire by Friday evening. A prize was on the line.

Although, Isabel could simply lie and touch herself all she wanted once she was home. But that ruined the fun, didn't it? Already, her online fling with a stranger in New York was the most sexually adventurous thing Isabel had done since losing her virginity. *In retrospect, that wasn't super adventurous, but it was* exciting *at the time.*

While Isabel resumed her afternoon work at her desk, a text buzzed on her phone. She half-expected it to be Alexis messaging her from across the office to ask if Isabel wanted to go out that night. Or, even worse, attempting to hook her up on a blind date. Alexis somehow had a laundry list of queer women in her contacts, and they were all looking for love.

Too bad Isabel wasn't half as interested in them as she was the woman on her own phone.

"You've been such a good sport this week, my Beauty," Dominique said. *"I have a special surprise for you. Do you know where the Black Diamond Building is in Seattle?"*

Isabel's heart stopped. Had Dominique figured out who 'Beauty' was and where she worked?

But before the desire could drain from her veins, she realized that it was an innocent question. The Black Diamond Building was one of the most well-known landmarks in the entire Pacific Northwest region, even among people who had never been to it.

It also boasted plenty of services to the public, which became more apparent with Dominique's next text.

"I had a package sent to the front desk. It's for 'Beauty Smith.' The password is 'dreamer.' You can pick it up anytime after lunch. They said they'll hold it until tomorrow, but I would very much like you to get it tonight. I promised you relief, didn't I?"

Isabel glanced around the room to ensure that none of her coworkers were watching her. *"I know where it is. The front desk, you said?"* It was staffed by one or two people, depending on the time and day. But she'd had no idea they would accept and hold packages for some random person in New York. How much power—and how much sway—did Dominique hold?

Isabel had to wait until she finished work before running down to grab her package. Naturally, Alexis and a couple of others asked if she wanted to go out for drinks, but she cheerily informed them that she had "other plans." Alexis immediately wanted to know what they were. When Isabel slyly suggested she was going on a date with her online lover, Alexis backed off, but not before offering her best wishes.

Still, Isabel had to wait for most of her work friends to depart before grabbing her things and taking the elevator down by herself. The surge of people exiting the Black Diamond Building shortly after five p.m. made it difficult to cross from the elevators to the front desk, let alone get the attention of the busy woman staffing it.

"Uh, hi." Isabel finally made eye contact with her. "I'm here to pick up a package for Beauty Smith. I was told it would be waiting for me here at this desk."

The woman was in no hurry to hand over the package. "So you were also told about the password."

Wow, this is actually happening. Isabel felt like she was in a thriller. A sexy, suspenseful thriller. "Dreamer. Short for BeautifulDreamer."

With a labored sigh, the receptionist reached beneath the desk and pulled out a small package that was featherlight in Isabel's hands.

"Thank you."

A smile struck her face as Isabel backed away from the desk, package pressed against her chest. She joined the sea of people floating toward the main entrance, her mind running wild with possibilities as she made her escape. She was almost at the entrance when she spotted the last person she expected to see.

Scarlett Black, sitting in one of the lounge chairs by the large glass revolving doors. Her gaze lingered on them as she watched the people entering the building. Who was she waiting for with such anticipation? Who was she expecting to walk through those doors?

Scarlett hadn't seen her yet. And Isabel wanted to keep it that way. She couldn't say why. She just had a feeling.

Isabel backed away, almost running into a man in a three-piece suit. As they apologized to one another, Scarlett looked in the direction of the disturbance.

Crap! Isabel ducked behind a pillar and caught her breath. *What am I doing?* So what if her boss saw her leaving at an appropriate time?

But something was off about Scarlett's presence. It was almost like she was a tigress lying in wait, hoping to catch a glimpse of something, someone.

Who was that someone?

It didn't matter. Isabel had to stop letting Scarlett Black consume so much of her attention. Even outside of work, Isabel would find herself thinking about her. *She's my boss. And she's a bitch.*

Why is that such a hot combination?

But Isabel and Scarlett were *not* going to happen. Beauty and Dominique? That was happening right now. And it was Dominique who commanded Isabel's allegiance, both in her personal time and outside of it.

She took one of the lobby's other exits that let her out

onto a side street. As soon as the crisp evening air hit her face, she forgot all about Scarlett Black.

There was only Dominique to occupy Isabel's mind.

~

Wow.

Isabel stood before her bathroom mirror, the only one in her studio with good lighting. *This is the most risqué thing I have ever worn.*

She knew from the lightness of the box that it was probably lingerie, but she hadn't anticipated something so *sexy.* Indeed, the royal blue bra and panty set was made of lace and not much else. Elastic in the bands? Metal in the underwire? That was about it.

And she loved every naughty inch of it.

How did Dominique know my size? Isabel hadn't told her. To be fair, the bra was a little tight, and the underwear created a hint of muffin top. The tags had said *S,* but Dominique probably should have sent her online lover an *M.*

Not that it mattered. It was comfortable enough for what it was.

There was one other problem. The labels on the lingerie read *Parker Black.* A brand owned by none other than Scarlett Black's sister.

Because the last thing Isabel wanted to think about while wearing lingerie gifted to her by Dominique was her infuriatingly sexy boss.

Pushing thoughts of Scarlett aside, Isabel combed her hair and put on some lipstick. She had no intention of showing her face that night. It wasn't like Dominique had shown off hers yet, either. But the little ritual made her feel sexy. And *sexy* was what she craved after a long week of teasing.

It was only when she turned around and caught her reflection in the mirror that she realized the underwear was *crotchless.*

Isabel stared at herself for a few more seconds, a strand of dark hair wrapped around her finger. She had never worn crotchless panties before. What kind of girl did that make her?

One who gets called all the best names in bed, I hope.

Isabel left the bathroom. *I can't believe I'm doing this.* She turned off all her lights, including the string lights hanging above her bed. With the blinds closed and only the glow of her laptop screen to illuminate her way, Isabel stretched herself across her bed and navigated to the Darkest Desires website.

Dominique was already waiting for her in the app's video chat, her sound and camera off. She sent a message explaining that both would remain off that night. *"This is what it means to be mine, Beauty. Sometimes, you'll be the one doing all the work, putting yourself out there and making yourself vulnerable for my entertainment. But I'm a fair Mistress. I'll always reward your devotion."*

Isabel propped her arms up on her pillow and kicked her feet up behind her. *"I'm guessing you want me to turn on my camera?"*

"What's the point of sending you a present if I don't get to see you in it?"

Isabel hesitated. *"There's no crotch in these panties."*

"Why would there be?"

Dominique had a point there. *"It's fine if I don't show my face, right?"*

"Whatever makes you comfortable. I'd love to see your face eventually. But for now, I'm content with simply owning your body. I'm so looking forward to seeing my possession."

Her possession. As Isabel sat up and wrapped her arms around her semi-naked torso, she imagined a world where she was nothing other than that. Where she didn't have to go to work every day. Didn't have to think about anything at all. Her life revolved around doing as her Mistress bade her, be it walking around in her underwear or showing herself off in bed. Mistress Dominique took care of everything else.

Such a sweet fantasy. And tonight could be a taste of that.

Isabel moved her pillow out of the way and turned on her camera. The preview allowed her to ensure that nothing was visible above her lips.

She started the video chat. She hoped that the room wasn't too dark for Dominique to see her.

"You're beautiful," said the message that appeared on both Isabel's laptop screen and phone. *"Now, show me what I've been missing all week. Open your legs for me. Let me see all there is to see."*

Isabel exhaled sharply. Dominique's command felt so... indecent.

So why did it make her burn all over?

"Don't be shy, my Beauty. Your body is safe with me."

Isabel hesitated. Dominique was asking for a great deal of trust. But Isabel knew she was genuine. She knew

Dominique was a real woman. What kind of woman? That remained to be seen.

But wasn't that what Isabel yearned to find out?

You only live once, girl. This is your moment to explore who you are. When will you have a chance like this again?

The world had presented the opportunity. She had to seize it for herself.

Slowly, she opened her legs—right in front of her webcam.

Isabel was a groomer, but not a shaver. And suddenly, she was self-conscious, wondering what this glamorous New Yorker would think of her body hair. Yet there was no going back now.

"*Exquisite.*" She had to read Dominique's message on her phone, since her laptop was too far away from her eyes. "*I've said that before, haven't I? It's true. Tell me, what kind of delicate blossom are you, my Beauty? The kind who responds to sweet words, or spicy? How naughty are you, really?*"

Isabel found herself unable to answer her. Sweet? Spicy? At that moment, words were meaningless. All she was aware of was her growing need.

"*Your pussy is the prettiest thing I've seen all year,*" Dominique tested. "*Go on. Show me more. It's mine, and I want the full tour.*"

Isabel's hand traveled down between her spread thighs. What exactly did *the full tour* imply?

"*Spread your lips apart. I need to see if you're wet for me yet.*"

Isabel was glad her face was out of view of the camera because she was sure it was bright red. She could feel the heat, the rush of blood, just like she could feel it between her legs. She ached for Dominique, as she had all week.

She closed her eyes before spreading her nether lips apart. Just how much could Dominique see through the camera? Did it please her? Undoubtedly. But even with Isabel reassuring herself that this was one of the most erotic things she had ever done, she couldn't help but quiver with apprehension. After all, she had never served herself up on such a platter before.

When she finally dared to check her messages again, she was greeted with, *"One day, I will tie your legs apart just like this. You'll be helpless to move as I have my way with you. How wet will you get? How easy will it be for me to fuck you until you're screaming my name?"*

Oh. My. God. Isabel's fingers twitched involuntarily, a sudden urge to slide them down to touch herself overcoming her. It had been so long now. And Dominique's words were only making her hotter.

But her Mistress hadn't instructed her to do that. Not yet.

"Do you know my name, Beauty?"

Isabel bit her lip. *"Mistress."*

"Yes. And do you know what I own?"

"My body."

"That's right. So, I give you two gifts, Beauty. The first is the gift to do with my possession as you please. The other is to finally relieve yourself of all that sexual tension you accumulated this week. I want to see how quickly you come when you touch yourself before my hungry eyes."

Isabel had known the command was coming. In fact, she'd been eagerly anticipating it. Yet she was still shocked to hear it coming from her Mistress's lips. Or rather, from her fingers to Isabel's screen.

"Touch your clit. Slide your fingers inside. Do whatever it takes to make yourself squirm. Oh, and Beauty?"

"Yes?"

"Put down the phone. Show me your breasts. Let yourself go."

Placing her phone on the bed was one way to alleviate some of the anxieties playing in her mind. No more fishing for responses. No more anticipating Dominique's words. Isabel was on display for her, exposed to her. And to the whole internet for all she knew, but it didn't matter.

It was finally time to succumb to the orgasm that had been building up inside of her all week.

Isabel lowered her bra straps. Her breasts already bulged out of their slightly too small cups, but without the support of the band to hold them up, the left one spilled from the lacy fabric while the other strained to be seen. She released them both. Her nipples had already hardened into tiny, firm peaks.

Did it please her Mistress to see how Isabel's body responded to her commands? Isabel wouldn't know until this was done. The phone was down. That granted her the freedom to use both hands on her body.

Isabel slid a hand down between her legs again. She didn't need to fantasize to get herself going. She was already on the edge, ready to explode from the first touch of her finger to her tender, wet folds. Sure, she was a little self-conscious. Dominique could tell her she was as fine as ambrosia, and it wouldn't help.

But perhaps her reticence—and the subsequent giving in—was what turned on Dominique.

She drew her finger up to her clit, sending a tremor through her body. The pleasure was almost too much. *I'll have to be quick. For my sake.* Too long, and the orgasm wouldn't be as strong. She only wanted to give Dominique her best.

A touch. *Shiver.* A stroke. *Tremble.* A dip of her finger. *Oh my God.* A hand grabbing her breast. *Yes!*

A faceless woman on the other side of the country, sitting in the dark and doing God knew what while Isabel brought herself to climax.

Had she remembered to turn on her mic?

It didn't matter. Isabel threw her head back, her hips rising into the air as her fingers made short work of all the sexual frustration accumulating in her body. When her orgasm finally hit her, it was a storm surging through her, consuming her entire being. Her gasp was louder than the hum of her desk fan, the groan following it threatening to blow out her mic. Assuming she had turned it on…

But her climax subsided as quickly as it arrived. She lay back in her bed, conflict swirling inside. *I really just did that. For a stranger.* She'd acted out a fantasy she'd never known she had.

And now it was no longer a fantasy. It was as real as the woman at the other end of her camera.

Isabel didn't wait for Dominique to give her an order. Legs still spread open before the camera, she let the bottom half of her face dip into view, then touched her hand to her lips, her tongue flicking against fingers coated with her essence.

"My Beauty." She could almost hear Dominique's satisfied chuckle as her response appeared on the screen. *"You might be a dirty girl yet."*

But as Isabel basked in her Mistress's praise, another message appeared.

"I'm going to log off now. You, however, are going to keep pleasuring yourself until you can't possibly take it any longer. Then you will repackage your soaking wet panties and take them back to the front desk at the Black Diamond Building. They won't know what's inside, but they will know where to return the precious package."

Dominique wanted her to send back her panties? The thought of shipping her used underwear to her lover on the other side of the country flooded Isabel with embarrassment.

But Beauty? Beauty adored the idea.

And Dominique wasn't done. *"You will also continue to touch yourself daily while thinking of me. Five minutes, at work, every day. Because we can't have you forgetting who you belong to. Now, what do you have to say, Beauty?"*

Still dazed from the sensations embracing her body, Isabel sent back the first thing to come to her mind.

"Thank you, Mistress."

For she was well and truly Dominique's now.

And it only made Isabel desperate for more of her.

Chapter Nine

"*I'm sorry, Mistress. I haven't had a chance to carry out my daily duties for you yet. I've had a very busy day.*"

That was the message that graced Scarlett's phone one fine afternoon as she sat in her office.

Beauty. My Beauty. How Scarlett longed to leave her office behind—along with her life, all her responsibilities—and spend the rest of the day with Beauty. Flirting. Teasing. Touching.

Because she couldn't be content with this online relationship forever. No, soon enough she would feel the need to be with Beauty in the flesh. Or at the very least, see her face to face.

For all Scarlett knew, she might have seen Beauty already. She'd camped out in the Black Diamond lobby on Friday afternoon, hoping to catch a glimpse of Beauty as she picked up her gift. It hadn't been a serious attempt to catch her, of course. Scarlett had only stayed in the lobby for ten minutes after returning from a meeting, and the place had been packed. She wouldn't have been able to pick Beauty out from the crowd even if she'd been trying.

No, Scarlett had simply been indulging in the fantasy, playing a game of *What If?* Spying on Beauty in real life would be a betrayal of her trust. Scarlett had already lied to her by saying she lived in New York, when in reality they lived in the very same city.

But it was all for the sake of privacy. Scarlett had too much to lose by trusting a stranger she met online. She needed to proceed with caution. She would continue to hide behind the veil of anonymity. Until she was ready. Until she was *sure*.

Of what, exactly? Scarlett didn't know.

She sent a message back to Beauty. *"The day isn't over yet, but time is running out. I'll be very disappointed if I have to punish you."*

Scarlett was tempted to follow up with a detailed description of the most wicked punishment she could think of, just to keep the little vixen on her toes. Instead, she set her phone aside. She, like Beauty, had her hands full with work. The crisis that Connect was in wasn't going to fix itself, and the clock was ticking.

Of course, there was an easy way to fix Connect's financial problems. After her lunch with her father, she'd put together a plan of action based on his recommendations. And like all things Phillip Black, it was pure, ruthless efficiency.

She opened up the folder that sat at the side of her desk. It contained said plans, outlined in meticulous detail. The social media team? Gone, folded into Black Diamond's social media subdivision. Customer service? Outsourced to one of Black Diamond's subsidiaries. All non—essential staff cut and team leads replaced with more experienced personnel where necessary. No more college grads running the show.

No more Ms. Diaz…

But Scarlett couldn't *gut* Connect like that. There had to be a solution that wouldn't lead to stripping the jobs and health insurance from more than a dozen people. She was determined to find an alternative.

Or perhaps she was simply delaying the inevitable.

There was a knock on her door, followed by Emmy's head poking through it. "Ms. Black? Your sister is here to see you."

Parker? What did she want? "Send her through."

Emmy nodded. "I'm going to grab a late lunch, but text me if you need me."

A moment later, Scarlett's sister appeared in the doorway. But it wasn't Parker. It was Bianca, the youngest of her sisters. She wore her waist-length blonde hair loose, framing her youthful face.

"Bianca. What are you doing here?" She'd never visited Scarlett at work before.

"Nice office." Bianca helped herself to a seat in an armchair by the window, inspecting the room as she did. "And hi to you too."

Scarlett got up from her desk and joined her sister, taking a seat in the opposite chair. "Let me rephrase that. What can I do for you?"

Bianca opened up her stylishly oversized purse and dug around in it. "Mom wanted me to give this to you. Here." She handed Scarlett a worn velvet jewelry box. Inside was a diamond necklace in an antique style. "She said she already talked to you about giving you this? Apparently, it's some family heirloom that Mom and Grandma wore at their weddings."

Scarlett narrowed her eyes at the necklace. Clearly, this was an attempt by her mother to guilt her into getting serious about her wedding plans.

All for a wedding that would never happen.

She snapped the box shut. "Tell our mother that I'd prefer it if she spoke to me herself instead of using you to deliver her backhanded messages. This is a new low, even for her."

Bianca gave her an apologetic shrug. "Sorry. I did tell her that, but she's been going on and on and on about how you keep dodging her questions about the wedding, and she managed to wear me down."

"I understand. Mom can be… persistent."

"That's an understatement. After everything with Parker, she's become obsessed with your love life. Mine now, too."

"Well, you can also tell her that my love life is fine." It was true. Scarlett's real romantic life was going swimmingly. Other than the fact that she and her lover had never even seen each other's faces.

But that didn't make their connection feel any less real, or fulfilling. As far as Scarlett was concerned, Beauty was everything she'd ever wanted. She hadn't looked at or thought about another woman in weeks.

Why would she, when she had Beauty?

"So things are good with you and Adrian, then?" Bianca asked.

Scarlett raised an eyebrow. "Sending you to deliver her

messages is one thing, but Mom has you trying to get information out of me too?"

"That's not what I'm doing. I'm just curious. I want to know what's happening in your life. That's why I agreed to bring you the necklace. It was an excuse to see you."

"You don't need an excuse to see me. You can talk to me whenever you like. You know that, don't you?"

Bianca nodded. "I know. It's just hard sometimes. You know, to talk about stuff."

"Is something the matter? Are you okay?"

Bianca scrunched up her face. "Ugh, you're just as bad as Mom. Nothing is *wrong*. I just wanted to catch up, that's all. I know we don't do that much, but…"

Scarlett felt a pang of guilt. "I know. And I'm sorry. I'm just so busy these days, between work and everything else."

"Right. Sorry, I shouldn't bother you."

Bianca started to get up, but Scarlett reached across and touched her hand. "No, I didn't mean it like that. Stay. I need a break anyway."

That was a lie. Scarlett did *not* have time for girl talk with her baby sister right now. But Bianca seemed to have something important on her mind.

"Tell me what's been going on with you. How's school?" Bianca was in her final year of college now. Scarlett didn't know where the time had gone.

Bianca sank back into her chair. "It's fine. I've been thinking about grad school, actually. Most of the schools I want to go to are out of state, but even if I get in, I don't think Mom will let me go. She and Dad won't pay for it, anyway. Not if Mom doesn't approve."

Scarlett couldn't argue with that. To say that Vivianne

Black was overprotective of her youngest daughter was an understatement. Bianca was old enough to drink now, and their mother still babied her. It didn't help that Bianca had been diagnosed with type 1 diabetes as a child, which had their mother convinced she was fragile as a china doll.

"You can't let Mom stop you from living your life. You should apply to school wherever you want to go. You can worry about dealing with Mom after you get in." Scarlett was well aware of the hypocrisy of telling Bianca to defy their mother. Here she was, living a lie, all for the sake of her parents.

But her mother and father had very different expectations of their oldest daughter than they did of Bianca and Parker. Scarlett didn't have the luxury of rebellion.

Bianca slumped deeper into her chair. "I guess. I just don't know how I'm going to convince her to let me go. She doesn't *listen* to me. She dismisses everything I say like I'm still a little kid. I keep trying to tell her things, but…"

"Things like what?" Scarlett studied Bianca's face. It was clear that there was something else on her mind. "Is something going on?"

Bianca let out a dramatic sigh. "It's nothing. You wouldn't understand."

Scarlett winced. While their age difference meant that she and Bianca had never been close in a sisterly way, Scarlett liked to think her little sister saw her as someone she could confide in. It stung to know that Bianca felt she couldn't trust her with whatever this was.

Not that Scarlett could judge anyone in her family for keeping secrets.

"I'm sorry," Bianca said. "I didn't mean that. I'm just tired of Mom's crap."

"Again, I understand. Mom has that effect on everyone."

"She's really been stressing me out lately. I wish I could be more like Parker. She takes everything in her stride, even Mom."

"She really does, doesn't she?" Bianca wasn't the only one who was envious of the middle Black sister.

"Well, I should let you get back to work. Thanks for talking to me. I appreciate it."

Scarlett gave her sister her warmest smile. "Any time."

She watched Bianca leave, unsure of whether their conversation had actually achieved anything. The girl was so hard to understand sometimes. The two of them were from different generations, and it showed.

She couldn't help but wonder what could be causing a rift between Bianca and their mother. While Bianca was closer to their mother than Scarlett and Parker were, that didn't mean their relationship wasn't a rocky one. Vivianne Black wasn't exactly the maternal type. She saw her children more as accessories than daughters. Sometimes, Scarlett felt like she was more of a mom to her sisters than their actual mother was. Sometimes, it felt like she was the one holding her entire family together.

She was carrying the weight of the Black family name on her shoulders. And it was getting heavier by the day.

Scarlett took the jewelry box containing the necklace and returned to her desk, shoving it deep in her bottom drawer. She had work to do. Pen in hand, she dove into her folder of plans again, cross-referencing them with Connect's financial reports, looking for something—anything—that could save her from enacting the plan she'd laid out. There was a solution somewhere. She just needed to find it.

But as she scribbled in the margins of the previous year's financial report, all that appeared were gouges in the paper. She dug around her desk for another pen, but the few she found were empty, too. And Emmy was at lunch, which meant Scarlett would have to take a trip to the supply closet herself.

With a deep sigh, she got up from her desk and left her office. She earned her share of sideways glances as she made her way to the supply closet, the worst of which she put a stop to with a firm look. Scarlett didn't require friendliness from her employees, but she did require respect. She was under no illusions about her popularity at Connect. She didn't care about being liked by those who worked for her. All she cared about was getting the job done.

Which wasn't easy, when the entire office was hostile toward her.

She reached the supply closet. As her hand touched the door handle, the door swung open. Someone barreled out of it, almost running into her.

Isabel Diaz.

"Whoops!" Her face was red and flushed, the heavy roll of drafting paper she held in her arms almost falling to the floor. "I'm sorry!"

Scarlett looked her up and down. "Hard at work, I see?"

"Just trying to get the new UI design finished before the deadline."

Scarlett nodded. But Isabel had already fled in the direction of her desk.

Hm. Perhaps I'm working her a little too hard.

As Scarlett returned to her office, a box of pens in her hand, she received a message from Beauty.

"It's done, Mistress."

Scarlett leaned back in her chair, a smile tugging at her lips. Beauty never failed to deliver, and right when Scarlett needed it. How she longed to have Beauty serve her in person…

Patience. Besides, even if Scarlett wasn't yet ready to meet Beauty face to face, she still had her ways of taking things between them to the next level.

Chapter Ten

More lights turned off in the office hallway. Already, Isabel struggled to see the notebook before her, but she wasn't in a hurry to turn on her desk lamp.

Instead, she stared blankly out the window at the dark Seattle skyline. The deadline for the UI redesign was fast approaching, but what she was facing inspired more dread than a deadline could.

Creative block. The bane of her artistic existence.

While Isabel had ideas in spades, none of them translated to the paper, let alone the screen. She had hoped that having the office to herself after the sun went down would jostle her imagination. *Oh, it did.* Instead of configuring a new desktop and mobile layout for Connect, however, she doodled.

For Isabel, 'doodling' was more complex than shapes and lines. 'Doodling' meant putting everything, every thought and feeling that haunted her mind all day, down on paper. More often than not, that meant people. Portraits of them, filtered through her creative process, but still recognizable.

Her current subject? The woman who consumed her every waking moment, and most of her dreams.

She didn't really know what Dominique looked like, of course. And while Isabel could still recall the lingerie she'd worn, and that striking red hair, she chose to focus on the slender shoulders and delicate collar bones that entranced her every time she closed her eyes. Perhaps the portrait she drew didn't even look like Dominique. But she was the woman of Isabel's dreams, and that was what alleviated the crushing sensation wrapped around her heart.

"... If he says he can't come, then he can't come, Mother."

Isabel's peace was shattered by someone marching through the office's main entrance, heels clicking on the linoleum floor. Scarlett Black, her phone glued to her ear and her mouth running a mile a minute.

"What do you want me to do about it?" The exasperation in her voice was barely contained. "I'm not Adrian's keeper. And you have to stop sticking your nose in our business. Sending Bianca to do your dirty work? Really?"

Isabel froze in place as her boss approached. In the dim light, it took Scarlett a few seconds to realize someone else was still in the office.

She gave a small start, but retained her composure. "I have to go. Something's come up. No. I said, *no*. Surely even you know what that word means."

Scarlett hung up the phone. *On her own mother? I would never.* If Isabel treated her mom like that, she wouldn't hear the end of it. And in multiple languages. Isabel's Spanish was limited to a few select phrases like *"¿Dónde está el baño?"* but she could understand her mother's curses clear as day.

She could only imagine what Mrs. Black was saying

right now. Then again, maybe the woman was used to her daughter talking to her like that.

Scarlett turned toward Isabel. She was dressed as if she were ready to go home, not come back into the office. Yet not even her sleek black coat could hide the body that only a personal trainer and dietitian could buy.

There I go, making assumptions about her again. But Scarlett probably did the same toward her all day long. That was if she even gave Isabel a second thought.

"I'm sorry," Scarlett said. "I didn't know anyone else was here tonight. It's quite late, Ms. Diaz."

Isabel leaned back in her chair. "I'm just working on the new UI design. I'm not finished yet."

"I suppose the deadline is coming up. But I thought you were moving to the final stage? Those drafts you turned in last week were more than adequate."

"What can I say? I'm not happy with them. My name might not be on the website, but I want the design to be something I'm proud of. Like I am of the old layout." *That's right. I actually* like *the current layout, Ms. Black.*

Scarlett pursed her lips. "I suppose it can wait another week. I'll extend the deadline for you."

"Oh." Isabel wasn't expecting leniency from Scarlett Black. "Uh, thank you. That would really help."

"I don't want you tiring yourself out. It's not good for your creativity, and we pay for that as much as we pay for your skills." Scarlett's eyes wandered toward Isabel's notebook. "That's a lovely portrait. Anyone I know?"

"No," Isabel stammered. "She's not anybody in particular." She closed the notebook, suddenly aware of how much the portrait of Dominique resembled Scarlett. Was it because both irresistible women had waltzed into her life at the same time, causing the two of them to fuse in her mind? She hoped Scarlett hadn't noticed. "Sorry, I was just doodling to get the creative juices flowing."

A small smile appeared on Scarlett's face. *Have I ever seen her smile before?* It was pretty. Like pale pink icing on a white birthday cake.

"Why don't you go home, Ms. Diaz?"

Isabel nodded. "Sure."

But when neither of them moved, Scarlett continued. "I should apologize for being so tough on all of you since taking over here at Connect. It's certainly not my intention to cause so much stress for everyone. I'm in an impossible position, having to balance Connect's profits while keeping everyone who works here and has made the company what it is happy. But that's not an excuse. I'm simply offering an explanation, because I know I'm not popular around here. I really do apologize."

Isabel held her notebook close to her chest as if to stop it from falling to the floor and exposing all her naughtiest desires for Scarlett to dissect. "People don't like change, that's all. There was a lot of change when Evan sold the company."

"Yes. I understand. I wish things could be more like they used to be, for the sake of all of you."

Isabel raised an eyebrow. "Do you? Because—"

"Yes, I do." Scarlett cut her off. "I have to get going. I have work to finish. Have a good night, Ms. Diaz. And I really did like your drawing."

Scarlett strode off to her office, opening the door with a flick of her wrist. She didn't look back at Isabel.

Was it because Isabel was inconsequential? Or was it because she felt that same current as well?

That subtle but undeniable charge of budding respect—and attraction?

~

"Sorry it's taken so long to reply," Isabel typed into her phone. *"I had a long day at work today. I only just got home. I'm beat."*

She lay down on her back on her bed and lowered her phone to her chest, closing her eyes. The latest album by her favorite female singer-songwriter played in her earbuds. The slow, ethereal melodies matched the folksy, lovelorn lyrics, lulling Isabel into a dreamlike state.

Songs about love lost to the wind... That was how Isabel felt, wasn't it? But instead of 'lost love' it was 'love never had.' Love had always seemed just out of reach for her. Now, it felt closer than ever.

Too bad it was with a woman on the other side of the country.

Dominique responded a few minutes later, the message buzzing Isabel's phone against her chest. *"I had a long day, too. What was so long about yours?"*

Isabel had no reason to hold back how she really felt, not with Dominique. *"My boss is a bit of a bitch. We're all overworked and hate the changes made in our office. I know I shouldn't put all the blame on her, but she's who I think about when I'm upset about my job. She's the one passing down the orders, after all."*

"That's unfortunate. But I thought you liked being bossed around?"

Isabel grinned. *"I do, Mistress. Just not like that. It makes me feel like my work isn't valued. It's hard to hide my imposter syndrome when I feel like I lucked into my position to begin with. She just makes it worse."*

As the woman in her earbuds lamented yet another great love slipping through her fingers, Isabel rethought her words.

"That's unfair to my boss, honestly. She's just doing her job."

She was starting to sympathize with Scarlett more and more. Maybe she wasn't the cold, heartless corporate suit that Alexis and the others made her out to be. Maybe Scarlett was just another person trying to stumble her way through life, like all the rest of them.

Isabel could relate to that. And she couldn't help but wonder what her boss was like behind the stone veil she wore. She had seen a glimpse of it earlier that night, when Scarlett had smiled at her. It had felt so genuine, and it had made Isabel's heart flutter…

But just thinking about Scarlett like that felt *wrong*. Isabel only had eyes for one woman. And that woman was Dominique.

"It's not really her fault that I'm in my position." Isabel continued. *"It's just that, all this change has me questioning what I'm doing with my life. I don't want to spend the rest of my days in an office, sitting behind a computer. I want to create. I want to make art."*

"I can see why that would bother you. You have an artist's soul, Beauty. I can sense it in you."

Considering Isabel spent her days designing app layouts for her corporate bosses, calling herself an artist was a stretch. But art was something that was embedded in her being.

It had been for as long as she could remember. She'd grown up feeling like she was different on some fundamental level, and she'd had to find ways of coping with that.

And art had been one of those ways.

For Isabel, it was more than just a passion. It was her refuge, her solace, the one thing in the world that made her feel like she was in her element. Art was simple. It was shape and color, form and texture and light, combinations of them all in infinite permutations. It made sense to her in a way that the rest of the world often didn't.

"What kind of artist are you?" Dominique asked.

"I draw and paint. Watercolors and oils, mostly. I just love to create."

"Which do you love the most?"

"Depends on my mood. Right now, I'd kill for a decent set of watercolor pencils. I haven't played with any since college. It feels like so long ago now."

"So why don't you pursue it? Being an artist?"

Isabel snorted. *"I don't know if you know this, Mistress, but being an artist isn't exactly a high-paying gig unless you get lucky. Nobody's paying artists in anything but exposure. I could go it alone and hustle, but I'm tired just thinking about it."* She let out a heavy sigh. *"You're older than me. Does everything have to be about selling your soul just to get ahead? Because that's how it feels right now."*

But as soon as Isabel pressed send, she regretted it.

"I'm sorry. I don't mean to be a bummer. I didn't mean to unload on you..."

But before Isabel could finish typing her sentence, Dominique's reply appeared.

"No. You shouldn't have to sell your soul. None of us should."

Both an answer and a non-answer. Somehow, it made Isabel feel a little better. *"I can't even draw much now at all. I've lost the spark that got me into college. Every time I sit down to sketch or paint, I just... everything is completely blank in my mind. All I think about is work, and my responsibilities, and how over everything I already am."*

"That's such a sad thing to hear, my Beauty. I'm sure you haven't lost the spark inside of you. Life has this way of crushing you down. It starts when we're children, doesn't it? We get put in these little boxes, assigned these roles, set on paths we have no choice in. Forced to conform to who this world wants us to be."

Isabel could understand that feeling. While it probably wasn't exactly what Dominique was talking about, Isabel had spent her whole life being shoved into boxes she didn't fit into. Everyone else seemed to fit into them just fine. But she never had.

"As for me," Dominique continued, *"my life was chosen for me since birth. I didn't get to explore hobbies and passions. Sometimes I wonder if there's an artist deep inside of me as well."*

Isabel began to reply, but Dominique was still typing.

"You know what? I don't want you to turn into me. You should make art. You should create. Do it for yourself. Do it for me."

Isabel hesitated. *"For you, Mistress?"*

"Yes. Draw something for me, and only me. When you're finished, show it to me."

"What would you like me to draw?"

"Anything you'd like. Whatever I spark inside your imagination."

As far as inspiration went, Dominique certainly sparked Isabel's imagination. Already, an idea was forming in her mind.

"I have to go soon," Dominique sent. *"I'm afraid I'm falling asleep."*

"Okay. You are three hours ahead of me, after all."

Dominique didn't respond to that. *"Are you available Friday evening?"*

"Yes. Why?"

"Good. Let's make a date so we can have some fun together. I know just the thing to give you the experience of having your Mistress right there with you."

She couldn't wait. But at the same time, a part of her wished Dominique was closer so they could have a real-life date. Isabel yearned to be with her Mistress in person, but it made her nervous all the same.

One day. One day, Isabel would get to meet the woman of her dreams in the flesh.

Chapter Eleven

As soon as the clock ticked over to 5 p.m., Isabel hurried home. *No staying late tonight. Sorry, guys!* Alexis wasn't thrilled that, once again, Isabel wasn't going out with the rest of their coworkers that night. *"This is what happens when people get significant others,"* her friend had quipped.

While Dominique was thousands of miles away, this budding relationship of theirs certainly felt real. Didn't Isabel check her phone every five minutes just to see if Dominique had messaged her? Didn't they both stay up late at night exchanging messages about nothing at all? Didn't she feel the giddy thrill of blossoming romance every time Dominique affectionately called her *"my Beauty"*?

She was falling for a woman whose face she'd never seen, whose voice she'd never heard. But in a way, the anonymity added to the thrill of the fantasy.

As soon as she got home, she threw some leftovers into her microwave. Dominique had wanted her to check in at six. While Isabel had left the office on time, it had taken her almost an hour to get home.

As she waited for her super-heated leftovers to cool, she opened Darkest Desires to see a message from Dominique.

"Are you ready, my Beauty?"

"I'm ready, Mistress," Isabel sent as she shoveled the hot food into her mouth, burning her tongue. *Thank God Dominique isn't here to see me like this.*

She blew on her food some more, scrolling through her phone as she waited for a response. When it finally arrived, it contained a link to a map location.

"Go to this address," Dominique instructed. *"What you're wearing right now doesn't matter. You're expected within an hour."*

Isabel examined the map closely. The address was one block from the Black Diamond Building.

You have got to be kidding. She had just come from there!

"I assume that's enough time for you to get there? I don't know where in Seattle you live."

"I can make it. Just finishing up dinner."

"I'd say 'take your time,' but time is of the essence, my Beauty. Besides, I'll be very sad if you miss your connection. I have so much planned for us. I've taken great pains to make everything perfect. Tonight, my Beauty, will bring us one step closer."

There was only one way to find out what that meant. And that was by moving forward.

As Isabel polished off her dinner as fast as she could, another message from Dominique appeared.

"Before you leave, pick a safeword and send it to me. I have quite the naughty night in store for us. I need you to know you have an out if you feel things are getting a little too... hot."

A safeword? Why would Isabel need a safeword if they weren't going to meet in person?

What did "too hot" mean?

She finished off her dinner before responding to Dominique's message.

"My safeword is 'inferno.'"

～

Trusting in Dominique's words, Isabel headed straight to the rendezvous point in the same clothes she'd worn to work. *At least they're cute. And warm.* Alexis had complimented her blouse and skirt earlier that day. Hopefully no one would notice the run that had formed in the pantyhose.

But who was Isabel expecting to run into? What did she expect to see? Certainly not an unmarked black car idling by the sidewalk, a crowd of people walking by and paying it no mind.

The driver got out as soon as he saw Isabel.

"Are you Beauty?" he asked.

How did he know? Surely Dominique didn't know what she looked like.

It must be because I'm sitting here gaping at the car like a confused fish. "Y… yes?"

"Excellent." The driver rounded the front of the car and opened the back passenger side door. "I have been instructed by Ms. Dominique to take you to your next location."

Excitement flitted inside Isabel's chest. *This is so dangerously fun.* She wasn't the most spontaneous of people. If anything, she was the opposite. She rarely broke from her mundane routine.

So why was she climbing into the car with a complete stranger? For all she knew, she was about to be kidnapped and taken across the nearest border.

Once inside, the driver lowered the privacy partition to inform Isabel that their destination was only a few blocks away. "Strap in, but don't get too comfortable."

A dozen possibilities raced in Isabel's mind as they looped around the next block. *A restaurant? A theater?* A hotel was next on her list, but she arrived at a five-star resort hotel before the thought was fully formed.

A message arrived from Dominique. *"Tell the receptionist that your name is Beauty Smith, and you're here under the reservation of Dominique York. They won't ask questions. They won't even ask for your ID."*

"What if they—"

"No questions. Just go."

Isabel was about to put her phone in her pocket when one more message arrived.

"I'm so eager for you."

~

The room was more spacious than Isabel had anticipated. As she flicked on the light, a single king-sized bed caught her eye. But the gorgeous view from the twenty-third floor quickly stole her attention, inviting her to peer at the city skyline and the airplanes soaring by in the distance.

I feel like I'm really in the city. Oh, she always had, but this was one of those rare instances when she had the chance to experience the full extent of what Seattle had to offer. A chauffeured drive through the city streets. A personal suite in a five-star high-rise hotel.

A boutique box awaiting her on the end of the bed.

How had Dominique put all of this together? It was one thing to be able to afford it all, but arranging for the help to deliver a box of whatever this was? Putting together all of these pieces, just for *her*? Isabel could hardly comprehend it.

And how did Dominique know Seattle so well? She seemed to be a well-traveled woman, so perhaps she'd spent time in the city. Besides, a detail like that didn't matter. Not when Isabel was living out the kind of fantasy that only existed in fiction.

"This is incredible," Isabel sent to her Mistress. *"All that's missing is you. I wish you were here with me."*

Apparently, Dominique didn't have time for sentimentality. *"Open the box, my Beauty. You can admire everything else later."*

Isabel set her phone on the bed and opened the large box lid. As she folded back the delicate tissue paper within, she imagined another set of lingerie underneath.

Instead, she found a black babydoll dress. It fanned out from the chest and didn't leave much to the imagination below the hemline.

"Put it on," was the message waiting for her when she picked up her phone again.

There was more than just the dress, thankfully. Another pair of panties that were almost identical to the last, and a bra that was more function than style, but Isabel soon discovered that function was optimal for a dress like *this*. As she ignored the Parker Black logo on the tag, she scrambled to put on the lingerie. It fit her better now that Dominique knew her true size.

The dress was next. It flowed down her body in a flattering way that accentuated her lifted breasts and added volume to her hips. Isabel smoothed the sheer black fabric against her stomach. The only reason she didn't panic about showing off so much thigh was because the box also contained a pair of knee-high boots that would steer any eyes in the right direction.

They were a little snug. Probably because Isabel hadn't told Dominique her shoe size.

"Send me a picture when you've finished dressing."

Isabel pulled her hair back into a ponytail and snapped it into place. She was quite pleased with her silhouette in the hotel room mirror. Pleased enough to show a hint of her cheek in the body shot she sent her generous Mistress.

It's like playing dress-up for my sugar mama. Alexis and the others definitely weren't doing anything this wild tonight.

"You are scrumptious as always, my Beauty. Now, open the smaller box."

Isabel had almost missed the small box inside the big one, barely larger than her hand. Was it jewelry?

She opened it up.

What in the world?

"Do you like your new toy?" Another message from Dominique. *"Go on. Tell me what you think as you put it inside of you."*

Isabel picked up the small, U-shaped vibrator. The box announced that it had 'State-of-the-Art Bluetooth and WiFi Capability.' Sure, she knew what it was. While she wasn't the most adventurous woman in the world, she'd heard of things like this before. She simply hadn't expected to receive one, gifted to her in a box like jewelry.

Because it wasn't just any vibrator. It was a remote-controlled vibrator. The kind girls like her were instructed to insert by someone who wanted to control their every desire.

She wants to know what I think? Isabel stood in front of the mirror, hiking up the short skirt of her babydoll dress. As she hit *record* on her phone camera, she made sure of two things.

First, that her face was still out of the shot. Second, that she didn't hold back the hiss between her teeth as she rubbed her clit to get a head start on inserting the bulbous end of the vibrator. The other end of the attachment perked up, sending more vibrations buzzing against her clit.

This seemed incredibly dangerous. Not to her safety, but to her sanity.

She sent the video to Dominique.

"Very good. Now, shall we go?"

∼

The privacy partition was up in the car as Isabel and the driver rode down another downtown street. That was good, because before Isabel could ask for mercy, the vibrator came to life inside of her.

"Ah!" She clutched the handle above her head, nearly bursting from her seatbelt. As the vibrations subsided within her, she received an expected message on her phone.

"Does it work? I hope it does."

Isabel took a moment to catch her breath before responding. *"The driver could have seen!"*

"Honey, where you're going, everyone's going to see."

"What?"

Suddenly, another jolt of pleasure surged through her. Her eyes clamped shut, and she dropped her phone to the floor of the car, her message unsent.

~

It didn't take Isabel long to realize what kind of club she had walked into. If the muted red lighting and the dark, sensual decor didn't give it away, the crowd did. Their outfits covered the entire spectrum of kink attire, from leather and latex to corsets and lingerie. Some brandished whips and riding crops. Others sported cuffs and ball gags like they were accessories. A few, like Isabel, were simply dressed for a night out.

As a new member, she was granted a tour of the club. From the basement level hosting an orgy room to the third floor that was reserved for private play and parties, the entire converted walk-up was a paradise of erotic pleasure.

She was starting to understand why Dominique had asked her to choose a safeword. *Things are definitely getting hot in here.*

What exactly did Dominique have in store for her tonight?

Left on her own, Isabel wasn't sure where to begin. She used her drink token on a cosmopolitan that was more cranberry juice than vodka. She was fine with that. The last thing she needed was to get too tipsy while she navigated a

BDSM club by herself. She wasn't a fan of noisy, crowded bars and clubs, but this one wasn't too loud or busy. Unlike at other clubs, the clientele here had priorities other than dancing and drinking.

Dominique had warned her before she went in that she was forbidden from using her phone inside, but there were ways around that. Drink in hand, Isabel ducked into the ladies' room and found a secluded corner where nobody would care that she was checking her text messages.

Sure enough, she had one from Dominique. *"Now that you're inside, use the earpiece I gave you. I'm going to call you, Beauty. That's how we'll dance around this nuisance."*

Her heart began to race. She was about to hear Dominique's voice?

Isabel pulled the Bluetooth earpiece out of her purse and stuck it into her ear, then let down her ponytail so her hair would cover the device. Almost immediately, a call came through her phone. Could Dominique read her mind from a distance, or was she just *that* good at anticipating Isabel's every move?

Is she here somewhere?

But the thought evaporated when Dominique's voice came through the earpiece. "Don't say a word. That would ruin the fun. Just listen."

Isabel frowned. *That voice...* Why was it so familiar? Why did she feel like she'd heard it before?

But as she left the bathroom, the music and sounds of revelry in the main rooms of the club made it difficult for her to hear the sultry voice at the other end of the line clearly. She had to concentrate to make out Dominique's words.

"I looked at the club's event schedule," Dominique said. "There's a girl-on-girl BDSM show tonight. That's why I wanted you there."

A BDSM show? Isabel stayed close to a wall as she sipped her drink, trying her best to appear casual. But inside her, curiosity burned.

"Go to the back room, where everyone is salivating over a pair of lady-kinksters. Find yourself a seat. In the back, the front row, between two horny people… I don't care. The point is to look but not touch. We're going to pretend I'm there with you, my Beauty."

Isabel combed her hand through her hair before realizing she was about to expose the Bluetooth device in her ear. It was just in time, because one of the bouncers dressed in all black nodded to her on his way by. After taking a moment to collect herself, Isabel caught the eye of a waitress who she meekly asked the way to the "show" in the back.

The waitress was more than happy to direct her. Clutching her cosmo to her shoulder protectively, Isabel entered the showroom. The music was much lower there.

Instead, the air was filled with needy moans from only a few yards away.

Was someone having sex? Right there in *public*? While Isabel knew it was allowed here, thanks to the generous tour earlier, she was still shocked to hear such unbridled cries of arousal.

But as her eyes fell upon the scene playing out, she realized that the couple on the elevated platform that served as a stage weren't having sex. However, what they were doing was just as erotic, at least in her eyes.

Before the watching crowd, a tall woman with bushy hair and a Venetian mask cracked her paddle against her bare thigh as she approached her partner, a petite, blindfolded beauty in a short pixie wig. The lucky woman was in the stocks.

Actual stocks! It's like something from a kinky fantasy. But Isabel didn't have time to stand around gaping. She'd been given orders, and her Mistress was waiting.

Isabel slipped along the wall toward a seat at the back of the room. At the same time, the masked woman raised the paddle. As it whistled through the air, Isabel sank into the large plush chair, her breath held. She didn't release it again until the woman in the stocks cried in what sounded less like pain and more like pleasure.

Heat shivered through Isabel's body, lips parting silently. She glanced around, self-conscious. But in a place like this, she didn't need to be self-conscious. Expressions of lust and desire, displays of sexuality, were everywhere.

Dominique still silent in her ear, Isabel watched everyone around her as they took in the show. There were singles like her, along with plenty of couples. Most were men and women, but there were lots of same-gender couples, like the pair of men sitting nearby. One of them was dressed in a fine suit and wouldn't have looked out of place at a business meeting, unlike the collared, bare-chested man at the end of the leash he held.

And it wasn't just couples. There was a striking trio of women sitting nearby, a tall, umber-skinned woman and a shorter pale brunette flanking a third woman with strawberry blonde hair, who seemed to be their submissive. *Two Dommes?* Isabel could barely handle one.

As she looked on, the brunette grabbed her submissive by the curls and whispered into her ear, a hand creeping up her thigh as she kissed her hard. Isabel turned away, her cheeks growing hot. It was so intimate, wasn't it? Watching people do this.

In public...

Touching each other...

Kissing...

And God knew what else. She was pretty sure a couple was having full-blown sex in the far corner of the room.

"Do you like what you see?" Dominique purred in her ear. "I've watched these two perform before. I'm so jealous you're there and I'm not. Or am I there? You never know."

Isabel's pulse sped up. Her gaze fell on the nearest woman. She sat a few feet away, auburn curls spilling around her face. She was alone, it seemed, her attentions solidly on the scene playing out on the stage. Every time the paddle met naked skin, the woman would sigh. And the way she wet her bottom lip when the handle of the paddle eventually found its way between the legs of the woman on stage was *art*. Isabel longed to sketch her. She longed for her to be Dominique.

She longed for any woman in the club to be Dominique, just so they could be together in the flesh.

"Can you imagine me doing that to you, my Beauty?" Dominique asked.

Isabel closed her eyes, trying to do just that. But for some reason, when Dominique spoke, she found herself transported back to her office. Perhaps it was because her Mistress's commanding manner made her think of another woman who commanded her life, at least during work hours.

But that was the only connection. Dominique's voice—with its sensual undercurrent, the sweet but subtle melody that played on every syllable—sounded nothing like Scarlett's.

"It doesn't matter whether I'm there with you or not," Dominique said. "It doesn't matter whether I'm touching you or not. Your pleasure is mine to command. I am the maestro of the moment."

A low hum echoed in Isabel's ear. Not a heartbeat later, warm waves of pleasure emanated from deep in her core, claiming her whole body.

The vibrator. So, this was it. The moment the maestro had been waiting for. Dominique was going to make Isabel come before an audience of people.

The thought made Isabel hotter more than the vibrations inside her did.

Their intensity increased. She jerked in her chair, her eyes squeezing shut as she held back the cry threatening to burst from her.

"Don't fight it, my Beauty. Fall into it. Embrace this moment, the here and now."

Isabel drew in a deep breath and opened her eyes again. She couldn't deny the power of the room. While those around her lost themselves in hedonistic bliss, she was helpless to fight the current sweeping her up with them.

Just as the woman on stage was granted release by her own Mistress, the vibrations increased within Isabel once again, sending shockwaves through her clit and deep into her center. She couldn't keep her eyes open any longer. Nor could she hold back the rising tide of pleasure inside her.

As it crescendoed in a frenzy, so did Dominique's voice. "Come for me, my Beauty. Let the whole world know that you're mine."

Isabel had contained herself for too long. Her head slammed against the back of her chair, her mouth open wide as ecstasy consumed her. She gripped onto the arms of her chair, holding on for dear life as she rode out the waves rippling through her body.

She swore she didn't make a sound. Yet half the room was looking at her when she regained corporeal consciousness.

And Dominique was beside herself in delight.

Chapter Twelve

The foggy skyline was the closest thing Scarlett had to a lover that Monday morning. It embraced the Black Diamond Building like an old friend, one who knew exactly how to kiss her dew-drop lips and nestle its promises within the crook of her neck.

Wouldn't it be nice if the fog brought her Beauty?

When had Scarlett become so sentimental? *It's Beauty who's doing this to me. She's the best thing that's ever happened to me, and I've never laid eyes on her.*

And yet, she felt closer to Beauty than ever before. Although Scarlett hadn't been to her favorite club that Friday night, she had lived vicariously through Beauty's awe and devotion. *I couldn't hear much. Not even the music.* It hadn't mattered. Scarlett imagined it. And when Beauty returned to the hotel shortly after her thrilling climax, Scarlett had been more than happy to offer her another round with the vibrator still inside of her.

What Beauty hadn't known was that 'Dominique' had a vibrator of her own. Scarlett hadn't come like that in years.

Certainly not with Adrian. Or any woman she had been with, for that matter.

And after both of them were spent, she'd given Beauty the suite for the rest of the night and the morning, revealing to her that there was one final gift waiting for her in the nightstand—a set of premium watercolor pencils.

The pure joy in her grateful reply left Scarlett feeling even more blissful than the orgasm had. Because nothing was sweeter than Beauty's happiness.

"Beauty," she tested to the silence in her office, to the city beyond its windows. "My Beauty." Ah, the way that name caressed her lips was divine.

Which must have been why the universe saw fit to smash her daydream to pieces.

"Ms. Black?" Emmy said from the doorway, prompting Scarlett to spin around in her chair. "Your father is on line one. He says it's urgent."

As the door closed again, Scarlett pushed a button to accept her father's call, putting him on speaker.

"I hope I'm not interrupting anything," he said, continuing without giving his daughter the chance to respond, "but we have a Code Bianca."

That caught Scarlett's attention. "Is she okay?"

"She's fine. She had to go to the hospital. Apparently, her blood sugar has been all over the place lately, and it dropped this morning. The doctors have assured me she will be fine and can come home soon enough, but it's your mother I'm worried about. She's absolutely hysterical right now. Could you go with her to the hospital? Try to keep her calm?"

"But I—"

"I know you're busy. Unfortunately, I'm stuck in an

important meeting all morning. Trust me, if I could take care of this, I would." His voice took on a serious timbre. "You're the only one I trust with this, Scarlett. I know I can count on you. Besides, it's family. Believe it or not, family comes first."

"All right. I'll take care of it." Scarlett hung up the call and gathered her things. The clock read 10:45 a.m. *I'm supposed to meet with Isabel at 11:30 to go over the redesign proposal.* It couldn't be pushed back another day, either. Scarlett had already pushed it back a week.

But as her father said, family came first.

Once she had gathered her things and logged out of her computer, she informed her secretary that she had personal business to take care of. Emmy knew what that meant. None of the other employees did, however, so Scarlett didn't bother taking her coat for a trip up the elevator. She didn't want the Connect crew to think she was leaving.

Scarlett left the office with confidence and entered the elevator with her shoulders sagging and her mind desperately wishing she could return to her daydreams. *Anywhere but here.*

The elevator lurched upward. Only in her family did she go *up* in the elevator from her office to go home.

~

"This place is absolutely dreadful," Vivianne spat over the phone. "You would never guess we have a wing named after your grandmother. The way they've treated your sister since she got here is a travesty to the family name!"

Scarlett lay across her couch, one hand holding her

phone up to her ear while the other rubbed her forehead. She could feel a headache coming on, which was why she hadn't bothered returning to work that afternoon. After heading into the hospital with her mother, they'd checked in on Bianca, who seemed none the worse for wear. They'd spent a few hours by her bedside while her mother fretted over her youngest daughter until both Scarlett and the doctors managed to convince her that Bianca was not, in fact, on the brink of death.

Her job done, Scarlett had said goodbye to her sister and headed home. As much as Bianca would probably appreciate having her "level-headed" sister watch over her, there was too much work to be done.

Besides, my mother will insist on fussing over her. Bianca was the quintessential Mama's Girl, and had been from the moment she was born. *I was a teenager back then.* Scarlett had been struggling enough with having a misbehaving little sister who was eight years younger than her. Then her mother had announced her surprise pregnancy, and Scarlett suddenly had *two* younger sisters.

The age difference was the main reason that she and Bianca weren't close as far as siblings went. But their mother? She still viewed Bianca as the baby she'd been two decades ago. And she treated her that way, too. She was probably sticking a straw in Bianca's mouth right now.

Her mother sniffed. "You can hear the person in the room next door. They won't stop crying. It's *very* disconcerting."

Scarlett bit back an exasperated sigh. "You're in a hospital, Mother. Not the Hilton."

"Yes, and we pay for amenities that will keep us calm

when we have to come here. Like decent walls. Clearly, something that has fallen by the wayside. I should like to talk to the hospital director about…"

There was a knock on the door. Before Scarlett could be grateful for the distraction, she remembered who she was expecting.

She peered through the peephole before opening her door, coming face to face with Isabel Diaz. And what a fine face that was. The faint flush on her cheeks was the same color as those luscious lips. And she hadn't worn her sweater up to Scarlett's floor. *Hello, arms.* They were nice, weren't they? The way they held that portfolio against her waist almost made Scarlett forget what was happening at the hospital a few blocks away.

"Sorry, Mom," Scarlett said. "I'll have to call you back. There's business I need to take care of."

She could almost hear the fire shooting from her mother's mouth. "How could you hang up on me like this? While your sister is in the *hospital?*"

"She'll be fine. And I have full faith that you'll handle it." Scarlett hung up and slipped her phone into her sweater pocket before greeting the woman standing in the hall. "Hello, Ms. Diaz. I'm glad you could stop by under such precarious circumstances."

She stepped aside so Isabel could enter. Delicate footsteps padded against the hardwood floors. As Scarlett closed her front door, something skittered in her chest.

Stress. It must be all this stress.

Isabel followed her into the living room, where Scarlett directed her to the couch, offering her coffee as she set her portfolio on the clear glass coffee table. Isabel declined.

"My apologies for the change of plans." Scarlett took a seat in the armchair catty-corner to where Isabel sat on the sofa. "I had some personal business to attend to."

"No need to apologize," Isabel said. "Things happen. Although I didn't expect I'd be coming to your apartment."

"You had no problems getting up here?" Scarlett had instructed Emmy to lend Isabel her swipe card, which permitted her access to the building's top floors. They were restricted to members of the Black family and their trusted staff.

"No. I had no idea you lived in the building."

"I'd appreciate it if you didn't tell anyone. My family likes keeping everyone and everything close together, but I try to hold on to some semblance of privacy."

Isabel nodded. "Everything's okay though, right?"

Scarlett removed her cobalt blue sweater. Was it warm in there? She must have turned up the heat without realizing it.

She draped her sweater along the couch. "My sister had a bit of a health scare, and it sent my mother into overdrive. Normally, my father would take care of her, but he's very busy today." Once Scarlett saw the concerned look on Isabel's face, she realized she would have to further explain. "No need to worry. My sister has type 1 diabetes. She had to be monitored this morning. It's more of a formality than anything for us to worry about, but you can't tell my mother that."

"I'm so sorry."

"About what? My sister, or my mother? Or my sister having to deal with our mother while in the hospital?"

It took Isabel a moment to realize she was allowed to

laugh at that. Scarlett found her concern endearing. She had taken Isabel's sensitive nature for naivety when she first met her. But working with her at Connect had changed that. Over time, Scarlett had learned that all her best employees shared one thing in common—their passion. They *cared*, in a very real way.

That included Isabel, who heard that her boss's sister was ill enough to go to the hospital and immediately fretted on her behalf.

It would be sweet if it wasn't so disarming. With everything that was going on, Scarlett had a tempest of worries brewing within her, and if she wasn't careful, they would all spill out.

"I'm sorry you've been so stressed out lately," Isabel said.

"Is it that obvious?"

"It has to be tough, that's all. Dealing with family and our office."

Scarlett felt compelled to brush her hair against her face. Was it to conceal the blush on her cheeks? To hide the fact that the brave front she put up was at risk of crumbling from nothing more than a few words from her young employee?

"It's difficult at times," she admitted. "My mother is a professional housewife, but she doesn't do the best job of it. It's always fallen on me to be the glue that holds our family together. I suppose that's what happens when your mother has you in her early twenties and then waits almost a decade before having the rest of her kids. Even with nannies around, some part of you is now their mother, too."

"That can't have been easy."

"Well, couple that with the fact I'm also the heir to my

father's entire legacy. He will never be satisfied unless I'm just like him." Scarlett didn't know why she was telling Isabel all this, but she couldn't stop. "I have to learn every angle of the family business, running it with the same ruthless efficiency as him. Which is exactly why he decided to test me by putting me in charge of a tanking startup that is hemorrhaging money because the man who founded it only ever saw it as his personal cash cow. Factor in the hostile employees who would rather see me dead, and…"

Isabel's eyes widened.

Scarlett cursed internally. She had just revealed that Connect was courting financial ruin. Because of course Isabel didn't know. No one did.

"Connect is failing?" Isabel stammered.

Scarlett sighed. The cat was out of the bag. It was better to tell Isabel the truth than to let her go tell all of her coworkers what Scarlett had said without context.

"It has been since before I came on board," Scarlett confessed. "Your magnanimous Evan Albright never cared as much about the business as you thought he did. He didn't care how much money he was wasting, as long as Connect grew. All so he could sell to a large corporation like mine."

"Yeah, I figured that out when he moved to Hawaii to live on a superyacht with bikini-clad models."

That made Scarlett chuckle. For all Isabel's sweetness, she could be refreshingly blunt at times.

"So you can also imagine what the books looked like to my father when all was said and done. That's why I'm here, Ms. Diaz. I'm my father's fixer."

She knew how it looked from the outside. Ruthless ice queen Scarlett Black went from company to company in her father's name, crushing them under her heel so they could be swallowed up by Black Diamond.

"I *don't* sweep into new acquisitions for the purpose of ripping them apart and selling them piecemeal. I do it to keep everything afloat. Sometimes, the answer to our financial straits is to sell everything off and fire all non-essential employees. But that's the worst-case scenario, and I always try to avoid it. Believe it or not, I want Connect to succeed. I don't *want* it to fail. If that happens, everyone loses their jobs. That's a heavy weight on my shoulders."

Isabel shook her head in disbelief. "Wow. I had no idea things were so dire."

"That's the truth of it. My father is putting immense pressure on me to fix everything. I've delayed lay-offs and department mergers for as long as I can, but he's not going to take it much longer. My family didn't get rich from supporting floundering companies. And corporate greed aside, the reality is that Connect's business model just isn't profitable as it is."

"I... I understand."

But while that may have been the truth, Isabel was clearly demoralized by the reality of the situation.

"I'm sorry," Scarlett said. "This must be hard to hear. I know that Connect means a lot to all of you. And I understand why everyone is hostile toward me and the changes I'm making. After all, I swooped in with my corporate bullshit, spewing it all over your progressive ideals. I don't mind if people in the office hate me. It's not the first time. What frustrates me is that I have to fix this company while my own employees stand in my way."

Isabel nodded. "I get it. And I'll do everything I can to

help you. Whatever you need. I don't just want to keep *my* job. I don't want *anybody* to lose their jobs. You're right about one thing. Connect is important to us. It's more than just a job. It's a family. We built Connect from the ground up, together. And that's what Connect is all about, isn't it? Community?"

She stopped short. Perhaps she was as surprised by the fervor of her speech as Scarlett was.

"I just think that's where some of the animosity is coming from," Isabel continued. "I believe in the mission of Connect. We all do. People are assuming that Black Diamond wants to tear it apart and turn it into something else, something that goes against what Connect stands for."

"That's not what I want," Scarlett said. "My focus is on making Connect thrive. Trust me, if everyone works *with* me instead of *against* me, I can make that happen. My goal is to put Connect's vision in the spotlight, but changes need to be made for that to happen. That was true under Evan Albright, too. You just didn't know it."

"But I'm guessing you don't want me sharing all this?"

"No. It might make things worse. Just know that I don't want to tear Connect apart. I don't want to fire anyone. I *won't* fire anyone. You have my word."

Scarlett could see the weight lift from Isabel's shoulders. "I'm glad to hear that."

"As for your redesign proposal..." Scarlett picked up the portfolio and handed it back to Isabel. "I don't need to see it. You've checked in with me every step of the way, and I've signed off on everything. I'm sure it's fine. Connect needs a fresh, modern update to the app to attract more investors *and* users. You work on attracting people to your vision. I'll handle the investors." Scarlett forced a smile. Not because she didn't have one to spare, but because stress often suppressed the warmer part of herself. "You do good work, Isabel. I mean it. Your talent and your passion show through in everything you do. I'm glad I've had the opportunity to witness that."

The compliment turned Isabel into a stuttering mess. *I suppose that's not surprising. She's in my apartment, on my couch, with me leering over her.*

But the designer's flushed cheeks and shy gaze didn't speak of discomfort. She didn't seem to mind Scarlett's gaze on her at all…

Scarlett cleared her throat and stood up to lead Isabel to the door. The sooner she got her out of there, the better. Because Isabel had a magnetic pull about her, one that spelled trouble for someone in Scarlett's position.

Stick to anonymous flirtations. She didn't need to pursue something with Isabel. Not with Beauty in the picture.

But the fates were mocking Scarlett that day. Because as she showed Isabel out of the apartment, something caught the young designer's eye.

There, on Scarlett's kitchen table, was the box from Beauty. The one containing the returned panties.

My trophy from our time together, even though we are apart. The lid was mostly closed. There was no way Isabel could see inside from that far away.

Yet she hesitated, tripping over her own feet as she crossed from the living room to the front hallway. Scarlett steadied her with a hand on her arm and asked if she was all right.

Isabel blinked. "Yes, I just…" She shook her head. "Never mind."

Scarlett urged her toward the door. "Take care, Ms. Diaz. I won't be returning to the office today, but I appreciate the hard work I know you're going to do."

Isabel left without another word.

Alone now, Scarlett went back to her kitchen table and closed the box properly. *This should be in my bedroom.* She had been careless leaving it there like that. What if Isabel had seen inside? It would be most unbecoming for their professional relationship.

And the last thing she needed was for her real life and the life she led in secret to collide.

Chapter Thirteen

"I don't *need* you here." No mother liked to hear that, but to Vivianne Black, it was kryptonite. Especially coming from her youngest daughter, who was currently slumped across her couch.

Vivianne continued to fuss over her like a mother hen. *As if she knows what that's actually like.* Scarlett kept her distance. She had learned a long time ago to not get between Vivianne and her current obsession.

"Mom, seriously." Bianca burrowed deeper into her hoodie and the throw blanket she kept on the couch. "The doctor said I could have gone home hours after I was admitted. That was *two days ago*."

Their mother scoffed. "Who is going to take care of you if you have an episode? I don't like you being here by yourself. You need to come up to the family penthouse, at least. Your old room is just the way you left it."

"I *know* it's how I left it! It's like a weird shrine of all the kid stuff I don't want here. You know, here in *my* apartment?"

Scarlett decided to intervene before her mother's feelings were irrevocably hurt, because a hysterical Vivianne Black was the last thing anyone needed right now. "She's right, Mother. Bianca has been surrounded by doctors and nurses for days. She needs some privacy to unwind. *Real* privacy. You'll only be a floor above her." She shared a glance with her younger sister. "I'm sure Bianca will have no problem checking in with you every couple of hours until she goes to bed. Over the phone, that is."

It took a few more minutes, but eventually, Scarlett escorted her mother out of the apartment, to Bianca's obvious relief.

"Someone should check in on her every so often," Vivianne said as they headed toward the elevator. "What if she falls ill?"

Scarlett rubbed her mother's back. "I know you worry about her. I live right across the hall, so I can check on her, too."

The doors chimed open. Reluctantly, Vivianne stepped inside. Scarlett didn't return to her own apartment until she was sure her mother really was heading upstairs.

As soon as she walked through her front door, Scarlett let out a sigh of relief. Finally, a chance to check in with Beauty. They hadn't exchanged more than a few messages in as many days. Between her job and her family, Scarlett's every waking moment had been consumed by her real-life responsibilities.

But her dreams, and those twilit moments before the sweet embrace of sleep took her, were dedicated to Beauty.

She settled into her couch with half a glass of red wine.

"I'm sorry I've been so preoccupied, my Beauty. Life gets in the way. How have you been?"

The three dots that followed seemed to linger for far too long.

"I've been well," Beauty finally wrote. *"And I've finished that drawing you asked me to do. The pencils you gave me helped."*

"I'm glad. Let me see it."

Scarlett sat back in her armchair and waited. She didn't know what to expect. After all, she had simply told Beauty to "draw something." It could have been a kitten. A self-portrait. A landscape painting of the British countryside.

And when the image appeared on Scarlett's phone, her heart stopped.

"I drew you."

Beauty's words barely registered in Scarlett's mind. She had known who the woman was the moment she'd laid eyes on the drawing. 'Dominique' lounged across creased sheets, naked body bared proudly, from her full nipples to the neatly groomed fuzz on her mound. *I've only shown her a hint, yet she remembers me so clearly.* But while the woman's physical resemblance to Scarlett was uncanny—even the parts of her that Beauty had never seen—that wasn't what resonated with her. The figure was sketched in pencil, grayscale, with one exception—her hair. Watercolor flames in an arresting shade of red danced and flowed down her body and onto the sheets beneath her. The crimson locks were so captivating that Scarlett almost missed the opaque veil that shrouded half the figure's face. Only two lips peeked out from beneath.

It's me. It's the real me.

It was like looking into a mirror that reflected her soul.

It was exactly how Scarlett saw herself in her mind's eye. The veil—it was everything she wished she could let go of. All her responsibilities. All her inhibitions. The woman underneath that veil longed to break free, like the scarlet flames leaping from behind it. They were everything she held inside, every part of her that she only let out for Beauty.

No one else in Scarlett's life had ever seen that in her. Not her family, not Adrian, not her friends or lovers. But Beauty?

Beauty *saw* her.

It took Scarlett a moment to realize there was another message waiting for her. *"What do you think?"*

"I don't know what to say. It's beautiful."

"So you like it?"

"I adore it. I'm simply lost for words. Beauty, you have no idea of the gift you've given me."

"No, I should be thanking you. You inspired this. You inspired me. After you told me to draw something for you, I felt compelled to create something magnificent."

It was undeniably magnificent. Such attention to all the little details, like the bow of her lips and the arch of her shoulders. Beauty had put her all into this picture. It dripped with imagination and poured with creativity. It was strikingly raw and vulnerable, just like Beauty herself.

Had Scarlett done this to a wayward artist? Had she become a muse?

"It isn't just my art that you inspire," Beauty wrote. *"Being with you is so freeing. When we're together, I feel confident in everything, from my desires, to my art, to who I am as a woman. I*

don't have doubts and insecurities. I don't have to pretend to be someone I'm not, or hide parts of myself. With you, I can just be."

Warmth swelled in Scarlett's chest. *"I understand, I think. I feel that when I'm with you, too. As you've probably guessed, Dominique is just a pseudonym. But she's more real than the woman I am in my everyday life. She's the part of me that I long to set free."*

Scarlett paused. Was she really ready to open up to Beauty like this?

She continued to type before she lost her nerve. *"The truth is, the version of me that everyone else sees is so different. You wouldn't recognize me if we passed each other on the street. Straight-laced. Dour. That's me. It's tiring. I spend my days—at work, at home—being whoever everyone needs me to be, all at the expense of my own dreams. But being with you has allowed me to live some of those dreams. Every moment we share is more precious to me than you could ever know."*

It was the most honest she'd been with Beauty since they first started speaking. It was the most honest she'd been with anyone, maybe ever.

Beauty's reply came swiftly. *"That's where you're wrong. Maybe I don't truly know you, or what you're going through. But I understand it. Because I feel it too. And I'm glad we can share in our dreams with each other, if only from a distance."*

Something stirred in Scarlett's stomach. Beauty's drawing alone was proof enough of her words. She knew Scarlett deeply, in a way no one else did.

So why were they still playing at this game of shadows and false identities?

Because Scarlett wasn't ready yet. She wasn't ready to

cast aside the veil of anonymity. And she didn't know whether Beauty was either.

But that didn't mean they couldn't be together in person. Face to face. Skin to skin.

Flesh to flesh.

Scarlett sent her message before she could regret it. *"I have something to tell you. I'll be in Seattle for business next week. I want to meet up with you, to express our desires in person. It's time. I can't stop thinking about you and what we could accomplish together. That means something. It means we should be together, even if it's only for one night."*

Beauty was typing. But Scarlett didn't wait for her to finish.

"It will be completely anonymous. I'll find a way. We'll keep the fantasy alive. Do you trust me?"

Beauty stopped typing.

Scarlett held her breath as she awaited a reply.

"I trust you, Mistress. I can't wait for you to touch me."

What Beauty couldn't possibly have understood was how much Scarlett yearned to touch her, too.

Chapter Fourteen

It wasn't Isabel's first visit to the BDSM club, yet she was far more nervous than last time. Tonight was going to be different.

Tonight, she was meeting Dominique.

It all feels so real now. Her Mistress had given her detailed instructions for their meeting, along with the gift she carried in her cross-body bag.

It was a masquerade mask, dropped off for her at the Black Diamond Building like everything else Dominique sent her. *"Tell me the color of your dress,"* she had texted earlier that week. *"I need to know what you'll be wearing so I can send you something to go with it."*

There was only one real option in Isabel's closet. No, it wasn't the black babydoll her Mistress had sent her last time. *I couldn't possibly wear the same thing twice.* Not for Dominique, the most discerning woman in the country.

Tonight, Isabel was dressed in a fitted purple velvet dress with spaghetti strap sleeves. Dangling from her ears were a pair of 'sapphire' chandelier earrings she'd bought at a thrift store earlier that year, along with the matte black heels she wore. She'd been nervous about what Dominique would think of her cobbled-together outfit, but when Isabel sent her a picture of the ensemble earlier in the week, she received a message containing only the word *"Beautiful"* in return.

And just a day later, Isabel had received the masquerade mask in the same shade of violet as her dress, only with gold trim.

"Mask, please." The bouncer at the front door pointed to Isabel's face. In her anxious state, she had forgotten all about it. She slipped it on and headed inside, paying the cover charge. Dominique had offered to pay it for her, but Isabel insisted on covering it herself. It was just one thing she could do to assert her agency over what was sure to be an exhilarating night.

She entered the main room. Everything was exactly like last time, except tonight, all the club's patrons wore masks. Some were Venetian-inspired like Isabel's. Others wore bandit masks, threatening to 'steal' away their targets for a night of erotic play. One woman simply wore a 'mask' of white face paint, with red lips and rosy cheeks. *She looks like Queen Elizabeth.* It was impossible to make out the woman's identity underneath it all.

Was there a better place or time for an anonymous liaison? The club was already dark and loud, and sexually charged was the order of the day. And the masks? They were enough to conceal the identities of the wearers, to maintain the veil of secrecy that defined Beauty and Dominique's relationship.

How had her Mistress picked such a perfect place from

three thousand miles away? The idea—the feeling—that Dominique was closer to Isabel than she'd said kept niggling at her mind.

But it wasn't surprising that a worldly, well-traveled Domme like her was already familiar with this club. And the calendar of events was on the club's website. Isabel had looked it up after the mask she'd received, along with Dominique's instructions, had left her with a dozen questions.

She could be here right now. Isabel glanced at an older woman sitting at the front bar, one bare leg slung over the other as she sipped her martini, a Venetian mask over her eyes. *That could be her.* Isabel knew it wasn't... but what if?

That was the wild game Isabel played as she went deeper into the club. She knew where to go. She knew who was waiting for her. Dominique had arranged everything in advance, including reserving them a private room on the third floor. If Isabel remembered one thing from her tour the last time she was here, it was that the third floor was for premier members, who could reserve a room to cater to their fantasies. All Isabel had to do was head upstairs and give her name to the hostess taking care of guests at the front of the room.

That was easier said than done. For one thing, Isabel had to wait behind a couple who could barely keep their hands off each other. She swore she recognized the man as a local sports star. Was the woman his wife? Girlfriend? Did Isabel care? Was she only trying to distract herself from her nerves?

What if she doesn't show up? Or worse. *What if she's not who*

I thought she was? This could have been one big catfish scheme the whole time.

"Can I help you?" A silky voice to go with the satiny mask on the hostess's face.

"I... I have a reservation," Isabel stammered. "It's under the name Dominique York. She told me to go ahead inside. She's..." Isabel had been promised she wouldn't have to show her ID to claim the reservation, but surely this woman had to verify her somehow. A club like this didn't stay in business while catering to Seattle's kinkiest fiends without ensuring their safety and privacy. "She is my Mistress. I'm sorry. This is my first time doing something like this."

The hostess offered her a reassuring smile. "Of course. Your Mistress has reserved the Marquis Room. I can take you there."

"Thanks."

Isabel followed her down a long hallway that grew increasingly darker the farther back they went. Rooms with names written on the doors—some subtle, some more obviously erotic—stole her attention, until she almost bumped into the hostess, who was stopped in front of a small door.

It read *The Marquis Room.*

The hostess unlocked it and showed Isabel inside. "I'll let her know you're here."

"She's here already?" Isabel asked.

The hostess didn't respond. As soon as Isabel was inside, the woman closed the door. Isabel was alone.

All she could do was wait.

The room was smaller than she expected. Small, but practical. A full-sized bed took up most of the space, the only illumination coming from dim lights on the wall that tinged everything with red. She could barely see her hand before her, but she could see everything on the walls.

Now she understood why only premier members were allowed to reserve these rooms. They came with real BDSM tools and implements, the kind the club probably didn't want strangers without social insurance to use. Isabel recognized some of the things neatly arranged on the walls, such as the paddles and crops. After all, they were the subject of so many of her fantasies, and she dreamed of the day that Dominique would use them on her. But what the hell was the thing with the rubber spikes on the side?

She wrenched her eyes away from them before they made her lose her nerve. Instead, she examined a petite bowl beside the bed. It contained condoms of various types and sizes. A small sign beside it said, *"Please be safe, men, women, and all folks alike."*

A friendly reminder that she was hooking up with a relative stranger. Because that was exactly what Isabel needed right now.

She sat down on the edge of the bed, sheets rustling beneath her, squeezing her knees beneath her palms. She would have played with her hair, but it was tied up in a tight bun. It was a look she rarely wore. It had taken her multiple attempts to get it right.

But Dominique had requested she do something different with her appearance. *"Go outside of your comfort zone. Wear less clothing if that does it for you. Or do something different with your hair."* The latter had won out.

Slowly, the seconds turned into minutes. Slowly, Isabel began losing her mind. Since no one was around to see her, she braved a look at her phone, but there were no messages. Then again, she had no service in the room.

Suddenly, the door handle turned.

Isabel's breath caught in her chest. She smoothed down her dress and sat up straight. She wanted her Mistress to behold someone ready to make her dreams come true.

Instead, it was Isabel who saw her dreams manifest before her.

Dominique.

The world stopped as she entered the room, a mesmerizing apparition in an emerald-green dress and heels. A Venetian mask obscured her eyes, and her lips and hair were so red that they outshone the lights in the room.

My Mistress. The Dominique to her Beauty.

She closed the door behind her and twisted the lock before sweeping toward Isabel on the bed.

Isabel's heart skipped a beat. "I—"

She hadn't heard a sound from the moment Dominique had stepped through the door. And she heard nothing now as a finger pressed against her anxious lips.

"No need to speak," Dominique said. "Unless it's your safeword. *Inferno*, correct?"

Isabel nodded. *Dominique's voice, low and smooth like smoke and silk...* She had heard it before, whispering into her earpiece in a noisy club. But she hadn't anticipated how arresting it would sound in person. Perhaps she should have, given Dominique's penchant for the dramatic.

As her fingers tipped back Isabel's chin and promised her the world, another woman came to mind.

Doesn't Ms. Black sound just like this?

No, not quite. Scarlett's voice was higher and more

clipped in its authority. Dominique's voice was soft. Deep. Secure.

Passionate.

"I have a gift for you." Dominique placed a small bag on the end of the mattress. "Close your eyes, my Beauty."

My Beauty... Hearing those words straight from Dominique's lips was enough to set Isabel's soul alight.

She shut her eyes. She wanted to show Dominique that she was ready to follow orders, no matter what they were. Besides, she trusted this woman whose touch was like silk, whose commanding voice reminded her of the latent desires lurking deep within her.

A satiny scrap of fabric wrapped around Isabel's face, knocking her mask slightly askew. Her fingers gripped the mattress as Dominique tightened the blindfold behind her head.

She stroked Isabel's hair with gentle fingers. "Hair as dark as night. I adore it."

My hair's not that dark. But Isabel didn't correct her. Her hair probably looked darker in this room, where anything that wasn't bright or neon was nothing more than a shadow.

"You may speak when your Mistress demands it. As I am now." Beyond Dominique's velvet tones was the faraway thrum of a bassline. Music was a constant presence in the club, and her Mistress's voice was but another instrument tonight. "Tell me you trust me, Beauty. That's all I need from you."

Isabel trembled, but not because she was afraid. Through her conversations with Dominique, they had learned each other's limits, both explicitly and implicitly. She knew that

Dominique would never do anything she wasn't comfortable with.

No, her pulse raced and her whole body quivered because her excitement had reached fever pitch. Every inch of her was ready for Dominique.

"I trust you, Mistress."

Those words took the last of her sanity. Isabel didn't know whether she fell backward onto the bed because she'd lost her grasp on the world, or because Dominique eased her down onto it. It didn't matter. Dominique was there to catch her.

All Isabel had to do was accept her fate.

She relaxed into the bed, offering herself up to her Mistress. Dominique positioned her spread-eagled, something Isabel was only familiar with from the videos and books she consumed when nobody else was looking.

How did she know? Drop by ephemeral drop, Isabel's lifetime of fantasies spilled from her mind and flowed into the farthest extremities of her body, consuming all her senses. Her fingertips were electric. Her head spun from Dominique's perfume, the scent of musk and spring rain enveloping her. Even though her eyes were covered, Isabel had the sight of her Mistress entering the room seared into her mind.

A soft hand ascended one of her legs, teasing the inside of her thigh beneath her dress. "You say you're not a virgin," Dominique purred. "But when I fuck you, you're going to feel like one. You've never experienced pleasure like this before."

Just those simple words made Isabel wet. She had been

ready, *waiting*, for so long now. When Dominique's hand disappeared, she immediately longed for it to return.

And when it did?

Isabel gasped.

Handcuffs clasped around her wrists. The little O-rings that she had seen around the sides of the bedframe were now getting their use. One by one, each of her limbs was cuffed to a corner of the bed. First, her wrists. Then, her ankles, but only after Dominique had stripped off Isabel's heels and panties. Dexterous fingers swept along her bare feet and sensitive toes. Somehow, it didn't tickle. It only made her shiver with delight.

Isabel had a feeling that Dominique was a mistress of extremes. Her touch was tender now, but in a few minutes? Isabel hoped she would be screaming in exquisite pain mixed with pleasure.

Bound, blindfolded, and silenced, she urged her Mistress on in her mind. *Kiss me. Taste me. Breathe me in. Sample me to your heart's content.*

Devour me until there's nothing left.

Slowly, Dominique pulled down the front of Isabel's dress, pinching both nipples with slender fingers. Then her lips replaced them, one after another.

Isabel groaned. But her groan was nothing compared to the sound she made when Dominique reached between her plaything's legs. It took her exactly one second to find Isabel's clit. The reflexive curling of her muscles to draw up her legs and bend her knees was foiled by the cuffs holding her ankles to the bottom corners of the bed.

She was helpless to do anything but whimper in fevered acquiescence as one, then two fingers entered her.

Dominique was gentle at first, testing her, making sure that her possession could handle her at her full intensity, before giving Isabel just that.

She bucked uncontrollably, overcome. *She hasn't even kissed me yet.* But Isabel didn't need a kiss. She needed her Mistress's mouth right where it was, pulling one nipple into its warmth before going after the other, tongue swirling, lips sucking. Isabel twitched and writhed as climax threatened her. Every finger inside of her was another excuse to rattle her handcuffs and thrust her useless thighs against the hand staking its claim.

But Dominique wasn't permitting her to come. She had already proved to be more than willing to withhold pleasure, and tonight was no different. As soon as Isabel began to shudder with an impending orgasm, Dominique withdrew her hand and pressed her wet fingers against Isabel's thigh.

"Stay right there, my Beauty." Dominique's weight left the bed. Isabel was left breathless—and bereft. Her need to hold Dominique against her was almost too strong to handle.

Anything could happen now. A kiss. A touch. A silent reminder that they were never that far apart, even at those times when three thousand miles separated them.

Instead, something hard and smooth touched her slit.

"I've been dreaming about doing this for so long," Dominique said. "Ever since I first saw your irresistible body."

Heat rushed into Isabel's core. *Is that what I think it is?* She had never done this before, but she'd fantasized about this particular aspect of lesbian sex many times before.

Dominique parted Isabel's lower lips with her fingers. "There's something about your suppleness that begs to be tested."

Those words tantalized Isabel's eager ears. She bit her bottom lip in anticipation of *it*, of what lay between her Mistress's legs. Although she had toys at home, using them on herself was a completely different experience from having someone else use them on her.

Especially when that someone had free rein over her blindfolded, bound body.

She pulled against both handcuffs holding her to the bed, bracing herself. But as Dominique entered her, she couldn't believe how easily her body welcomed her Mistress. Nor could she comprehend how good Dominique felt inside as she surrendered to her with a soft gasp.

Apparently, Dominique couldn't believe it either. "You're not my first lover, Beauty." Her voice was huskier than before, breathing life into every neuron in Isabel's body. "But you're by far the most satisfying to tease and taunt, if only because I can tell how badly you want me. You've been ready for me since the moment we met. That's what I think."

Another sweet inch entered her, drawing a long, needy moan from within Isabel's chest.

"But there's one question on my mind," Dominique crooned. "Just what kind of girl are you, Beauty? Are you a princess? Or a slut? Go on, tell me. Here's your chance to speak."

Isabel was torn between the physical sensations flooding her being and the tantalizing relief blooming in her subconscious. She had been waiting for so, so long to have someone understand what kind of girl she was.

"I'm a slut, Mistress," Isabel whispered.

Dominique chuckled softly. "That's right." She drove her hips forward, filling her completely as she grabbed hold of Isabel's waist. "You're my sweet slut. And now you get what you've always deserved."

Isabel couldn't respond even if given permission. Dominique's thrusts came hard and quick, her practiced rhythm honed down to a science.

No, not science. This was art, *music*. Magnificent, spellbinding music.

Dominique had no further words, let alone instructions, for her. The subtle dance beats beyond the walls matched the rhythm of the squeaking bed and the rattle of Isabel's handcuffs against their rings. She let it fade into the background, focusing on the sound of Dominique's breath, the feel of her Mistress against her and inside her as she strove to bring Isabel release.

Her climax was inevitable. What brought Isabel to her knees was how hard it hit her.

She made sounds that had never fallen from her lips before. She writhed against her handcuffs, wordlessly praising Dominique for being so attuned to her body's desires. As her back arched and she trembled uncontrollably, her Mistress didn't stop, only angling the strap-on so it not only matched the curve of Isabel's body but hit her in just the right spot, sending her pleasure soaring even higher.

God, it was almost too much!

But nothing was too much with her Mistress, who

remained inside of her long after her orgasm passed. As soon as Isabel caught her breath, a pair of delicious lips came for hers.

Their first kiss. And it was *after* the foreplay and main event.

No, it *was* the main event. Still bound to the bed, Isabel rose into Dominique's hungry, aching lips, a desperate murmur welling from her chest as her Mistress consumed her. It was all Isabel could do not to lose herself entirely in the other woman. Dominique tasted like cinnamon and chocolate and red wine. She felt like a summer breeze brushing against Isabel's weary body.

And when she pulled away, it was like a sunset that crowned a summer horizon—it stole her breath, but it was over much too soon.

One by one, each of Isabel's limbs was freed from their restraints. Dominique encouraged her to sit up with a gentle hand before lifting the blindfold from her face, suggesting to her that she hold onto it as a keepsake of their time together.

But before Isabel's eyes could adjust to the light so she could behold Dominique in all her glory again, the woman turned around and prepared to leave, her strap-on returned to a bag that now hung at her side.

"Wait…" Isabel protested.

Dominique looked back over her shoulder. "I have to go, my Beauty. I adored spending this night with you. I can't wait to do it again."

"But—"

"I'm sorry, but it's for the best. If you need anything, you know how to reach me."

Dominique reached for the door handle. Her red wig was slightly askew now, giving Isabel a glimpse of the hair underneath.

Svelte. Silky. Brown.

Instantly, Isabel was reminded of someone else. Someone she also felt inexorably drawn toward.

In the afterglow of such a heady night with Dominique, all she could think about was Scarlett Black.

Chapter Fifteen

"*I can't stop thinking about you, Mistress. I can't stop thinking about what we shared.*"

Isabel was supposed to be responding to all the work emails piling up in her inbox. She wasn't paid to flirt on her phone, after all. Yet here Isabel was, struggling to stay on task.

"*You consume my thoughts like no one ever has before. I know I'm not as experienced as someone like you, but I just know that nobody could ever compare to you.*"

She almost regretted accidentally quoting Sinead O'Connor. Almost. But the sentiment had been too accurate.

Isabel was falling in love with a shadow.

"*Please tell me we can meet again soon. My need for you is growing like you can't believe.*"

Another shadow soon appeared next to her.

"Hey," Alexis said. "Are you off in La La Land again?"

Isabel turned off her phone's screen and shoved it in her lap, face down. "Nope. Perfectly behaved over here."

"Mmhm." Alexis grabbed one of the nearby rolling chairs and sat down next to her friend. "I don't believe you. You've been acting super weird lately. And it's been even worse this week. Even Ned has noticed and has been gossiping about it. Now, tell me what's going on so I can correct him the next time he insists you must be terrified about the state of your job."

Isabel laughed uneasily. "It's nothing like that. Things are going well in that department." Since the meeting in Scarlett's apartment, Isabel's working relationship with her boss had changed. Now, Scarlett seemed to trust her enough to not feel the need to micromanage her. Once or twice, she'd even asked Isabel for her opinion on important matters relating to Connect.

But Scarlett hadn't been in the office much lately. Isabel had incorrectly assumed it had to do with Scarlett's family, but a memo had gone out earlier that week that Scarlett would be "meeting with important shareholders, so please keep all public areas neat and tidy."

"Sooo, what's up?" Alexis said. "Are you on drugs? Because I want what you're having."

Isabel bit back her words by chomping down on her lip. That only made things worse. Alexis was perceptive enough to know that Isabel was hiding something.

"It's that woman, isn't it?" she asked with knitted brows. "The one you're talking to online."

There was no point hiding it any longer. Pretty soon, Alexis would figure out that her friend's lover was more than just some casual online fun.

Isabel nodded. "Things are going well between us. In fact…" Oh, to hell with it. She needed to get this out! "She came to town for business last weekend. We met up. And, um... I can confirm that she's a real person and not a catfish looking to scam me out of my hundreds."

Both Alexis's brows unknitted to fly up her forehead. "No way. You two banged?"

Isabel shushed her loudly, her face growing hot. "Could you keep it down?"

"Sorry. I guess I'm a bit shocked. Isn't that out of character for you? I mean, you're not one to meet up with strangers from the internet. That's more my poison."

Isabel giggled. Her phone almost slipped out of her lap, but she caught it at the last second. "What can I say? I've been feeling adventurous lately. Besides, we don't all have a million potential lovers waiting for us on Tinder."

"Who said anything about Tinder? I'm picking up guys on Reddit now."

Isabel's face fell. "Please love yourself, Lex."

"At least you know what you're getting with them. Besides, not all of us are lucky enough to attract hot, rich lovers from New York. Some of us have to make do with 'Cameron the tech bro.'" She patted Isabel's arm. "I'm glad that things are going well for you. Maybe this woman is good for you, after all. You do seem more confident lately. More comfortable in your skin."

She's right, isn't she? Isabel had really come into her own since she started talking to Dominique.

If only she didn't make me think of my boss.

There was a time, when Isabel was in her bed on the brink of sleep, when she wondered if Scarlett and Dominique were the same person. But that was ridiculous.

For one thing, Dominique lived in New York. Plus, Scarlett was straight and engaged to a man.

"She might be changing me a bit. No, it's more like she's bringing out parts of me I've always been too afraid to let out. It's not just about sex, you know. There's so much more to her. She has me drawing again. I'm suddenly infused with so much inspiration that it's like I can't make my pencil stop once I'm home. I even forgot to eat dinner last night! I think..." If she admitted it out loud, it would make everything real. Was Isabel ready to face that? "I think I'm feeling more than lust for her now. I think I might be falling in *love* with her."

Alexis sat back. "Whoa. That's the big time."

Yeah... Isabel realized how preposterous it sounded the moment she said it. How could she love someone whose name she didn't know, whose face she'd never seen clearly?

I'm sure she's beautiful. But was the anonymity still worth it? It had been thrilling at first, had added to the mystique of their torrid encounters. But what was between them went beyond kink now. While it had become a staple of their relationship, she wanted more. She wanted that pure, unadulterated intimacy that came from knowing someone inside *and* out.

But before Isabel could negotiate her own feelings with herself, Scarlett reappeared in the office, stopping purposefully by Isabel's desk.

"Ms. Diaz," she said, still in her thick coat and scarf. "Has the new UI gone live on the test site yet? I was hoping to beta test it before my meeting in half an hour."

"Oh!" Thank God, someone was here to distract Isabel from thoughts of Dominique. "Yes, Ms. Black. I forwarded it to you half an hour ago." It had been the last thing she did before she started chatting with Dominique. "The comment boxes in the margins aren't part of the final version, don't worry. They're for you to leave your thoughts. Let me know when you're done and I'll take a look at the feedback. Unless you wanted to meet about it?"

Scarlett's subtle smile grew. "I don't think that will be necessary, Ms. Diaz. I'll go look at it now."

Once her flurry of footsteps disappeared into her corner office, Alexis turned back around in her chair, one eyebrow now reined in while the other remained on her forehead.

"What was that about, hm?" she asked.

"What do you mean?"

"You know. Getting cozy with the boss? The woman who is single-handedly driving this place into the ground and will probably fire us all as soon as she has the chance?"

"I think you have it all wrong. Scarlett isn't like that at all."

"*Scarlett?*"

Whoops. I might as well own it. "Yes. You know, I think people are being too hard on her. She seems to really care about the success of the app. Believe it or not, you can be a capitalistic heiress *and* want to take care of your workers. Just because she isn't fanatical about the message of the app doesn't mean she wants us out on our asses."

"Wow. You sound like her little lackey already."

"Don't do that, Lex."

"No. It's fine." Alexis stood up. "Good luck with everything you've got going on, Miss Cloud Nine. Let me know how things go. I've gotta get back to my desk now that the boss is here and glaring at everyone with that fake smile of hers."

Isabel couldn't disagree with that. She had seen Scarlett's real smile, and it was nothing like the one she occasionally wore at work. It was just as reserved, but it was warm, sweet, soft…

She swatted the butterflies in her stomach away. There was only one woman who commanded her fantasies, her heart. And Isabel was still waiting for a response from her.

She picked up her phone and checked her conversation with Dominique.

She had been left on read.

She frowned. It had only been a few minutes. But Dominique hadn't even acknowledged the message. No reaction, no reply. Suddenly, Isabel was questioning her newfound confidence.

Had she come on too strong? What if Dominique wasn't that into her after all? What if she had been lying about being single, or about who she was?

What if had no intention of making someone like Isabel her girlfriend?

What if?

Chapter Sixteen

Scarlett took a deep, meditative breath before stepping out of the elevator.

Here we go.

Once a month, the Black family met up for dinner. That was one of the ironic things about her family. Even though all three daughters lived a floor or two down from the penthouse where they grew up and where their parents still lived, it took an act of God—or in this case, Vivianne Black—to get everyone at the same place at the same time.

Can you blame any of us? Even their father was often 'too busy' to sit down to dinner with his family. Parker, the middle child, had her own business to oversee, and a relationship to occupy her time. As for Bianca? She was a spoiled girl in her early twenties. She would rather party with her friends or flirt with boys than spend time with her family.

But they were all here, in the restaurant on the fourteenth floor of the Black Diamond Building. Every month, the Black family booked a private room in the back, and every month Scarlett dreaded asking Adrian to join her. Because he always said no now.

That was the question in Vivianne's eyes the moment Scarlett walked through the door. She was the last to arrive. Her parents were already well into their drinks at the head of the table. Next to their mother, Bianca sat, fiddling with her phone. At the other end of the table were Parker and her girlfriend Julia, a young woman who spent most of her days at a cat rescue.

Scarlett liked Julia, if only because she'd had the guts to go toe-to-toe with their mother the very first time they met. Something had happened between then and now to mellow Vivianne out when it came to Parker's relationship. Was this a sign that their mother was now more open to her daughters being on the gayer side of the Kinsey scale?

No way. If any of us can have a girlfriend, it's Parker. Scarlett lived on another level of expectations.

"Scarlett! Where in the world is Adrian this time?" Not even a hello. All her mother cared about was fussing over the future son-in-law who would never be.

Scarlett draped her sweater over the back of the chair next to her father. "He sends his regards, but he's busy with work. Banking never sleeps."

Her father snorted. "I have it on good authority that it sleeps after five p.m."

But his wife didn't share his humorous disposition. "We haven't seen him in *so* long. I'm starting to think that he's seriously ill. Or that there's something going on between you two."

Their personal waiter appeared to take Scarlett's order, which had been exactly the same for the past six months.

But that only granted her temporary respite from her mother's interrogation.

"I know he's alive because I was talking to his mother in the salon earlier this week. Oh, did I tell you that Betty Holt has fully embraced her gray hair? I should say white. *Stark* white. But she looks beautiful. You should see it, Scarlett. Invite us to dinner with you and Adrian so you can see it."

"Mom." Scarlett barely had a chance to pull her napkin across her lap. "Can we not tonight? I've had a long week at work and want to relax. Adrian's not coming. That's all there is to it."

"But—"

Phillip shot his wife a look. "When they're married, you can harass them all you want. Right now, Adrian belongs to the Holts first and foremost."

"That's just it, Phillip! They *still* haven't set a date for the wedding. It better happen *soon* if I am to get grandchildren…"

Scarlett tuned her out. *This is why I haven't told her the truth, told anyone the truth.* So much rested on Scarlett's shoulders. From the moment she got her first A in school, her destiny was to not only take over the company one day, but to be the perfect heteronormative empress of the Blacks' financial nation.

Chairperson. Wife. Mother. She was destined to be the woman who had it all.

But Scarlett had never had the chance to figure out who she was. Since hitting puberty, her mother had pushed her toward every good-looking boy. And the kicker? Scarlett had liked a lot of those boys. That had never been the question.

But she'd always liked girls, too. She would never forget the first time she saw a Paula Abdul video or witnessed Selma Blair on the big screen. However, her interest in women had never been allowed to flourish. She'd buried it deep in an attempt to forget about it, because it reminded her of everything she was never allowed to have for herself, simply because of who she was.

"Are you even listening to me?" Her mother was still talking. "You're almost forty, Scarlett. Your womb is about to shrivel up—"

Scarlett's hands curled into fists under the table. "This conversation is *not* happening." Her mother could never let a single dinner go by without sinking her teeth and claws into one of her daughters. *I'm not martyring myself for the monthly grilling this time.*

Sensing this, Vivianne set her sights on her middle child. "How are things with *you*, Parker?"

Scarlett's sister—sporting short bleached hair and a pantsuit—was more fascinated with her minestrone than anything her mother had to say. "Things are well with me, Mother. Thank you for asking."

Vivianne sniffed at her daughter's sarcastic response. "And how about you... Julia?" That pause before her name was almost too intentional, even for Vivianne. "Are the cats doing well?"

Parker let out a snort of amusement. Scarlett stifled one of her own. Even their mother's attempts at being cordial came across as ridiculously patronizing.

Julia nodded. "Things down at the shelter are great. We've just taken in twenty kittens from one of the shelters over in Spokane. They had a—"

"Have you two decided to get married yet? How about kids?"

Julia's mouth gaped open mutely. Scarlett merely shook her head. Apparently, the fact that Parker was in a relationship with another woman did not absolve her of her womanly duties in her mother's eyes.

"We have *not* talked about that yet," Parker said. "Not with any sincerity. We've only been living together for a few months."

Her mother huffed. "Well, at least I have Scarlett to give me the wedding of my dreams soon."

Scarlett gritted her teeth. *I could tell them all right now.* About Adrian. About Beauty.

Sweet, sweet Beauty.

Scarlett hadn't thought of anyone since the past weekend. She barely remembered that Adrian existed. There was only Beauty on her mind.

Beauty, who made her feel things she'd never felt before.

Beauty, who had asked to see her again.

Beauty, who clearly wanted more.

That frightened Scarlett. And she didn't know if it was because it was too much, too soon, or because she was afraid of the repercussions if she followed her heart for the first time in her life.

Because her mother was right. Scarlett was almost forty. She was old enough to make decisions for herself.

But until that point in her life, she'd had so many choices made *for* her that she almost didn't know how to ask for what she wanted—let alone take it. She made all these weighty decisions on a daily basis—at work, for her family.

Yet she couldn't make this single decision for herself.

No, it wasn't Beauty's intensity that was pushing her away. Or the fact that Beauty lived in Seattle and was deliriously like someone a little closer to home to Scarlett.

I've been lying from the very beginning. Not just about where I live. About who I am. Dominique was a woman who took life by the horns and brought it to its knees. Scarlett Black? She was so afraid of challenging the fate cast upon her that she couldn't even look the bull in the eyes.

So here she was, engaged to a ghost, playing at the perfect life.

Dominique was a lie. But not as big as the lie Scarlett was living.

Scarlett didn't say much throughout dinner. Not even to her sisters who, in her defense, did not say much to her either. All Scarlett had the energy for was deflecting her mother's comments. And the best way to stay under the radar was to not say anything at all.

Mercifully, dinner that night didn't descend into a verbal brawl, which wasn't uncommon when it came to their family dinners. Not that Scarlett stuck around for the entire thing. She left dinner as soon as she had the opening. Her plate clean and her water gone, she said the obligatory farewells to everyone and apologized for having to leave early. Vivianne wasn't happy, but she was distracted by the fact that Bianca had gotten up to go to the bathroom five minutes ago and hadn't yet returned.

And it was Bianca who Scarlett bumped into in the hallway on her way out.

"Can I talk to you for a second?" she asked.

Scarlett had been so focused on getting out of there that

she was taken aback by her sister's request. "Of course. What's going on?"

Bianca hesitated.

"Is it Mom?" Because it always was. And Scarlett had sensed some tension between them during dinner. *More tension than usual, that is.* It wasn't a family dinner if Vivianne Black didn't get on everyone's nerves, even those of her favorite daughter.

Bianca started to speak, then shook her head. "It's not about Mom. Not really…"

Scarlett frowned. What was going on with Bianca lately? It was clear she had something on her mind.

But what she said next was completely unexpected. "I was just wondering when you're going to tell everyone you're not going to marry Adrian."

Scarlett was too shocked to gasp. "What?"

"Yeah, I figured it out. This wedding is never going to happen. You two are over."

Fix this, Scarlett. The truth couldn't come out now, not yet. Not like this. "What are you talking about? Adrian and I are fine."

Bianca rolled her eyes. "Come on. Don't treat me like I'm an idiot. I'm smarter than everyone thinks."

Scarlett's bag almost slipped from her sweaty fingers. *How the hell do I fix this?* "I told you. Nothing's wrong. Adrian is a busy man, you know. He can't come to every…"

But the look on Bianca's face told her that she didn't believe a word coming out of Scarlett's mouth.

"Fine." She lowered her voice. "Yes, we're over. We've been over for a while now. How did you know?"

Bianca shrugged. "Like I said, I figured it out. It wasn't

hard. Mom won't stop going on and on about how you *still* haven't set a date for the wedding, and you refuse to even talk about it. Plus, the few times I've seen you and Adrian together lately, there's no spark there. At first, I thought you were just going through a rough patch, but it's obvious now. You don't love him anymore."

Scarlett sighed. There was no point in keeping it all in any longer. "It's true. We fell out of love some time ago. We've both moved on."

"I'm glad you admitted it. That's the first step to finally telling Mom and Dad." Bianca put her hands on her hips. "Because you know they're going to find out, right?"

"I know. And I'm working on it. Just keep this to yourself, will you?"

"Sure. Just warn me before you break the news, okay? I want to be prepared for the fallout. 'Cause it's gonna be massive, and Mom is gonna *freak.*"

With a flip of her hair, Bianca returned to the family's private dining room, leaving Scarlett standing dumbstruck in the middle of the hallway. As the waiter gently pushed by her, she tried to shake the intrusive thoughts that had wormed their way into her head.

Beauty isn't a ticket to freedom. She's your death knell.

The thing about intrusive thoughts? One couldn't simply shake them off.

Not even Scarlett Black.

Chapter Seventeen

Another late night at work. While Isabel was getting used to the grind that the corporate takeover of Connect had brought, that didn't make it any easier.

Especially with everyone feeling the crunch.

"It's Friday," she heard Connor bemoan from all the way across the room. "Freakin' Friday night, and we're all stuck here, doing work for something we don't even believe in anymore. How is this fair?"

It's not fair, but it's how it is. Isabel was one of the first to parrot "life's not fair" whenever her coworkers had a commiseration party in the breakroom, but her matter-of-factness did *not* endear her to her coworkers.

The difference between them and me? I still believe in Connect. But that didn't mean Isabel wasn't suffering as much as the rest of them. She was running on just five hours of sleep. Plus, her coworker was right. It was Friday. Not only were they not out at happy hour together, but they'd be lucky to make it home with enough time to shower and unwind before the night was over. Some of the older employees had kids, never mind pets that needed walking and feeding.

But it was all hands on deck. Scarlett had imposed a firm deadline for the prototype of the new app so that everything would be ready for an upcoming meeting with potential investors. Apparently 'investors' was now a dirty word in the office. Isabel didn't understand it. Even when they were a plucky startup, they had courted and recruited investors.

Isabel slipped on her headphones, smooth melodies playing through them to drown out the sounds of the office. *I can't get dragged down by their negativity.* She was feeling overwhelmed enough as it was. Since that night at the club with Dominique, she hadn't heard back from the woman who had changed her life so much in so little time.

I still can't believe it. The club. The blindfold. Dominique, in the flesh.

And now, nothing.

Isabel knew that her online lover had a lot on her plate. But ghosting her? That wasn't like Dominique.

Was it?

"Ugh, can you believe this crap?"

Isabel slid off her headphones, turning to see Alexis slumped in the seat next to her, her eyes bloodshot from staring at a screen all day. *All damn week, most likely.* Everyone was looking a bit ragged. Some more than others.

"You guys are here late too, huh?" Isabel asked.

"Of course. Her Majesty has the social media team completely revamping everything from Facebook to Twitter. Oh, did you hear? As of this week, we're ditching Instagram for TikTok, so yours truly has been fidgeting with filters and algorithms on yet another site." Alexis groaned. "This whole time I thought I'd get to pretend that TikTok doesn't exist. It's making me feel *old*, and I'm not even 30 yet. It's too new to have been a part of my curriculum, so I'm learning everything from scratch."

"Isn't that part of your job, though? You've got to stay on top of the latest social media sites, right?"

"Yeah, whatever." Alexis sighed. "I'm just so damn tired. Doesn't help that the team decided I should be the 'face' of the account, mostly because I'm a woman."

"How do you even advertise Connect on TikTok?"

"What do you think our meetings this week have been about? Doesn't help that Tzarina Black won't let us leave until we have a plan mapped out so we can enact it starting Monday morning. Ned's in there right now, crossing his fingers that what we've put together is good enough for her. I told him that was a fool's errand." Alexis shook her head. "Ever since she took over, we've been working double for fewer rewards. At some point, there's gonna be a revolt. Why work ourselves to the bone for a sinking ship? I'm already looking for another job."

While Alexis could do whatever she wanted in regard to her professional and personal lives, Isabel was getting tired of the constant complaining. "You sure you're not just mad about having to work for once?"

Alexis rolled her eyes. "Oh, God. Here we go."

Isabel hadn't meant to be so snippy, but she couldn't take it anymore. Alexis had crawled under her skin and was nibbling at every last nerve in her body.

"You're acting so immature about this," she said. "Guess what, Alexis, work happens. Not everything is ball pits and sandwich bars, afternoon naps and happy hours that start thirty minutes early. Those days are over. And Scarlett knows what she's doing with Connect. How do you think she got to where she is?"

Alexis jerked upright in her chair. "Do you hear yourself? Going to bat for the woman who was literally *born* into her position?"

"Sure, but what can you do about it? None of us can control where and how we were born any more than she can. What *is* in her control is what she does with her opportunities. I know nepotism is rampant in this country, but do you really expect her to become an ascetic and renounce it all? No, don't answer that. Of course you do, because nuance is dead and everything only exists in nice shades of black and white."

Isabel slammed her fist upon her desk with that final statement. Alexis's jaw dropped. She was staring at Isabel as if she wasn't sure if she should yell back at her or try to shake out whatever demon had possessed her.

But Alexis was saved from making that decision when behind her, Ned popped out of Scarlett's office with relief on his face.

"Looks like you're going home." Isabel pulled her materials together, preparing for her turn in the principal's office. "Congrats. Meanwhile, I have to keep trucking."

Alexis was still speechless as Isabel prepared for her meeting. It wasn't until she logged out of her computer and stood up from her chair that Alexis said anything at all.

"I guess I have been a bit whiny lately." She shook her head. "Sorry. You're right. We've all been blasting Scarlett for just doing her job. Can you blame us, though? It's a lot to adjust to after the way things were."

Isabel's shoulders sagged empathetically. "I'm sorry, too. I'm just as tired and cranky this week, and I took it out on you. Let's get drinks sometime this weekend. Just, somewhere quiet."

Alexis smiled. "Yeah. Let's."

Isabel patted her friend's shoulder before heading toward the boss's office. Along the way, she passed Ned, who was announcing to his team that they were cleared to go home for the weekend. As his voice receded behind her, she heard him mention that he was looking forward to catching the tail-end of his nephew's birthday party.

Wow. People are really making sacrifices. She would keep that in mind the next time she lashed out against the negativity around the office.

Isabel reached Scarlett's office, giving the assistant stationed outside her door a nod. As she waited to be invited in, her phone buzzed. She pulled it from her pocket. She had a message from Dominique.

"I need to tell you how sorry I am for disappearing on you like that. My personal life has been taking its toll on me. Of course I'd love to see you again, my Beauty."

A smile spread across Isabel's lips. She had just finished typing out her response when Emmy signaled for her to enter Scarlett's office.

And, send. Phone in one hand, files in the other, Isabel pushed the door open with her shoulder and stepped inside.

Immediately, Scarlett held up a finger. "Just one second, please. I have to finish up this message."

"Of course." Isabel remained at a respectable distance as

Scarlett typed something on her laptop. Her large two-in-one was on the other side of her. Was it her personal laptop? It wasn't any of Isabel's business, but what was there for Scarlett to worry about in her personal life that she couldn't do on the company computer?

Scarlett shut the lid of the laptop. As she prepared to accept the files from her employee, Isabel's phone buzzed loudly again.

"Oh." Isabel placed her folder on Scarlett's desk. "Sorry. I normally put it on silent when I'm at work." Nevertheless, she stole a peek at Dominique's response to her message. It was spicy enough to make a girl blush. "Wow," she muttered, completely forgetting that her boss was just a few feet away.

But when she looked up, the expression on Scarlett's face was more than enough to bring her back to reality. Scarlett wasn't impressed. In fact, she looked downright shocked. All color had drained from her face, and her body was stiff. It was as if she *had* just been shocked.

"W-what is it?" Was she really that mad that Isabel had interrupted their meeting with her phone before it had even started? "I'm sorry, I'll put it—"

"It can't be," Scarlett said softly.

"What do you mean?"

But Scarlett remained frozen in her chair. What was going on? What was the uneasy feeling in Isabel's stomach?

Why was her boss looking at her that way?

When Scarlett finally spoke, it was a single word, whispered like something between a question and a prayer.

"Beauty?"

What? An invisible force knocked Isabel back a few feet, her phone slipping from her hand. She crouched down and picked it up, her head spinning. Did that name really just fall from Scarlett's lips? The same red lips that had taunted and teased Isabel since the day she'd walked into the Connect office?

No. She misheard. She must have...

Scarlett rose from her seat, her hands gripping the edge of her desk as she stared at Isabel, brown eyes piercing her. "*No.* It's impossible."

But her words weren't spoken in Scarlett's professionally distanced voice but Dominique's deep, seductive melody.

Oh. My. God.

Isabel's heart plummeted into her stomach. Suddenly, she was transported back to a moment just weeks ago, in her boss's apartment. *The box. It looked just like the one I sent—*

"*Dominique.* You're... you're..."

Dominique, who lived in New York.

Dominique, who had consumed Isabel's every thought since that fateful evening so long ago.

Dominique, who Isabel had made love to. Had fallen for.

She was here, in the ethereal flesh.

She was Scarlett Black.

Before she knew what was happening, Isabel was at the door. This was all too much for her. Her mind couldn't process it.

As she raced out of the room, all she was aware of was the adrenaline pumping through her veins and the disbelief clouding her already tenuous judgment.

Chapter Eighteen

*B*eauty...

She was gone before Scarlett could say another word. As soon as she realized who Isabel really was, seconds, minutes, had escaped her.

And so had Beauty.

My Beauty...

The woman who had captured her heart through a screen. The woman who had illuminated her imagination and made her realize what life could be.

The woman she was falling in love with.

Right here. In my office. Isabel had been Beauty the whole time.

Hadn't Scarlett known it, even if subconsciously? Perhaps it had seemed too good to be true. Because it *was* too good to be true. What were the chances of fate blessing her like this?

But she didn't have time to sit around calculating the odds. Isabel had fled the coop.

And like a wolf, Scarlett went after her.

Beauty!

She was all that Scarlett cared about. *Connect. Black Diamond. Isabel.* None of those words meant a thing to her when all she could think of was *Beauty, Beauty, Beauty.* Emmy barely noticed Scarlett flying out of her office. And Scarlett barely noticed her as she searched for that head of dark hair, that eager visage that she now considered hers.

But others noticed. The stragglers from the social media team were readying to leave, and Scarlett almost bowled one of them over as she rushed to Isabel's desk. *Empty!*

"Whoa…" Connor leaped aside. "Where's the fire, chief?"

"Isabel." Scarlett was almost out of breath. Was she out of shape, or was the panic of the situation reaching her lungs? *"Where is Ms. Diaz?* I need to know where she went."

Connor pointed toward the double doors leading out to the elevator. "I saw her running that way. What happened?"

Scarlett didn't have time to explain, let alone make up an excuse for their behavior. She rushed through the glass doors and looked down the hallway—

—As the elevator doors closed before Isabel's reddening face.

Scarlett cursed to herself. They were high enough in the building that taking the stairs wouldn't get her to the lobby any quicker. She would have to try her luck with the other elevator.

She didn't have her sweater. Nor did she have the appropriate shoes for sprinting across hard flooring. But none of that mattered. As she slammed her thumb against the down button and watched the numbers above Isabel's elevator tick down toward the lobby, she pushed her hair out of her face and willed her chest to stop heaving with labored, anxious breaths.

"Beauty," she whispered. *No.* She couldn't lose her now. Not when they were so close.

To what? To finally living out their dreams in the real world? To being a part of each other's worlds?

The doors to the second elevator dinged open. Scarlett rushed inside it and pressed the button for the lobby. As it began its downward lurch, she prayed that Isabel's elevator was stopping at other floors, picking up passengers. Because Scarlett was using one of the few privileges she regularly indulged in at work.

My override card. All top Black Diamond employees and family members–of which Scarlett qualified as both–carried a card that allowed them to override the elevator so that it didn't stop at any other floors. While it was mostly useful for getting places in a hurry, Scarlett had a new use for it now.

Getting her to the lobby before Isabel.

I'll never forgive myself if this is how it ends. In her mind's eye, Scarlett didn't separate the woman who worked for her from the one who had waited for her in the BDSM club that night. As far as she was concerned, Beauty was Isabel, and Isabel was Beauty. Wasn't it natural that the lover who made Scarlett feel things she thought impossible was the same woman she felt inexplicably drawn to whenever they worked alongside each other in the office?

Wasn't that destiny?

One of Connect's most talented employees and the most

incredible lover Scarlett ever had. She couldn't lose them both at once.

After the slowest descent to the lobby she'd ever suffered, the doors opened.

Isabel's elevator had already reached the ground floor.

"Isabel!" Scarlett's voice carried across the empty lobby. Only the night concierge and a security guard lingered in the place that usually boasted dozens of people as they came and went from the Black Diamond Building.

And Isabel. She was there.

And she was pointedly ignoring Scarlett as she shot toward the main entrance.

Where was she going? Who was she running from? What was in that head of hers?

How could Scarlett make everything okay again?

"Isabel!"

She was still running. Soon, she would be at the door. Then what would Scarlett do? Run out into the cold of the Seattle night and hunt her girlfriend down like she was her prey?

If that's what it takes.

"Isabel!"

But raising her voice only served to make Isabel walk faster.

Scarlett stopped in her tracks and drew in a deep breath.

"Beauty."

Isabel halted. And as she turned to Scarlett with flushed cheeks and tears of confusion in her eyes, the world halted with her.

But not Scarlett. She kept walking, aware that anyone could see them.

I don't care.

She would be damned if she let Beauty get away from her again.

She didn't see the employee who had redesigned an entire app as many times as Scarlett had requested. Nor did she see someone who vented with her coworkers about what a tyrant the new boss was.

All Scarlett saw was the woman who had sat on that bed and waited for Dominique to kiss her prize.

Beauty. Scarlett took her by the hand and pulled her into a heavy embrace. *You are who you are. And I don't care who that is.*

Isabel was limp in Scarlett's arms, but only for a moment. As soon as her hands wrapped behind Scarlett's shoulders, a kiss erupted between them.

Scarlett didn't know who kissed who first. All she knew was that it was the sweetest thing she had ever tasted. She was a woman who had sipped the finest wines, supped on the most flavorful meals.

But none of them compared to the lips of Isabel Diaz.

∼

"Let's get out of here."

Scarlett vaguely remembered speaking those words down in the lobby. She had kissed Isabel and declared she would never let her out of her sight, before remembering how dangerous it was to be caught together, as they were, in a public place. They both had images to protect.

"Let's get out of here."

Her override card. She'd used it once again, allowing the

elevator to project them up toward her apartment. As soon as the doors closed, she pushed Isabel against the wall and kissed her so hard that a muffled cry of warning drummed into her ears. A request to back off. Just a bit. For a *moment.*

Enough to press her lips against the nape of Isabel's throat. *I'll let her breathe, but not without leaving my mark on her somehow.*

This was the curse of Scarlett Black. Once she laid claim to something—someone—they were hers forever.

And her darling Beauty cried out to be branded.

The doors opened much too soon. She took Isabel's hand and pulled her down the hallway. As the elevator doors closed somewhere behind them, Scarlett fished her key out of her pocket and shoved it into her lock.

Isabel didn't waver. She didn't hesitate. Her need-filled gaze and sweat-sheened skin only asked one thing of the woman who pulled her into the dark apartment.

"Let's get out of here."

'Here' wasn't a place, not in the physical sense. It wasn't the lobby of a building owned by Scarlett's family. It was a state of mind.

'Here' represented all the trappings that prevented two women from fully embracing the world they had constructed in their hearts.

In her desperation, Scarlett almost pushed Isabel down onto the couch in the living room. *No. She's better than a quick lay in front of the TV.* Instead, she drew Isabel down the hall and burst through the bedroom door.

There were so many things that could have gone wrong. She could have had an unexpected visitor. *Adrian. My mother. One of my sisters.* Only two of those people let themselves into her apartment, even if Scarlett wasn't home. But her mother was the last person she wanted to think about right now.

She pinned Isabel down onto the bed, reveling in the halo made by her dark hair and the gasp on her lips. "Do you know why I came after you? Take a wild guess, my Beauty."

Isabel shuddered beneath Scarlett's weight. *Just like the other night in the club.* She would never forget the feeling of Isabel climaxing under the power of Dominique's carnality. *Raw and unrefined.* Just the way she liked it.

"Because you're mine," Scarlett growled. "I don't care who you really are. The last time we were together, I *made* you mine. Do you understand? The fact that our relationship is much more than we ever anticipated doesn't change that."

Isabel's lips parted, the only sound to emerge from them a delectable whimper.

"You could be the Princess of Sweden for all I care." Scarlett's hands were slick around Isabel's wrists. Were they both sweating? Was it Scarlett's desire seeping through her skin, or was it Isabel's adrenaline manifesting? "I'd still make you mine. Because, if you haven't noticed, I'm used to getting what I want." Her mouth came dangerously close to Isabel's. "And I want you, Beauty."

A flurry of words slid from Isabel's lips.

"What was that?"

Isabel discovered her voice, hidden in the depths of her wondrous throat. "I want you too."

That was more than enough for Scarlett, who dove into the abyss of her aching desire.

It had been too long since she'd lost herself completely in sex. The last time she was with her Beauty, everything had been scripted. Hot, but scripted.

This time? As she tore off Isabel's clothes, uncovering the woman hiding beneath, Scarlett was ruled by passion alone as she crashed against Isabel, their bodies colliding in a blaze of lust. Her own clothes? Gone. Scarlett needed to feel her, flesh against flesh. She immersed herself in Isabel's supple, pliant body, kissing and touching, claiming her in a way that only a lover could.

Fucking. Fornicating. Making love. I don't care what we do or how we do it. It was all the same to her, no matter what connotation was assigned to it. Isabel was Beauty. Beauty was Isabel. It was as simple as it was divine.

Scarlett found her religion again in that breathless moment. Isabel was her vessel, receiving Scarlett and everything she had within her flesh and form. The physical was the metaphysical as Scarlett planted her lips on every part of Isabel within reach, her hands either holding down her Beauty as she begged for more or fucking her with relentless hunger. It wasn't a scene in a club. It was real.

Raw and unrefined. Like Beauty. Like Isabel. Everything was perfect. *She* was perfect.

Those primal gasps.

Those eager fingers digging into Scarlett's skin.

Those inner walls squeezing and yearning.

That way she quivered and trembled as Scarlett brought her to an orgasm that made the entire bed quake.

The way that didn't stop her pleading for more, more, *more!*

And Scarlett's own pleasure? Isabel never had the chance to kiss Scarlett's nipples, to touch her folds. Not when Scarlett was so in control that she would tie Isabel down if she put up enough fuss.

But that didn't mean Scarlett went without. She extracted her pleasure from Isabel's, drinking it from the perfect chalice that she was. Her thighs twined with Isabel's, hips and fingers thrusting as hard as her mortal body allowed. There was no finesse. Just pure, unbridled lust. And a willing woman calling her down into the sweetest level of hell.

No, not hell. Paradise.

As for where they were now? It wasn't heaven. Nor was it purgatory, promising them redemption if they behaved. *This is as human as it gets. This is how you know you're alive.* At that moment, Scarlett's heart rushed with a need to impart to Isabel one simple thing—that, no matter what happened to them now, they would always have each other.

This time, when Isabel reached a climax, she took Scarlett with her, falling into a state of such transcendental bliss that Isabel was unable to say anything but Scarlett's name, over and over. *Scarlett. Scarlett. Scarlett!* The hypnotic music of her cries echoed through Scarlett's being as they lost themselves in endless ecstasy, and each other.

"You're mine." A whisper, from deep in Scarlett's chest. She paid no mind to the exhaustion coming over her as they returned to earth. Her body only slowed instead of stilling. Her arms were as strong around Isabel now as they had been before.

Like hell I'm ever letting her go.

"You were mine before you knew who I was," she said. "You're still mine, and you always will be."

She didn't let Isabel respond. She was the queen of her domain, and her princess would do as she said.

That included taking every ounce of her love.

Chapter Nineteen

The hurricane that was being whisked up to Scarlett Black's bedroom and all that followed had Isabel disoriented. She was aware of the change in scenery, the softness of the mattress, the woman who treated her to a whirlwind of otherworldly sex. But she was barely aware of herself as she floated in a sea of pleasure.

Not until the hour grew later, and Isabel sat up suddenly on the bed, her mind connecting the dots between herself and the woman lying beside her.

Scarlett. Dominique. They were one and the same. And they were right here next to her.

Scarlett stretched a tentative hand toward Isabel. "Is everything okay?"

"Yeah. Sorry." She hadn't meant to pull away. If anything, she yearned to be drawn into Scarlett's gravitational pull.

My brain and body are at odds. Yet she couldn't say that. It would only come out the wrong way.

She relaxed back onto the bed. "I'm just trying to wrap

my head around everything. I mean, this is real. What do we do about this? What happens now?"

Scarlett let out a reluctant sigh. "I suppose we should talk about this. I was simply hoping that we could pretend for a little longer."

"But now that we know the truth, how could we possibly pretend? And how did neither of us realize who the other was? Especially after the night at the club?"

"To be honest, I had an inkling, but I brushed it off. The coincidence was too great."

"I did too! But you told me you lived in New York."

Scarlett grimaced. "A white lie, to obscure my real identity. I'm sorry. I have a lot to protect in my personal life. I couldn't risk anyone stumbling across my profile online and putting two and two together."

"Well, you had me fooled. What drives me crazy is how different you sound. As my boss, you're so reserved and professional. You're like a robot with excellent programming."

Scarlett laughed. "I suppose that's not inaccurate."

Isabel's cheeks grew hot. She hadn't meant to be so blunt. The events of the past few hours had disarmed her. "What I mean is, as Dominique, you're so much more… unbridled. I could hear the lust dripping from your lips the first time you spoke my name. Was that on purpose? So people wouldn't recognize you?"

"It wasn't intentional. Not on a conscious level, at least."

Scarlett sat up, sheets falling away from her naked breasts. *No matter how much I try not to stare, I'm always distracted by her otherworldly face.* Her hair was somehow lighter in the faded shadows of her room. Isabel could count every transition of light to dark brown in the waves of her tresses. It was as if she were seeing Scarlett through an entirely different lens.

Isabel longed to draw her, to capture her in this moment as she was, unveiled and unashamed. But she had too many questions on her mind.

"Speaking of how I sound at work," Scarlett began, "you had a lot to say about your 'bitch' of a boss in your messages. I had no idea you felt that way about the real me."

Whoops. "I…" How was she supposed to respond to that without offending the woman she had inadvertently fallen for? "I'm sorry. It was out of line, I just—"

Scarlett placed a reassuring hand on Isabel's shoulder. "Don't worry about it. I'm well aware of how much of a hardass I've been since I took over at Connect. I've been under a lot of pressure to get things done to my father's standards. But that's nothing new. It's the story of my life. I was born carrying all of my parents' expectations."

Hadn't 'Dominique' said as much? That her life was chosen for her from birth? *We get put in these little boxes, assigned these roles, set on paths we have no choice in. Forced to conform to who the world wants us to be.*

"When it's not my father controlling my career and my professional life, it's my mother, with her obsession with my personal life. I'm required to be the perfect daughter at all times, the perfect personification of the Black family name. It's why I've had to be so careful about letting my identity get out there. I couldn't have my family, let alone the public, discover that I was having kinky sex with other wom—"

"Oh my God!" Isabel yanked off the covers and hopped up on her knees, her hand over her mouth. "You're engaged!

To that man! Adrian Holt. Isn't that his name?" The flash of guilt that appeared on Scarlett's face was all the confirmation Isabel needed. "You're cheating on him with me, aren't you?"

She should have known. From the very beginning, this was too good to be true. How else could a woman like Dominique—like Scarlett—have crashed into her life and swept her off her feet like this?

Isabel was *the other woman*. She had been all along.

"Beauty. Isabel…" Scarlett held up her hands. "Just let me explain. It's been over between Adrian and me for years. Literally *years*. But we're the only ones who know it."

"What are you talking about?"

"It's… a long story."

Scarlett lay down on her back, arms behind her head, body still bared to the warm light. But Isabel couldn't bring herself to ogle. She was too concerned with how painfully naive she had been.

"I've known I like women for a long time, but I've never really come out. I've never *allowed* myself to come out. It doesn't help that I've always liked men, too. Maybe not quite as much as women, but these things aren't always black and white. I suppose you would call me bisexual? I mean, I *am* bisexual." She chuckled to herself. "I don't think I've ever said that out loud before."

"But that's not an excuse to cheat on your fiancé!"

Why was Scarlett still laughing? "You don't get it. The only reason Adrian and I got together is because our parents made it happen. We were pushed together. I'm Phillip Black's oldest daughter. Adrian, he's the oldest son of, well, his family are the Holts. The big Seattle bankers. It was a match made in heaven if we got along. And we did. We'd been friends since we were young. And things weren't bad the first few years together. I don't know what happened, exactly. We drifted apart. Our sex life evaporated. I grew more interested in women. And so did he, because one day I found out there was someone else he fancied in his life.

"But instead of being upset, I just felt guilty. Here I was, wanting to be with a woman, and here he was, trying to stay true to a woman who didn't love him like that anymore. The solution was obvious. We had to break up. But when you have families like ours, it isn't that simple. So I told him to go be with that woman if it made him happy, and I would have my own relationships independent of him. At first, we told ourselves that we were simply pursuing an open relationship, but we eventually accepted the reality that there was nothing left between us anymore. So we separated, but maintained the facade of being a couple so we wouldn't upset our families."

"So you're just pretending to be together to appease your families? How old are you guys again?"

"Forty. We're both almost forty." Scarlett shook her head. "Is Adrian forty already? He might be. Time goes by so quickly."

"You've got to be able to stand up to your families by now."

"Don't you think we know that? It's just not that easy. So much rides on our relationship. I'm the oldest in my family. I'm the heir. My father might not care what I do in my personal life, but he cares how it looks to our business associates. Most of them aren't as young and open-minded as some of our own peers."

That was a good point. It wasn't as if there weren't plenty of narrow-minded people Isabel's age.

"And my mother, bless her heart, she's a mess. She pushes heteronormativity like it's her religion. You should have seen what happened when my sister Parker came out as a teenager. Absolute holy hell was unleashed upon us all. I envy her, you know. Parker. She's always so confident in who she is and doesn't let our family hold sway over her. I could never be as brave as her."

Isabel opened her mouth to speak. Scarlett placed a finger on her lips.

"I know, my Beauty. I can't keep doing this forever. Even when I was meeting women in secret, I knew it couldn't last. Each one made me crave freedom just a little more. The woman before you made me realize how much I wanted that *forever.* But you? Isabel, ever since we connected, I've burned to be with you. To make you mine. To make *you* the fiancée that I show off to the world, not caring who says anything about it."

Her fiancée? This wasn't just moving fast—it was a semi-truck veering wildly out of control on a steep mountain pass.

"I..." Isabel shook her doubts out of her head. Now wasn't the time. "The thought of you *not* being confident is just so foreign to me. At work, you're so in control. And as Dominique? I've never met a woman who made me think 'how high' when you merely mentioned the word 'jump.' Like... damn. If you're not confident and secure in your sexuality, then you've really hidden it well."

Scarlett avoided Isabel's gaze. "A side effect of growing up in a family like mine. All of us children have learned to cope with the pressure in our own ways. Mine was to wear a mask that hid how I really felt. But it's exhausting. It's eating me away."

Isabel's stomach churned in sympathy. She placed a hand on Scarlett's arm, curling against her shoulder.

"I need to tell everyone the truth," Scarlett said. "I could probably deal with my father, but my mother? She's already got one gay daughter. The thought of having two—and she *will* call me gay, no matter what I say—will send her over the edge. I've been the 'decent' one my whole life. I followed the script. I did what was expected of me. All that's missing is the big wedding and at least one grandchild. Which my mother won't shut up about, because she wants grandbabies to show off to her friends."

"Really? That's what she cares about?"

A snort killed any lingering mood between them. "You don't know my mother. Everything is status to her. Regular old status, and status *quo*. She takes being my father's wife and the mother of his children seriously. Sometimes I wonder if she's ever had a life of her own."

Although Isabel nodded, she was struggling to keep up with everything Scarlett was telling her. *Between what happened an hour ago and now all of this information, it's so much to take in.*

"I had no idea that the woman I was with was going through so much," she said. "Although, I guess I had an inkling. Sometimes I could feel the way you were holding back, holding things in. As Dominique, I mean. It's why I drew you the way I did." She hadn't intended to, not at first.

But brushstrokes and lines weren't just how Isabel expressed her thoughts and feelings. They were how she processed them, too.

A wan smile grew on Scarlett's lips. "You were right. That drawing of me, it was like you'd captured all my vulnerabilities on paper, for better and for worse. You have no idea how much it meant to me for someone to see me as I am."

"You have no idea how much *you* mean to me. Being with you, as Beauty and Dominique, opened my mind *and* my world. It made me feel like I've finally found myself. I..."

Scarlett waited for her to continue, but she had lost her voice. She slipped her hand into Isabel's, comforting, coaxing, *beckoning*. "Tell me," she said, her perfume and breath one and the same. "I've spilled my heart out to you. I hope you feel safe enough with me to do the same."

"Well," Isabel began, "my life certainly hasn't been as dramatic or exciting as yours. But I can relate to the feeling of struggling with expectations that don't fit who you really are. It took me a while to come to terms with my sexuality, too. I didn't realize I was gay until college, because I'd spent my whole life subconsciously repressing my feelings for other girls. I just wanted to be 'normal.' To *feel* 'normal.' Because..."

Scarlett cocked her head. "Yes?"

"I've always been different. For most of my life, I thought I was broken, somehow. Like I was missing something everyone else had that made them understand each other and the world around them. It was like everyone moved through life so easily, whereas for me, everything was difficult. Well, almost everything. Art. That was one thing I always found easy. It made me feel like I was in my element. But the rest of the time, it was like I was an alien from another planet, or someone displaced from another universe. I used to wonder if that was the case as a kid..."

Isabel trailed off. She hadn't meant to share such a silly thought out loud. But Scarlet just squeezed her hand in wordless reassurance.

"It was like no matter how hard I tried, I didn't fit," Isabel said. "Not anywhere, or with anyone. Then when I was in college, I started seeing a therapist and she told me she suspected I was autistic. At first, I thought she was wrong. I guess my idea of autism was based on all the usual stereotypes, and they didn't fit me. But I looked into it, and I'd never felt so validated in my life. It explained everything I'd ever felt, everything I'd ever experienced. A lot of autistic girls never get diagnosed as kids because we're good at blending in. But when I finally did get that diagnosis, it was like everything fell into place. For the first time in my life, I understood myself. And since then, I've realized that the only way to be happy is to embrace who I am. I'm not broken. I never have been."

"Oh, Beauty." Scarlett reached up, caressing Isabel's cheek with her fingertips. "It pains me to think that you ever felt like you were broken. How could something so perfect be broken?"

Isabel's heart skipped. "So, this doesn't change how you see me?"

"Of course not. Nothing could change that. You'll always be my Beauty."

She let out a sigh of relief. "I'm not used to talking to people about this. A part of me worries that people will treat me differently or won't understand. But also, it's because it's taken me long enough to work out what being autistic means for me. I think I'm coming to see it as just another part of me, like everything else. My race, my gender, my sexuality. It's a big part of who I am, but it's not *all* I am. It's just one of the many things that combine to make me, well, me."

"Like the facets of a diamond," Scarlett said. "Together, they make the whole thing shine."

Isabel smiled. "Kind of like that."

"And you shine so beautifully, Isabel Diaz."

"I can't take all the credit. You're the light that makes me shine. At least, that's how it feels when I'm with you. When I say you helped me find myself... I've spent most of my adult life trying to figure myself out and find where I fit in the world. You've given me the confidence to explore who I really am, to *embrace* who I really am. And not just by putting me in touch with Beauty and all my desires. You're the muse that inspired me to create again, to make art. You've given me life."

"I understand. I feel the same way."

Although Scarlett was vulnerable in that moment, her words carried the same reserved tone that Ms. Black's voice held at work. *That's right. They're the same person.* The controlled corporate businesswoman and the unrestrained Domme.

Their alter egos had collided with their real-life selves. There was no turning back now.

Isabel tucked a stray strand of hair behind her ear. "So what do we do now? This whole situation is crazy. I don't even know where to begin."

"Honestly?" Scarlett said. "I don't know either."

"This is just a big mess."

"It doesn't have to stay that way. In fact, this has given me the push I sorely needed." Scarlett drew Isabel into her arms. "I'm going to stop living a lie. I'm going to free Adrian, and myself. I'm going to tell my family the truth. They don't need to know the details of my sex life, but they can at least know that I have someone as bright and wonderful as you in my life. They'll get over it. They'll have to."

She allowed a brief kiss to hover on Isabel's lips. Isabel's pulse fluttered. *We're so close to slipping away again. So close to losing ourselves in each other again.*

"I want to be with you," Scarlett said softly. "Knowing you've been so close to me this whole time only makes me want you more. But we have to keep it quiet for now. This is a delicate situation."

"I know. I can't go around blabbing to everyone at work that I'm sleeping with the boss. It would ruin us both if they found out now."

"Then it's settled. You let me handle this. In the meantime, at work we will be as we always have been. Professional. Respectful. Nothing more."

Isabel nodded. What choice did they have?

"And perhaps it's best if we put a pause on your daily trips to the supply closet for now." A sly smile crossed Scarlett's lips. "I was wondering why you seemed so flustered when I caught you coming out of there that day."

Isabel buried her face in her pillow, an attempt to smother her embarrassment. That had been a close call.

But everything was out in the open now. So how was she

supposed to act like there was nothing between them while they were at work? How was she supposed to pretend that her heart didn't ache for Scarlett every moment they were together?

But she couldn't court those thoughts for long. Not when Scarlett kissed her the way she did.

Chapter Twenty

This is a mess.

A statement that could have applied to many things. Scarlett's personal life, for one. Having a secret romance with one of her employees certainly fit that description.

But was that what weighed on the mind of Scarlett Black, CEO of Connect, heir to the Black Diamond fortune, as she sat in her living room the next day?

No. The 'mess' was the folder before her and what it contained—all of Connect's financial records, from both before and after she came on board as CEO. Everything, from the expenditures to how little current members paid to access the app's benefits, was on display to her.

We're still hemorrhaging money. Her father was breathing down her neck. She had to do something. She had to cut off the fat so that Black Diamond could at least break even from the acquisition.

I have to figure this out. No more putting it on the backburner. Scarlett was going to salvage Connect, even if it killed her.

The financial reports weren't the only thing in the folder. It also contained the detailed plan she'd put together after that lunch with her father. That was a surefire way to salvage Connect. Ruthless cuts to employee numbers. Eliminating entire departments. Gutting Connect and turning it into a shell of its former self. A profitable shell, but a shell nonetheless.

However, Scarlett couldn't possibly carry out those plans. She'd been hesitant to do so before, but now she was certain. She couldn't tear Connect apart. It just wouldn't be *right*. The small, grassroots startup was just too important, to the community, and the world. And people's jobs, their livelihoods, were on the line.

That included Isabel's. Connect meant so much to her. And she was the reason Scarlett was putting her nose to the grindstone so soon after Isabel had departed that morning. If Scarlett could fix Connect's financial problems and set it on a path to becoming profitable, perhaps she could soften the blow when she inevitably told her family the truth—that she was formally breaking off her engagement with Adrian.

And that she was in a relationship with a woman almost half her age.

When I put it that way...

She needed help. Which was why, as soon as she heard the knock on her front door, she practically leaped off her couch and raced to answer it.

Scarlett opened her door wide enough for Parker to enter. "You're a sight for these sore eyes."

"My sister says she wants to catch up, and who am I to turn her down?" Parker said.

"Come on in. I just need to clean up some files."

Parker followed Scarlett into the living room, her hands in the pockets of her tattered jeans. Somehow, she still looked like a million dollars. Parker had always been the most bombastic of the three Black sisters. *I may be the most "sophisticated" according to the tabloids, but Bianca is the trendiest and Parker the most eye-catching.* This was a woman who could dye her short hair blonde and throw on a baggy sweater, and everyone swooned. Parker had that pull on people.

She stretched herself out on the couch, careful to avoid the folder sitting on the far arm. Scarlett was right behind her, collecting the confidential financial documents and returning them to the manila folder. Not that Parker would do anything with them. She had her own business to worry about. Then again, Scarlett suspected that her sister didn't concern herself too much with her lingerie brand's financials. That was someone else's problem.

"I appreciate you making time to see me." Scarlett set aside the folder on the coffee table and sat down next to her sister. "I know you're a busy woman, especially lately. How is Julia?"

"Even busier than me. Which is how she likes her life." Parker cocked her head in her sister's direction. "You know her well enough by now. There's never a shortage of cats that need homes, and Julia has made it her mission in life to put a cat in every home in Seattle."

"You mean like how one ended up in Bianca's? And yours now, too?"

"Actually, we have two. And we're fostering a kitten. What can I say? Julia can be very persuasive. The only reason you don't have a cat is because she can't pin you down long enough to make you choose one."

Scarlett propped her elbow up on the back of the couch. "So things are going well between you since she moved in?"

"As well as they possibly could be." Parker paused. "So, things are going well with this... app... thing?"

Scarlett raised an eyebrow. "Like you're interested in that." Given how Parker's eyes glazed over every time Scarlett or their father started talking business, it was a wonder that Parker's own company was doing so well.

She shrugged. "This is what I get for making trite conversation. You know it's not my forte. Cut right to the chase. That's how I like it."

"There's nothing to cut to. The whole reason you're here is so we can catch up."

"All right then." Parker crossed one leg over the other, a smile playing on her lips. "How's Adrian doing?"

Scarlett held back a grimace. "He's... fine. Nothing much changes with him."

"He could have been recently diagnosed with mesothelioma and you'd tell us he's *fine*."

"No, I wouldn't. I'd tell you he's due a structured settlement."

"Ah, yes, that thing all of us so sorely need because we don't have enough money," Parker said.

"I see that being with Julia has improved your sense of humor."

"She has that effect on me."

Scarlett cocked her head, studying her sister's face. "How

did you know it was her?" Realizing how vague she was being, she reoriented her thoughts. "What I mean is, how did you know that Julia was the one for you? You risked so much of our mother's fury when you introduced her to the family. You must have thought it was worth it."

"Worth what? Subjecting her to our mother? Oh, yeah, sure. I've spent half of my life looking for the perfect woman to throw to that wolf. You caught me. That's been my kink this *whole* time."

Why do you have to say that word in front of me? Parker shared her sister's hunger for the kinky side of life, but she didn't know that. And while Parker was the most progressive and open-minded of everyone in her family, Scarlett couldn't imagine how her sister would react if she discovered that Scarlett, the golden child of the family was as much of a sexual deviant as her.

I'm not so golden anymore.

"Fine. I'll give you a serious answer." Parker turned toward her, mirroring Scarlett's pose. "I *just* knew."

Scarlett couldn't roll her eyes hard enough to get her point across. "That's not an answer."

"Sorry. I forgot to mention the fireworks going off in my heart and the neon signs flashing above Julia's head."

Scarlet should have known better than to expect a straight *anything*, let alone an answer, out of Parker Black. Years of being the black sheep in the family had fostered an impenetrable shell around her, one that Scarlett was only occasionally allowed to chip away at. She was, after all, one of the very first people to know the truth about Parker and Julia's relationship. *She trusted me enough with that information. The least I can do is trust her in return.*

Because it was no coincidence that the woman most likely to understand Scarlett's predicament was sitting in front of her.

Parker had never been an idiot. She may have done foolish things with her life while acting out against the family, but she was perceptive. Scarlett would dare say that her sister was the smartest person in the family.

I don't know if I could have launched my own brand with little to no help. That was a bit of a falsehood. Scarlett was the one who privately loaned Parker some of the money she needed to start her company. Had Scarlett expected to get her money back? No. Certainly not as quickly as Parker made it happen.

"I'm sorry." This time when Parker spoke, it almost sounded genuine. "Sometimes I have a hard time turning off the sarcasm. Especially when it's such an arbitrary question."

"Don't worry. I get it."

Parker's gaze wandered the room, landing on a spot on Scarlett's living room carpet. "The truth is, Julia made it feel like it was all worth it. The pain. The strife. Everything with Mom."

Parker's vulnerability struck a chord in Scarlett's heart. "I see. She was really that special, huh?"

"Guess so. I went through all of that bullshit for a reason, and it wasn't just my pussy calling the shots this time. Guess my heart had some things to say, too." Parker's face turned red. "You're embarrassing me. It's bad enough when Julia makes me say this stuff."

"She must be a strong woman to put up with Mom's crap. Surely, you were attracted to how strong she was."

Scarlett had another thought. "Has Mom been bothering you two lately? Or has she finally backed off?"

"Mom is Mom. It's not like any of this is new."

"I know, but ever since you brought home a 'serious' girlfriend, she's really cranked up the homophobic comments. It's like she's accepted Julia as your partner, yet she's clinging to her homophobia even harder than before. It doesn't make any sense."

"Has Mom ever been a rational woman? I worry about her sometimes. She's so staunchly heterosexual it's affected all of us in terrible ways."

For a second, Scarlett's heart stopped. *Us?* "What do you mean?" Was Parker onto her?

"Sorry, I forgot that you don't have a gaydar. Not that Bianca is very subtle about it."

"*Bianca?* You think she…" Is that what she kept trying to bring up with Scarlett, in her office, then again after the last family dinner? If Vivianne Black ended up with three sapphically-inclined daughters, she might just have a heart attack.

"It's just a hunch. She hasn't said anything to me yet, not directly. I think she's still figuring it out herself. Or maybe she just doesn't see the need to 'come out' or define her sexual orientation." Parker shrugged. "You know how the kids are these days. I'm just concerned about the effect Mom is having on her. She's not used to our mother's bullshit. Unlike her, I've been dealing with it since I was eight, so I know how to handle it."

"Since you were *eight*? Really?"

Parker stared at Scarlett, incredulous. "Yes, really. The homophobia didn't start when I came out in high school. It started long before then. You don't remember? I used to scream about wearing those frilly dresses and going to finishing school. All because Mom was determined to turn me into an uber-feminine little lady instead of the wild tomboy I was."

"I remember all that, but I never made the connection."

Parker chuckled. "The signs that I was gay were there all the way back to my kindergarten days. I was obsessed with Cindy Crawford for a hot minute, and it wasn't because I thought she was cool and wanted to be like her. I was having inappropriate feelings for a five-year-old, let me tell you."

"And Mom realized it?"

"Mom realized it when I was making my Barbies marry each other instead of Ken. Like I said, it's been going on since I was a little kid. I'm used to it. It doesn't mean it's right, or that I should take it, but I'm used to it. So is Julia. We get by and live our lives."

Scarlett resisted the urge to hug her sister. *She doesn't need my too little too late.* Plus, given their relationship, it would only be awkward.

"I had no idea. I was so caught up in my adolescent bullshit during those times." That wasn't an overstatement. Scarlett's memories of high school and college consisted entirely of her tearing her hair out from stress over her future while ignoring her mother's matchmaking attempts.

"I'm envious of your ability to know and own who you are." Scarlett swallowed a lump in her throat. *Here we go.* So close, yet so far from revealing the truth. "You faced all of that pressure, including from our mother, and never backed down."

"What choice did I have? Besides, you reach a point where you realize that it doesn't matter. People can tell you to be one way all they want, but who the fuck cares? They aren't you. They aren't the ones living your life. What are you going to do, Scar? Let someone as unhappy as our mother dictate your life? She'll be dead soon enough. Then what? Will you be middle-aged and still kowtowing to some dead woman's ideals?"

Were these rhetorical questions? Or did Parker know more than she was letting on? It didn't help that she was looking Scarlett dead in the eye. *So serious.* So unlike Parker.

Scarlett averted her gaze. "If only it were that simple."

Silence filled the space between them. She thought back on all the opportunities she'd had to tell the truth. How she let them slip through her fingers. How she wasted over twenty years of her life being someone she wasn't. *How I dragged Adrian down with me.*

And now, she was at risk of dragging Isabel down, too.

"You know, now that I think about it," Parker said, interrupting her sister's thoughts, "it wasn't always so easy. Especially when I was a kid. Just because I knew who I was, it didn't mean I knew how to *deal* with that. Why do you think I acted out so much? I was always fighting for my identity and independence. I was jealous of my friends, be they rich or poor, who got to come out to their parents and were either supported or found ways to absorb the blows. It took almost thirty years for me to realize that none of that matters. I'll always find a way. I like to think Julia is my forever, but things can happen, things out of our control. If Julia dies in a car accident next year, am I going back to being the family punching bag?" Parker clenched a fist, pounding it into the palm of her other hand. "No. I refuse. I won't live for anyone but myself. It's not worth sacrificing my life for anyone, especially not Phillip and Vivianne Black."

Hearing her parents' full names startled Scarlett into something. *Something big.* It was right there, on the cusp of her consciousness. The answer, the perfect solution to all her problems…

Parker narrowed her eyes in Scarlett's direction. "All of these questions. Where are they coming from? Something's on your mind."

Scarlett blinked, her train of thought lost. "Hm? No, it's nothing."

A moment ago, she'd been prepared to tell her sister everything. But now, she had new food for thought. She had to rethink her strategy, both in how she introduced Isabel as her lover, and how she took control of her own life, for once.

"Why don't I get us that coffee?" she said, rising from the couch. "It's the new blend from Colombia. The one Father wants us to sample so they can send the notes back to the—"

"You're hiding something from me," Parker said. "And you know I'll figure out what."

"You're being ridiculous." Yet everything, from Parker's demeanor to her mannerisms, suggested that she might already know the truth about Scarlett Black, the heir to the Black Diamond empire.

The Parker of a year ago would have gone ahead and said it. *"I know you're screwing some woman, Scar. I don't know who she is, but she exists. Now that I've shocked you into submission, why don't you tell me your side of the story?"* But the

Parker of today? The person who was confident in her identity and her role in this crazy family?

She didn't say anything. She left it for Scarlett to divulge when she was ready.

As she turned the coffee pot on, Scarlett dreamed of a day when she could be as brave as her sister.

Chapter Twenty-One

I'm out of coffee again. Isabel stared into the bottom of her to-go cup, wishing she had sprung for a large instead of a medium. Who had she been kidding? She couldn't make it through the whole afternoon with only a medium coffee.

It was crunch time. The meetings with prospective investors were fast approaching, and Scarlett had made it clear, both in their pillow talk and text messages, that much was riding on the success of these meetings. Isabel had been a bit too distracted by feelings of giddy schoolgirl infatuation to fully grasp Scarlett's words, but there had been something about "potential solutions" and "new directions" thrown in there, beneath her breath.

I'm hopeless. I think about her breath, and I think about kissing her.

No. Isabel couldn't lose focus. Scarlett was counting on her to play her part, and as the head of graphic design, Isabel had a *monumental* part.

No wonder she had been out of touch with most of her

coworkers, who had their noses to the grindstone just like her. Everyone, from social media to customer support, was working overtime. Some of the IT department had even come in on Saturday evening to make sure the alpha build of the new app was functioning smoothly. They were the first in Scarlett's office that morning, running their presentation by her in the hopes that it was ready to go. Based on the grumbling, and one empty trash can getting kicked over, things had not gone well.

Scarlett wasn't playing favorites with Isabel either. When she'd swung by Scarlett's apartment on Sunday afternoon, it had been to go over a few final changes Isabel had made to the redesigned UI. There hadn't been enough time for fooling around.

However, the urge was always there. So they restricted most of their flirting to their phones, which constantly erupted with more promises of sexual delights.

Just as soon as things calmed down at work.

She's taking this so seriously. Isabel deeply admired Scarlett's commitment to Connect, not to mention her focus. This was a woman who turned down sex with her new girlfriend if it meant meeting her deadlines.

Isabel had to admit, it was kind of hot.

She stretched her arms above her head and rolled her cramped wrists in tight circles. *Need coffee.* She absentmindedly grabbed the cup, noting how light it was. *Empty. Right.* She already knew that. She needed caffeine badly.

Fortunately, with so many people in the office working themselves to the bone, the breakroom coffee pot was always full and hot.

Isabel got up from her desk, taking the opportunity to stretch out her tired body. No, the office no longer had nap pods and complimentary sandwich bars, but it had free coffee and plenty of space for stretching. It wasn't unusual to see Alexis or one of the guys using the yoga mats by the big windows overlooking the busy commercial streets. *Throw on a pair of headphones, and you can pretend you're in the mountains.* Easier to do when it was foggy, but a nice, clear day offered a substantial view of Mount Rainier. Today, it was mostly the building across the street.

Isabel entered the breakroom with a yawn on her lips. Her mind was filled with CSS and images of her boss's body as she scratched her head and looked around the room.

Uh... The breakroom was full of her coworkers, sipping coffee, munching on snacks. But as soon as she stepped through the door, everyone turned to stare at her.

Was her fly down? That didn't make sense. She was wearing a skirt.

So what was going on?

But no one was saying a word. A few people cleared their throats, and Ned from social media looked away with red cheeks. Alexis was by the counter, sipping coffee from a porcelain cup. Even she seemed to be dodging Isabel's quizzical glances.

Isabel joined her by the counter. "How are things on your end?"

Alexis pursed her lips. "You know. Tough."

"Right? I'm going to rethink my stance on chiropractors after this. My back is killing me from sitting at my desk for hours."

But Isabel's attempt to make polite conversation was falling on deaf ears. She felt a pang of guilt. *I know we haven't had much chance to hang out lately, but I swear I'll make it up to you, Alexis.* Crunch time and her relationship with Scarlett had dominated all of Isabel's waking hours in these past weeks.

But they were in the final stretch. Isabel had a good feeling about the pitch to potential investors. If anyone could sell Connect to middle-aged men in suits, it was Scarlett Black.

Alexis turned away. Any other day this week, their coworkers would have been chatting away in their chairs or power-napping with their heads on tables. Today? Nothing but awkward looks and shuffling feet.

And silence. Empty, foreboding silence.

Isabel placed her coffee cup on the counter. "What in the world is going on in here? Did somebody die over the weekend?"

Ned was the only one who would look at her. Yet his embarrassment was so intense that he scooted out of his seat and forgot his coffee as he hustled out of the breakroom.

"Izzy…" Alexis lowered her voice as she came closer to her. "I saw you two on Friday night."

"Hm?"

"You and Scarlett. I saw you in the lobby. *Kissing.*"

Something punched Isabel right in the gut. "W-what did you say?"

"I think you heard me just fine. But if you need details, I left the office on Friday night, but I didn't get far before I realized I left my charger at my desk. So I came back, and there you and Scarlett Black were, making out like a pair of teenagers in the middle of the lobby." Alexis crossed her arms. "What the fuck, Isabel? I thought you were going out with some chick you met online. Dominique?"

"I..." Isabel swallowed. *What do I do? Oh my God. Alexis saw us? In the thirty seconds we were down there?* What were the odds? "What if I told you that Dominique was actually Scarlett?"

"So it's true, then?" Although Alexis kept her voice too low for the others to hear, Isabel was well aware of their straining ears. Caroline practically crawled over the table to get closer to the action.

Do they all know?

"So it's true?" Alexis repeated. "You're sleeping with the enemy?"

"What?" Isabel shook her head. "The enemy? You're kidding, right?"

Alexis gave a derisive scoff. "I should have known. You've been so cagey about your personal life lately. I guess this is why. You were sleeping with that soulless *corporate hag*. Now I don't feel so bad about telling Ned what I saw."

Isabel's heart dropped. "You told Ned?"

"And he told the rest of us." Caroline took a sip of her tea, barely able to contain her salacious smile. "Seriously, don't tell Ned secrets. He can't hold on to them."

"Are you really sleeping with Ms. Black?" Toby from customer service asked.

"Bet she was sleeping with Evan, too," Caroline mumbled. "It would explain the promotion."

Isabel was too shocked to speak. For a moment, Alexis looked like she was going to come to her friend's defense.

But instead, all that came out of her mouth was, "How could you betray us like this? Whatever happened to solidarity, huh?"

"Betray *you?*" Isabel backed away from the counter. "You're the one who blabbed everything without knowing the whole story!"

"What more could there be to the story? It didn't look like she was forcing you."

Caroline smirked. "Now *there's* a juicy scandal."

"Shut the hell up, Caroline!" Isabel almost tripped over her own feet as she turned and lunged for the breakroom door. "What do you guys know? Nothing!"

Betrayal? Alexis dared to call it a *betrayal? All I did was live my damned life.* So what if Dominique was Scarlett? So what if Isabel was falling for someone almost twice her age who was engaged to some high-profile banker?

So what?

How is it any of their business? Isabel couldn't think rationally as she rushed back to her desk. But there was no solace there. Emmy looked up from her own desk and cocked her head in mild amusement. Two other coworkers glanced over their shoulders, immediately falling into fits of gossipy giggles.

They all knew.

With bile choking her throat, Isabel grabbed her sweater and sped to the double doors leading out of the office. No, she wouldn't run like she had on Friday night. She wouldn't give her coworkers the satisfaction of knowing they had humiliated her at work.

Instead, she marched to the elevator, holding back her tears and pulling her phone out of her sweater pocket.

The elevator doors opened. But instead of going down, she went up.

∼

"Isabel, what's wrong?"

But as Scarlett hurried to where she stood beside the apartment door, Isabel could barely form words. Scarlett had entrusted her with a swipe card that allowed her to ride the elevator up to the top floors of the building. However, she didn't have a key to Scarlett's apartment, so she'd waited outside, head resting on the wall behind her as she struggled to keep all her emotions from pouring out.

But now, she was moments from breaking.

"Come on." Scarlett unlocked her front door. "Get in here and tell me what's going on."

Isabel burst into the apartment before Scarlett could open the door all the way. Was there comfort inside? Yes, but not enough. Although she'd been to Scarlett's apartment more than once now, the lush furniture and the stunning views didn't feel familiar. Even when Scarlett escorted her to the couch, the pillows and carpeting were as foreign as they had been the first time Isabel laid eyes on them.

"Talk to me." Scarlett took a seat beside her and placed a hand on her shoulder. "Does this have to do with the tension in the office?"

So Scarlett had noticed it? Of course she had. Yet she hadn't even reacted. How was she impervious to everything life threw at her? Whenever anything went wrong in Isabel's life, she completely broke down.

"They know," Isabel said between labored breaths. "Everyone knows. Alexis... she saw us kissing on Friday night. She told Ned. He told everyone! What are we going to do?"

Scarlett took this news with as much decorum as Isabel had lost down in the office. Yet her gritting teeth and tightening jaw assured Isabel that she took it just as seriously. "I was afraid this might happen. But I have to say, I wasn't expecting it to get out so *soon.* Oh, Isabel."

Scarlett wrapped both arms around her, pulling her into a firm embrace. That was all it took. The dam inside Isabel burst and all the tears she'd been holding back broke through in a storm of sobs.

"It's going to be all right. You let me handle this, okay?" Scarlett stroked the side of Isabel's head. "I'll figure out what to do about this. As for those gossip mongers... You stay here for now, at least for the rest of the day. And tonight. I'll bring up your work laptop so you can keep at it if you'd like, and I'll have Emmy send out a strongly worded memo about professionalism and spreading rumors in the office. I'll see if I can get an NDA rolled out by the end of the day before anyone has the chance to tell the press."

"The press?" Isabel shrieked.

Scarlett nodded soberly. "That's my main concern right now. If my family hears about this... no, no. You let me worry about it. You've done nothing wrong. Never fear, my Beauty." She took hold of Isabel's shoulders firmly, piercing her with a determined gaze. "I'm in charge here. You have nothing to worry about with me at your side."

As much as Isabel wanted to believe the woman who planted a kiss on her forehead, holding her like she was never going to let her go, it was easier said than done.

Everything's falling apart. Not just everything Isabel had worked for in her short life. Everything that Scarlett had worked for, too.

And they had no one to blame but themselves.

Chapter Twenty-Two

A night's sleep wasn't the cure for Isabel's troubles, but it helped. When she woke up the next morning, she'd almost forgotten about the events of the previous day before they all came rushing back to her.

I'm okay, though. I'll get through this.

We'll get through this.

She rubbed the sleep from her eyes and stretched an arm above her head. Beside her, Scarlett stirred from her slumber. It was six in the morning. Late enough for dawn to touch the windows, but hopefully early enough for Scarlett to spare a few minutes cuddling her girlfriend before having to dash downstairs to the office.

Maybe I'll make us breakfast. What did Scarlett usually eat for breakfast? Did she go for eggs and toast, or did she graze on a grapefruit like so many busy businesswomen?

Oatmeal and coffee? Surely, Scarlett had oatmeal in her cupboards. *When I grow the will to finally get out of bed, I'll make us some, with fresh fruit too.* It was the least Isabel could do for the woman who had given her so much comfort the night before.

They hadn't even had sex. Isabel had been too upset to consider it. Apparently, she wasn't the kind of person whose anxieties were reassured with kisses and orgasms. She required a physical presence from the woman she loved, but in the end, a firm hug and reassuring words sufficed.

Scarlett rolled over groggily, facing Isabel. As she gradually awakened, she snaked her arm across Isabel's torso. "How are you feeling?"

She sighed into her girlfriend's arms. "A little better. Not sure if I could face everyone in the office today, though."

"I did as much damage control as I could yesterday. I even pulled Ned aside to have a chat with him about things. My goodness, I've never met a man who can go toe-to-toe with me in an argument, but as soon as my sex life comes up, he's more sheepish than a virgin on her wedding night."

Isabel laughed. A sharp pain in her throat reminded her that she hadn't drunk anything in several hours. *Not since I downed half a glass of wine to calm my nerves last night.* She was more than dehydrated. Her throat felt like she'd swallowed needles.

"I could use a shower," Scarlett said. "Would you like to join me?"

"Sounds great." Isabel kicked back the covers and pushed herself up. She'd worn everything but her skirt to bed. *I need a change of clothes. Guess I'll go home later to get some.* She didn't plan to go into the office that day. Everything she had left to do could be done here in Scarlett's apartment—or Isabel's. "Hang on a sec. I'm going to get a drink from the kitchen."

Scarlett kissed Isabel's parched lips gently before letting her go. "Glasses are in the farthest right cupboard. Above the toaster."

Isabel stumbled out of the bedroom, still gathering her bearings and trying her damnedest to wake up. *I get up around six every morning. You'd think I could handle this.* Yet the shock of the previous day had drifted over into this one.

Isabel made her way through the living room, shielding her eyes from the lightly clouded sun streaming through the window. She reached the kitchen and opened the cupboard, grabbing a glass and filling it with tap water.

The first sip was a balm to her blistered lips and dry throat. She gulped the entire glass down before filling it up again, then sat down at the island counter as she continued to drink. Strength returned to her. So did clarity.

This is a disaster. No, she couldn't dwell on it. The last thing she needed was to start her day with the same worries she'd gone to sleep with the night before. She was here with Scarlett. That was all that mattered.

Still, a distraction would be nice.

A manila folder caught her attention from the other side of the island counter. Isabel pulled it over to her, clearing her throat and rolling her head back and forth in a futile attempt to wake herself up. The folder was labeled *CONNECT Financial Report & Immediate Remedies.*

It was so like Scarlett to bring work home. Knowing her, she sipped her favorite wine while perusing these files late into the night. Isabel allowed a small smile to spread on her lips as she flipped open the folder. It was full of charts and figures, diagrams and tables, all outlining the company's financial past, present, and potential future.

Wow. Evan really dropped the ball, didn't he? Isabel had known it was bad, but she doubted anyone else in the company knew just how much the founder of Connect had blown on the sandwich bar and rideshares to and from work.

Scarlett had so much on her plate. Was it any wonder that she was stressed out about the upcoming meeting? Because Connect was in need of some serious cash.

She flipped through the pages, delving deeper into the folder. Soon, she reached the 'Immediate Remedies' portion of the document. It was packed with business buzzwords, mostly indecipherable to Isabel. But a few phrases jumped out at her as she skimmed the pages. *Restructuring... eliminate redundancies... non-essential staff...*

Her stomach churned. Those all sounded like codewords for firing people. But that couldn't be right. Scarlett had promised she wouldn't fire anyone, hadn't she?

But as Isabel turned to another page, her heart stilled in her chest. There it was, a bold heading right at the top of the page.

Employee Terminations.

Frowning, Isabel held the sheet of paper up to her face and read on.

Social Media: Ned Greer. Connor Reid. Alexis Sommers... The list went on. And a note beneath it, which read *Fold into Black Diamond Social Media subdivision.*

Isabel had to read that twice. Was Scarlett proposing that most of the social media department be laid off?

But it wasn't only the social media department who were on the chopping block. It was nearly everyone.

Accounting. Customer service. All were being assimilated into the monster that was Black Diamond Holdings.

Caroline Rose. Undetermined. Position appears to be superfluous.

Ouch. Although after her comments the day before, Isabel had little sympathy for the woman.

Isabel Diaz. Graphic design. Fold into Black Diamond Design subdivision.

Isabel blinked.

Was Scarlett planning to fire her?

Something tightened inside her chest. Isabel took a deep breath and scanned the words on the page again, searching for something—anything—that contradicted what she'd read, but it was in vain. And as she flipped through the pages that followed, she found figures outlining exactly how much money Connect would save for each employee cut from the roster. Under Isabel's name, the figure was tens of thousands of dollars per year. There was even a comment, handwritten in the margins in Scarlett's distinctive script. *"It's preposterous that Ms. Diaz even survived the merger. Black Diamond already employs a dozen more experienced designers we can use to do a much better job."*

Isabel set the paper down, heart in her stomach. These were Scarlett's words. They were so dry. So businesslike. A cruel reminder that corporate didn't care who they hurt as long as they made a profit.

That Scarlett didn't care...

"Everything okay out here?" Scarlett, in nothing but a baggy pajama shirt that should have made her look like the sexiest woman alive, appeared in the living room with both hands on her hips. "Thought I'd check on—" As soon as she saw the folder lying open before Isabel, she stopped in her tracks. "Why are you looking at that?"

Isabel sat back on her stool, her head hurting more now than it had the day before. "You're going to fire me?"

"What? No, I'm not. Of course I'm not. Those are just some old—"

Scarlett took a step forward. Isabel recoiled.

"So you *were* going to fire me? Before all this? Before us? Is that it?" The guilt in Scarlett's eyes was enough to confirm Isabel's suspicions. "What about everyone else? The social media department? Customer service! Who's next? IT? Because your Black Diamond guys can put together a better app?"

"It's not what it looks like." Now Scarlett was speaking like a stressed-out schoolteacher trying to keep her unruliest child in line. "Would you let me explain?"

But Isabel barely heard her. All she could hear were echoes of all the promises Scarlett had made. *"I won't fire anyone. You have my word."*

Her words were as empty as the air surrounding them.

"What is there to explain?" Isabel said. "Everyone was right about you. You're just another corporate shill."

Scarlett blanched. "*Beauty*—"

"No. Don't you *dare*."

Isabel slipped off the stool, avoiding Scarlett's gaze as she grabbed her sweater from the couch and pulled it over her arms. As for her skirt? *Scarlett can keep it.* Isabel's lined leggings and coat would be enough to get her home. She couldn't stand the thought of going back into the bedroom to grab that tainted skirt. *A trophy, so she can remember how she seduced one of her employees.*

Isabel shook her head. "Everything is just numbers to you. *We* are just numbers. You know that if you let your family's heartless cronies get their hands on Connect, you're undermining everything it stands for. But I bet you just don't care."

"Isabel..."

Hurt welled in Scarlett's eyes. Isabel ignored it, squaring up to her, arms crossed. "Did you know? This whole time, did you know who I was? I guess if you were just going to fire me anyway, you didn't think anything of getting under my skirt before I left. What was I going to do, right? Complain to HR?"

Scarlett's face twisted in disgust. "You have no idea what you're saying, Isabel. You couldn't possibly understand."

"You're right. I don't understand what it's like to have a heart of black diamond." Isabel didn't have the strength to storm out. She simply walked to the door, barely acknowledging the woman following at her heels. "Just leave me alone. I'm tired of playing in the big leagues."

Isabel wasn't offended that Scarlett didn't protest. All it did was confirm everything she already felt about her boss, the woman who had turned out to be so much more.

A soulless corporate hag. That was what Scarlett was. She had always been too good to be true.

As Isabel opened the front door, a thought emerged from her mind like a monster from the depths. "Just tell me one thing," she said, her back to Scarlett. "Did you target me because of how young I am, how naive I am? Did you get off on it? On making me fall for you?"

Scarlett shook her head. "No, I didn't target you. I swear to God. As for those files... Isabel—"

She already had one foot out the door.

"—They were just ideas, my father's ideas. Please, just listen to me."

Isabel paused in the doorway. *Maybe the old me would have listened to her. The new me?* The one born from one too many betrayals in as little as two days?

She couldn't be swayed by a beautiful woman's promises.

Women like her prey on women like me. Because I'm too stupid to know any better. She kept her gaze straight ahead as she marched down the hallway to the elevator.

She should have known better than to believe she could have something as wonderful—as normal—as love, real love. Let alone with someone like Scarlett, who had seemed so perfect.

But now, Isabel saw her for who she was. And she was rotten to the core.

Chapter Twenty-Three

Parker stood over where Scarlett lay on the couch, arms crossed and hip cocked to the side as she looked down at her older sister. "What hole have you fallen into now?"

Scarlett continued to stare at the massive catalog mockup on Parker's coffee table with unfocused eyes. It displayed women of varying ages, ethnicities, and body types modeling skimpy lingerie.

Isabel would have looked great in that blood-red number. Scarlett would have sniffed, but she had no tears to cry. She had tried to cry. God knew she *felt* like she should cry after what happened with Isabel that morning. Yet the only emotion she allowed herself to feel in her hollow chest was…

Well, nothing.

Isabel had been right. Scarlett had a diamond as black as coal where her heart should have been.

"Come on," Parker said. "Out with it."

"I don't know what you're talking about."

"Sure, Scar. You knock on my door at eleven in the morning when you're supposed to be in the office. You stumble to my couch. You faceplant in Julia's nice pillow. And you look like someone killed your best friend in front of you. Tell me again how great you're doing, and don't leave out any details. I'll stand right here and let you take up more of my time when *I* should be working too."

I'm not getting anything past her. Scarlett should have expected it in coming here. But she hadn't known where else to go or what to do when she realized that Isabel was *gone*. No, not just gone. Too disgusted with her to even look her in the eye.

So much had happened in a single day. Scarlett had canceled all her meetings. She couldn't even think about the upcoming presentation to the prospective investors. Her head was a ghost town, haunted by specters of emotions and thoughts.

Until someone came rolling through. *Isabel.* Every so often, Scarlett thought of her and felt something again.

Grief, mostly.

"It's been a crazy week, that's all." Scarlett sat up, pressing her face into her hands. Her flimsy sweater and baggy leggings were the first things she found to pull on after getting out of the shower. She probably should have attempted to brush her hair.

"You mean since I saw you last Saturday? Sweetie, this is the most we've seen each other in years."

Scarlett sighed.

"Is this about that girl you're screwing five ways to next Tuesday?"

It took Scarlett a moment to realize what her sister had said. Once it hit her...

"Excuse me?"

Parker sat down on the far side of her couch, bumping Scarlett's feet off it with her hip. "You heard me. You can't hide it any longer. Your dyke of a sister has you figured out."

"I... but..."

"Do us both a favor and don't try to deny it. That way, we can cut to the chase and get to the bottom of whatever all this is."

Scarlett was speechless. *She knew? She really knew?* Who else knew? Were her secrets spreading around like the flu? "How did you find out?"

Parker scoffed. As Scarlett swung her feet back up to the couch, her sister caught them and pulled both into her lap. "I didn't 'find out.' If there's one thing I can say about you, it's that you're the best in the family when it comes to hiding your secrets. And given how fucked up our family is, that's saying something. You don't just push your skeletons into a closet. You build a secret room hidden behind a bigger secret panel. Unfortunately for you, I'm very clever."

Scarlett had half a mind to kick her sister right in the stomach. "How long have you known?"

"Oh, let's see. First, I figured out that Adrian had solved your dead bedroom problems by getting his freak on with someone who wasn't you. You're much too sharp—unnaturally so—for him to cheat without you noticing, and you didn't seem bothered by it. So I figured he had your permission to see other people."

"Has it gotten out? That he's seeing someone else?"

"What? No. I just knew that he went from surly to

happy, but you were still surly. He was obviously getting some, but it wasn't from you. Then the same thing happened with you when you started having secret trysts with women, too."

"How do you know all this?"

Parker shrugged. "I've known you were into girls for a while. I've always been able to tell that you had some curiosity, at least. But I knew for sure about a year ago when I saw a familiar escort prancing about the hallway. You called her a 'consultant.' I called her Barbara the Saint because I knew first-hand how much she prays to Jesus when a talented woman makes her come."

Scarlett buried her face in her hands. "You *cannot* be serious."

"What, that we've banged the same woman? It's a small gay world. Some things have to stay in the family."

While Parker laughed at her off-color joke, Scarlett's face burned. *She's known this whole time. For how long? Who the hell was Barbara? Who else did she see me with?* Her mother would sometimes sniff her nose at some of the women Scarlett brought around, but she always bought the excuses and explanations.

Because there was no way Scarlett was *gay*. The idea was inconceivable to her mother. If she ever thought that, she probably chalked it up to paranoia because of Parker.

Yet Parker knew. She had known all along.

Scarlett's world couldn't be collapsing any faster.

"I only recently deduced that you were fooling around with one of your employees because of Julia. She came home one night swearing up and down that she saw you necking some woman in the lobby." A wicked smile grew on Parker's face. "How bold of you, Scar. It's almost like you haven't grown up in this family at all."

"I... shit."

"I thought that was why you invited me over the other day. I was waiting for you to tell me all about it. When you didn't, I tried steering you in that direction, but you just kept clamming up. I guess you could say I've matured a bit, because as much as I like watching you squirm, I figured it was best for you to come around on your own. Especially if there's another woman involved."

The couch pulled Scarlett into its depths. *Any farther, and I'll fall straight down to my office.* That way, everyone who worked for her could pick apart her corpse and gossip about what kind of underwear she wore.

"You're right," she admitted. "You're right about everything. I can't get anything past you."

"Not really, no."

"Who else knows?"

"Nobody, I'd hazard. Mom sees what she wants to see. Bianca is preoccupied with her own problems. Dad doesn't think it's his business as long as you're not causing a scandal. But I think he would have said something if he figured it out. He doesn't hold back."

Scarlett groaned. The thought of her father giving her what for about her predicament was almost as gag-inducing as their mother throwing herself into hysterics for the press.

"God." She rubbed her forehead with her fingers. "What a waste these past few years have been. No, it's been so much longer than that. Decades. Two whole decades of... *this*."

"I honestly can't imagine losing that much of my life to our family."

"You don't get it." Scarlett sat back up, twenty years' worth of pressure and warped logic coming back to her. "From the day I was born, I had to do everything our parents wanted from me. It wasn't something I ever questioned. You know me. Always the good student, the good daughter. If our parents didn't like my little boyfriend—or even my group of friends—I either did without or got a new one. If a teacher berated me for behavior or bad marks, I shaped up. I wasn't like you, Parker. I didn't know these things about myself from such an early age. I didn't even know I *could* like girls until college, and..."

"Let me guess. By then, you were in too deep."

Scarlett nodded. "Adrian wasn't too long after that. I actually liked him, you know. He really did make me forget about that 'nonsense' when we were first together. I told myself it had just been a phase. And even if I was bisexual, so what? I was still attracted to *some* guys."

"Can't say I can relate to that part."

"That's the point, isn't it? Better me than you. I'm the heir. The model daughter who learns the ropes and inherits the company. In the meantime, I get married to a suitable match and pop out a kid to keep things going. And that's the only way I get to have a relationship with our mother. I was always Daddy's girl. Mom has Bianca."

"And I've got me, myself, and I."

Scarlett didn't mean to keep pushing her sister in this unsavory direction, but she felt compelled to give voice to all the thoughts and feelings she'd kept buried inside for decades now. Just like Parker was *fast, fast, fast* right out of the gate, Scarlett had always taken her time coming around to new ideas. She really was her father's daughter.

"So what happened with Adrian?" Parker asked. "Just wasn't doing it for you anymore, and by then it had been a decade or something? I can't even remember how long you two have been together."

"It's been a long time. Even accounting for the past few years, when we could hardly be considered a couple, it's still by far the longest relationship I've ever had. But the years go by so quickly. You get busy, you blink, and your whole thirties have flown by."

"I'll keep that in mind."

Scarlett shook her head. "I don't want to keep living like this."

"So don't. Grab your new girlfriend and run for your life."

"That's the problem. Word got out at work that Isabel and I were having a secret relationship. And then she saw some notes I'd put together about Connect's future, and she got the wrong idea. She's mad. Probably not just at me, but how everything's going in her world. She's my polar opposite. Young. Sensitive. Strong, but in a beautifully vulnerable way." Something squeezed inside Scarlett's chest. "All this, it's crushing her."

"Didn't think about that when you started fooling around with her, huh?"

"I didn't care how old she was when it was just online. That was how it started. I didn't know who she was. Then things moved offline, and I realized she was the same woman I worked with every day. Then she was Isabel, not just Beauty, the username on my screen. And then everything went to hell..."

"So it did. Now, what are you going to do about it?"

"I don't *know*," Scarlett said. "I don't know if I can do this. I don't know if I can *fight* it all. Her. Our parents. My fate. Because Isabel and I were never meant to be."

"Seriously? You meet some woman online, fall head over heels for her, and it turns out she was right in front of you all along? If such a thing as fate exists, Isabel is *yours*."

"Maybe meeting her wasn't fate. Maybe it was the universe playing a cruel joke on me. Because I was never meant to have her. It was always supposed to be me and Adrian, or some other appropriate man who I could start a picture-perfect nuclear family with. That's the life I was always meant to have."

"Says who? Our parents?" Parker scoffed. "What the hell do they know? Are they going to be here decades from now when you're looking back on *your* life? No. They'll be *dead*." She leaned forward, locking eyes with her sister. "Our lives are our own, Scar. Who you love shouldn't matter. For fuck's sake, it's the 21st century. It's the old guard like them that keeps us from being happy over something as stupid as the gender of our lovers. Who says you can't have a strong marriage with a younger woman? Who says you can't have kids? Who says you can't *not* have kids?"

"Who says you have to avoid double negatives?" Scarlett murmured.

"Oh my *God*." Parker rolled her eyes. "You're such a nerd."

And just like that, the two of them were fifteen years

younger and sitting in Parker's teenage bedroom. "Not all of us can be bad girls who flaunt the rules like you," Scarlett said.

"Clearly you're no stranger to flaunting the rules. I mean, you're fingering your employee. Pretty sure there's a rule about that."

"Why do you insist on torturing me with these jokes of yours?"

"You want me to whip out the evidence I have that you're a kinky bitch? No? Then we'll keep it to fingering jokes."

Scarlett bit back her words. *I won't ask how she knows that, either.* Parker was dangerous, wasn't she? Between her sharp mind and devil-may-care attitude, she always had it in her to start WW3 in the Black family.

Instead, it might be Scarlett, who was building all the resolve she could to add to her personal arsenal of defensive weapons for use against Phillip and Vivianne Black.

"You're right." Scarlett sat up on the couch, fixing her slovenly clothes and fluffing her greasy hair. "I have to live my life for myself. Mom and Dad can't live it for me. As long as I'm not hurting anyone, who gives a flying fuck?"

Parker chuckled. "That's the spirit."

"I've got to make things right with Isabel. And Connect. And Adrian." Scarlett swallowed the lump threatening to choke her. "And our family."

This time when Parker goaded her, it was with nothing but affection in her voice. "Damn right. Grab the bull by the horns and show it who is going to be the boss of this family one day."

Scarlett wasn't even thinking that far ahead. She was thinking of the past, and the now.

I can't lose Isabel. Too much change was on Scarlett's fingertips.

And she would be damned if she let it slip through her fingers like ash.

Chapter Twenty-Four

Whether it was a testament to her maturity didn't matter. All Isabel knew was that suffering through work while everyone talked about her behind her back was the absolute pits.

"Apparently they've been dating since before the acquisition," Isabel heard while returning to her desk after her lunch break the next day. *"Now, I don't have any authority on this, but I hear Evan basically pimped her out to seal the deal. What a jackass, right?"*

The Isabel of one week ago would have risen against those baseless accusations, but what was the point now? People thought whatever they wanted to. While the NDA kept gossip in the office, there wasn't much Isabel could do to defend herself—or Scarlett. The best thing to do, besides avoiding the boss as much as possible, was keep her head down and focus on her work.

For as much as Isabel wanted out of this hell, she still had a job to do. She had bills to pay. The only way she was leaving Connect was if she was fired—not to protect her dignity, but so she could at least get unemployment. She was hurt and confused, but not *stupid*.

Avoiding Scarlett was easy at times, and an acrobatic act at others. Scarlett wasn't even in the office most of the time, but when she was? *I'm not here, I'm in the bathroom. I'm not there, I'm on break down in the lobby.*

So when Isabel reached her desk and opened her work laptop, she found a note stuck to the screen inside.

Can we talk? Let me know.

-D

D for Dominique. If Scarlett thought she was getting through to Isabel by using that name, she was crueler than anyone had taken her for.

Isabel tore up the note and tossed it into the trash, then put on her noise-canceling headphones. Usually, she used them to drown out the noise of the office so she could concentrate, but today, she used them so she didn't have to hear a single word out of anyone's mouth. The headphones also advertised that she was busy working so that her coworkers would avoid talking to her.

Or so she hoped. But it didn't stop someone from gently poking her in the shoulder.

Isabel closed her eyes and inhaled a deep, strengthening breath. If it was Scarlett, she needed to armor herself before she turned around.

But it wasn't Scarlett. It was Alexis, giving off the distinct impression that she had a tail tucked between her legs.

Isabel pulled off her headphones reluctantly.

"Hey," Alexis said. "Can we talk? I'm on break."

Isabel crossed her arms. "Came by to farm me for more

gossip-fodder, huh? Lemme guess. You want to verify whether Evan Albright was pimping me out in the old office?"

"Huh? No way. Who's spreading that around?"

"Emmy, if you can believe it."

"But she was..." Alexis's confusion spread across her face like freckles. "Never mind. Look, I came by to apologize." She reached into her front pocket. "Here. An olive branch."

It was chocolate from the lobby vending machine. *She remembered that Buncha Crunch is my favorite.* It was like they were about to go to the movies and were smuggling in snacks.

She pulled a chair over so Alexis could sit down. Isabel had only just finished her lunch of a turkey sandwich and potato chips, but with all the work she was doing, her brain needed fuel. Some chocolate would hit the spot.

"I'm sorry." Alexis opened the package and poured a few bites of Crunch into Isabel's hand before taking some for herself. "I shouldn't have told Ned about what I saw. I was just in so much shock when I came back on Friday night and saw you making out with the boss in the lobby. Like, right there in front of me."

Isabel shook her head. "It was stupid of us. We were caught up in the moment."

"After you left together, I just stood there, frozen. And then Ned came down, and he asked me what was wrong. Why I looked so pale, you know? So I just blurted it out. I never intended for... I'm so sorry, Izzy. I didn't realize what I had done until I came to work Monday and he had told *everyone*. They all got me worked up about it, too. Especially since I thought you were seeing this woman from the internet."

"I told you," Isabel said. "I didn't know Scarlett and Dominique were the same person. Not until a crazy coincidence made us realize we were dating each other. We didn't even know until the night you saw us together."

Alexis put a piece of chocolate in her mouth, eyes wide with disbelief. "It's like something straight out of a movie."

"It feels like it. Except this isn't fiction, Alexis. This is my life."

"I know. I'm sorry. I should have talked to you about it in private. Gotten your side of the story. And now we know to never tell Ned a single secret if our lives depend on it." Alexis leaned forward, elbows on her knees. "So… Scarlett Black. Is your girlfriend. Is Dominique. Not in that order."

"I still don't know what to think about it, either."

"'Cause it's crazy, right?" As if they were best friends again, Alexis offered more chocolate to Isabel, tapping the box into her hand. "It's bonkers. Who knew that the hot lady you met online was your boss? Wait, isn't she—"

"Straight and engaged?" Isabel's voice couldn't be flatter if she steamrolled it. "That's what I thought, too. It's also why I ignored all the signs that she was Dominique. Everyone knows Scarlett has been engaged to that banker for literally years. Apparently, it's complicated, but I shouldn't share her personal business. That's between us. Just know that her perfect life isn't as perfect as it seems."

Alexis grimaced. "I may have been unjustly negative toward her. I'm sorry. It must have been tough hearing me tear her apart while you were falling for her."

"Well, you weren't too far off the mark," Isabel muttered.

Alexis rattled the remaining chocolate in its box. "Huh?"

"Nothing." Isabel folded her headphones and set them on her desk. *Maybe I've been too harsh on Scarlett, too.* Since their fight the previous morning, she had kept a respectful distance from Isabel. *She's not defending herself, either.* She had asked Isabel to let her explain, but what was there to explain if Scarlett wasn't going to deny any of it?

Alexis offered the last of the chocolate to her friend. "You're really busted up about this, huh? I mean, beyond the stupid rumors going around."

"I guess so. I thought we had something special going on. But that's been a pipe dream with her. I… I don't want to get into the details. We had a fight, and I haven't talked to her since. I've been avoiding her while I'm at work."

The door to Scarlett's office opened. Isabel swiveled her chair around slightly so she wouldn't see the woman emerging from it.

"I don't know what to say," Alexis murmured. "Other than, I guess if you need to rant, or have a drink of commiseration, or hear about my dating woes for a change, I'm game. I owe you that much after the shitstorm I caused by telling Ned what I saw." She put her hand on Isabel's arm. "I hope you can forgive me, Izzy. You're one of my best friends, and I did a terrible thing."

For the first time in three days, a sense of comfort returned to Isabel's anxious heart. "Thanks. That's—"

"Ms. Diaz?"

The warmth in Isabel's chest evaporated. She looked up to find Scarlett's impassive gaze upon her as she loomed over her desk.

"Uh oh," Alexis mouthed, before scooting her chair out of the way.

Isabel swallowed. "I…"

"Could you see me in my office, please? It's important." But Scarlett didn't wait for her to respond, turning on her heel and marching back to her office, the door left ajar.

"What's that about?" Alexis asked. "Can't be about the new UI layout. I heard the meeting with the investors went well this morning. They were singing your praises about the design."

Isabel had heard that too, but she had been too upset to celebrate. *What is there to celebrate when we'll all be fired soon?* "I have no idea. Should I go?"

"Do you have a choice? She's your boss, after all."

Isabel stood up from her chair. "I guess so. Wish me luck."

She kept her head held high as she walked toward Scarlett's office, but she made sure to avoid Emmy, who had taken up Caroline's mantle as head of gossip after Isabel had snapped at her in the breakroom that day.

What do I do? Give Scarlett the silent treatment? Be professional? What if she's trying to get back with me? Isabel wasn't ready for this yet. She still needed time to process all her thoughts and feelings. But what else could she do?

She didn't bother to knock. She merely opened the office door the rest of the way and stepped inside. As usual, Scarlett sat at her desk, looking like the million dollars she probably had in her checking account. *An A-line office dress in her best color. Sensible three-inch heels. Simple jewelry that brings out her best features instead of stealing attention from them.*

And that hair. That soft brown hair that accentuated Scarlett's fine forehead and delectable neck. She had always been a vision, one that Isabel ignored for the sake of professional propriety. *But now that I know who she is...* She was more beautiful than Isabel could stand to look at.

Scarlett rose from her seat. "I know you don't want to talk to me, but before you decide to run out of here again, hear me out."

Isabel didn't give her the satisfaction of a response. But she didn't leave either.

"First, I want to apologize. You deserve more than what I've offered in the past few days. I really do care about you, you know. And I told the truth about the files. Those plans I put together were from back when I'd just taken over at Connect. But they represented only one possible option, not a definitive plan of action. And they were all based on my father's ideas, not mine. From the start, he wanted to go nuclear with the company. He brought me in to either turn things around in record time or to fire everyone and facilitate folding departments into other Black Diamond properties."

That might have surprised Isabel months, even weeks ago. But not anymore. The harsh truths of the world no longer shocked her.

"But I've long known that I could never bring myself to do that. Not then, not now. And I'm determined to make things right. With you, and with the company. We're going to make sure that not a single person gets fired. But to do that, we have to turn things around."

We? Isabel opened her mouth to speak, but Scarlett didn't give her the chance.

"I have a plan," she said. "But for it to work, I need your help. And if you won't do it for me, then do it for your coworkers." She sat up straight, clasping her hands together in front of her. "Do it for the vision you all have for this app. Only you can make it come to fruition."

Something stirred inside Isabel's chest. Was Scarlett attempting to manipulate her, tugging at her heartstrings because she knew how much Isabel cared about the plucky grassroots startup that had become her family?

Did it matter, if it meant saving Connect?

She closed her eyes for a moment, then looked Scarlett dead in the eyes. "Okay. What do you need me to do?"

She would work with Scarlett, if for no reason other than to save everyone's jobs—and the last of her hope.

Chapter Twenty-Five

Showtime.

Scarlett had never been so confidently nervous since entering her thirties. The butterflies in her stomach began to tear her apart the moment she saw her parents standing outside the executive conference room in the Black Diamond Building, an intimate but intimidating space where Phillip often met with his cohorts—both publicly and privately. As for Vivianne?

Nobody was more confused than her when she walked into the room late Saturday afternoon.

"Is this really necessary?" She pushed ahead of her husband as they entered the conference room. "I'm supposed to be at Gwendolyn Revere's garden party. Not that I *like* that shameless tart, mind you, but it won't look good if I don't go. And Saturdays are just so—"

"Thanks for coming." Scarlett motioned for her parents to sit on opposite sides of the table, as if they were at divorce arbitration. *That would be a shakeup in the family for the ages.* And maybe it would distract Vivianne enough to ignore her daughters' love lives.

Both her parents took a seat, barely acknowledging Isabel, who was setting up Scarlett's work laptop so it connected to the projector on the wall. Scarlett was to do most of the talking at the meeting, leaving Isabel as the 'assistant.'

"I know this is a busy day for both of you," Scarlett said. "Weren't you supposed to play golf with Adrian's uncle?"

That was directed at her father. *Even on a Saturday, he's wearing a suit.* Scarlett knew he owned khaki pants and polo shirts, but those were only for golfing. The man probably slept in his suits.

He shrugged. "We had an appointment to do so, but he didn't mind that I sent him a raincheck. The man is busy as well."

So Adrian used to tell me. Aside from Isabel, Adrian was the only person who knew about this meeting. *What a short but awkward conversation that had been...*

"By the way," Scarlett said. "Allow me to introduce you to Isabel Diaz."

Isabel popped up from behind the laptop sheepishly. *Look at her.* Cute, professional, and like a deer in headlights in the presence of Vivianne and Phillip Black. At the very least, she obviously knew who the latter was—and what kind of sway he held in Seattle's business world.

"She's the head of graphic design for Connect, and has been a huge help in putting together this presentation. Father, I—"

"What's Connect?" her mother hissed across the table. "Why am I here?" That was louder, and directed at her daughter. "Honey, I have nothing to do with this. You know I don't know business."

"She knows how to talk, though," Phillip muttered.

"Yes, well, I have other things to talk about as soon as I've finished discussing the future of Connect with Father," Scarlett said. "Why don't we begin so I can get you two out of here and off to where you need to go this evening?"

Phillip and his wife exchanged a puzzled look. "I do appreciate brevity," he said.

"Fantastic. Isabel?"

Isabel clicked a button that brought up the first of several PowerPoint slides. Right away, charts and graphs appeared on the wall for her father's perusal. Scarlett didn't say a thing as he sat back in his seat and studied the numbers.

Her mother? She grumbled about Gwendolyn Revere and her "pretentious shindig."

Scarlett continued. "I—with the help of Ms. Diaz—have come up with a plan to turn Connect around financially and help it fulfill its true potential to change the world for the better." She gestured to the slide on the wall. "Here we have our current numbers. Father, you'll be pleased to hear that the investors we courted this week are all-in with our vision. It helped that I had dinner with the head of the firm last night. He was *very* interested in our ideas."

"Our?" Phillip asked.

"Of course. I told you Isabel has been a huge help with this. Half of these ideas are hers, and I intend to make sure she's properly credited for every single one."

"Can you believe she had *fondue* at this time of year?"

Vivianne muttered, scrolling through her phone. "Honestly!"

Scarlett ignored her. "Our recent redesign has made the app functionally and aesthetically simpler. This is because we believe that the core tenet of Connect is simple. Communities come together, not just in times of need, but to build relationships and to help guide each other through changing norms. As we've often seen throughout our lives, people can be more than physically alone. There is a growing need, especially among the younger generations, for neighborly assistance and love that we can rely on at—"

"Scarlett," Phillip said, "I'm not your pitch. Get on with it."

"Right." She cleared her throat and motioned for Isabel to bring up the next slide. "When we acquired Connect, the plan was always to expand its reach. Take it nationwide and allow people to connect with others all over the country. But Connect is all about appealing to local communities. That's why, when you log on, all you're going to see is who is in your direct neighborhood. That goes for small businesses, too. When considering advertising, we knew it was inevitable, but how could we integrate it in a way that doesn't offend the sensibilities of our users? Nobody wants to log on and see corporate advertising. That goes double for *our* users."

Phillip said nothing, but his expression was critical.

Scarlett powered through. "That's why, in two years, when we take Connect not national but *global*, we will *only* allow small local businesses to advertise. The whole point of the app is to let people support those in their community. This is a fantastic opportunity for local businesses, from

Mom & Pop pharmacies to small bookstore chains, to reach their audience without having to compete against corporate budgets."

Right on cue, Isabel brought up the next slide. Scarlett already knew what her father was thinking.

"Yes, this will cost much more money out the gate. We're looking at a sizable investment to make this happen. But it *will* pay us back in the long term. All of my research projects that we're looking at double the gain compared to if we allow corporate entities to start advertising tomorrow. These projections take into account user feedback. The happier users are, the more they're willing to engage with local advertising. And the budget will be happy, too. We won't have to lay off a single employee. Besides…"

She looked to Isabel, who, for the first time in what felt like weeks, didn't avoid her gaze.

"We'll need every employee Connect currently has to make this happen on time. They're a crew that's dedicated to the message that Evan Albright preached. Even though he's gone from the company, his original vision lives on in the hearts of employees like Isabel over there."

Silence fell over the room. Scarlett turned back to her father, awaiting his response.

But she didn't have to wait for long.

"This is the exact opposite of what I asked you to do," he said. "Or have you forgotten how much money we're losing on this app every day?"

"Yes. You asked me to lay off people where we could, not spend *more* of our money," Scarlett said drolly. "Unfortunately, that wasn't going to work in the long term. I fully intend to see this current plan through. That's how much faith I have in it."

Her father's voice took on the tone he reserved for intimidating subordinates and business rivals. "Is that so?"

But Scarlett wasn't backing down. After all, she'd learned from the best.

"Didn't you bring me on as CEO to save this sinking ship? Haven't my plans worked out before? You wouldn't have trusted me with this project if you didn't think so." She matched her tone to his. "I've been acting in an executive capacity for over ten years, Father. I've been under your tutelage even longer than that. Have I ever once given you doubt? Haven't I pulled through with my plans *every single time*? I want this to succeed as much as you do."

Her father rubbed his chin, elbow digging into the conference table. "It's risky, this plan of yours. You say you came up with it with your employee there?"

"Yes." Scarlett nodded in Isabel's direction. "She's the one who came up with the idea that we should only allow local businesses to advertise in their neighborhoods. Fostering community is what Connect is all about. In fact, as of the remodel, it's our new motto."

Isabel clicked a button, revealing the company's new logo—a pair of hands holding the C for Connect. *Fostering Community* was written in serif font beneath it.

Phillip leaned back in his chair. "Like I said, spending money to make more money is always risky, and you'll have to prove to the board that they should release the funds necessary for this to happen. But…" He cocked his head to the side. "The logic is sound, and it's clear you've done the research. I don't see why you shouldn't try it."

Scarlett couldn't believe her ears. "Really?"

"Of course. As you said, you've been doing this for years now. I've taught you everything I know. And yours is the reasoning of a new generation. I can't pretend to always know what's best. If you think this is the route to take and you're willing to stand by it…" He gave her a firm nod. "Fine. Do it."

Scarlett could barely contain the smile threatening to explode on her face. Behind her, tension lifted from Isabel's shoulders.

"This is incredibly exciting and all," Vivianne said, slapping her phone down on the table, "but *why* did I have to be here for this? I'm sorry. I know how much this business stuff means to you two—God bless you both for it—but I am bored out of my mind. I could have been eating fondue instead of passing out at this table. *Why am I here?*"

The tension returned to Isabel's body. *You don't know the half of it with her.* But explaining Vivianne Black to Isabel could come later. Right now?

Things were about to get interesting.

Scarlett steeled herself. "I asked you here because I have something else to tell both of you." She turned her body toward her mother. The woman thrived on undivided attention. "Something I should have told you a long time ago."

That piqued even her father's interest. He leaned closer, undoubtedly wondering what else his daughter had up her sleeve.

"Oh, honey…" Stars lit up in Vivianne's eyes as she slapped her hand over her heart. "Have you and Adrian finally set a date? Oh! Oh, *honey,* are you pregnant?"

"What? No!" Scarlett squashed her mother's hopes before Vivianne could get the wrong idea. "Although this *is* about Adrian. It's about how we've broken up. I thought you should know."

The smile slid from Vivianne's face. Phillip's eyes grew slightly wider. It was perhaps the biggest expression of emotion he had ever shown.

"It was over years ago," Scarlett said, dropping all pretense. "So long ago that Adrian has dated more than one woman in private. Women who are *not* me. Don't get me wrong. He never cheated on me. It was with my approval. Likewise, I have been dating in my personal time as well. The reason I'm telling you the truth now is because I've found someone who makes me happy, someone who—"

"*What?*" Vivianne's sudden shriek was not unexpected, but Scarlett had hoped to cut it off before it grew in decibels. "What are you talking about? You and Adrian have... *what?*"

Scarlett gritted her teeth before addressing her hysterical mother. "Adrian and I have broken up and have moved on with different people. That's another thing I need to get out in the open right now, because we both want to move on publicly as well. You know, before we're fifty."

"But—"

"Like I said," Scarlett raised her voice, drowning out her mother, "I've found someone who makes me happy, and I plan on going public with the new relationship before the press gets a whiff of it. Because they *will*. People are already gossiping about it in this building. Probably because that someone is Isabel right here."

Scarlett's parents weren't the only ones stunned into

silence. It was Isabel who gasped the loudest. It wasn't like Scarlett had told her that she'd planned to do this. The past three days of them working together on the presentation had been completely platonic. Not once had Isabel insinuated that she wanted to get back together, and not once had Scarlett attempted to seduce her.

This is me going rogue. It was her grand moment, not only to stand up to her parents, but to take possession of the only person who mattered in her life.

Too bad her mother couldn't be happy for her.

"Are you *kidding* me?" Had she ever been that shade of red before? It was like every blood vessel in her face had burst. "What is going on? Is it 'give your mother a heart attack' day? Because that's what you are doing, Scarlett Abigail Black!"

"I'm not going to argue about this with you, Mother. Believe it or not, I've been attracted to women my whole life."

"My ass you have!" Cursing? That was new for her. *She's mad. Really mad.* "This is all Parker's doing, isn't it? Letting her get away scot-free all these years has put it into *your* head that this is acceptable. With Adrian Holt right there! Oh, you have to be kidding me. This is—"

"I am forty years old, mother!" Smoke flared from Scarlett's nostrils. "Close enough to it, anyway. And I'll be *damned* if I let either you or Father tell me how to live my life at this point in it. I'm nearly middle-aged and living a damn lie. What century is it? This isn't your day anymore. I'm not going to hide behind a man even when I'm in love with a woman. Let alone someone like Isabel, who I love more than anyone I *ever* have! Including Adrian!"

Isabel's hands fell limply over the laptop keyboard, closing out of the slides and accidentally highlighting half the icons on the desktop. Her face was so pale and her mouth open so wide that she looked like she had seen a terrifying ghost.

"Nothing has given me more joy these past few months than Isabel. What I feel in my heart when I look at her says it all." Scarlett turned to her. Isabel was backing toward the wall as if she could escape through it. "I love her. I *choose* her."

Isabel didn't say a word. She only stumbled over her feet, catching herself on the back of the chair next to Phillip before collapsing into it in shock.

"Do something!" Vivianne snapped at her husband. "It's bad enough we've got one daughter down this path! But Scarlett? The future chairwoman of your family's company? This is—"

Phillip slammed a palm on the table, silencing everyone in the room. Including Vivianne, who was stunned into that blessed quiet that her husband had undoubtedly been beseeching for the past forty years.

"Would you *shut up* for once? My God, Viv. Allow me to process this information without your *blathering* and screeching in my ear. Besides..." He turned his chair toward Scarlett, who prepared herself for her father's judgment. "Scarlett is right. This is her life to live. As long as she does it with intention and integrity, what is it to us who she's with? I'm so sick of you going on about things that no longer concern us. Adrian is out. And quite frankly, I'm glad of it. I haven't liked his father or uncle for years. I only put up with them because our children were engaged."

"But Phillip!"

"Have we not raised our daughter to be assertive enough to run this company? Have we not done everything in our power to give her what she needs to be her own woman? I didn't raise a robot when you handed her over to me, Viv. Robots don't run companies, people do. For fuck's sake!" Was this the first time he'd cursed like this in front of one of his children? Probably. "Let her live her life. Our daughters don't have to be as miserable as we have been."

Vivianne's mouth gaped open, over and over. She looked moments from passing out. "This is simply... but... *Adrian Holt...*"

Phillip stood up and straightened out his jacket. "I've known Adrian as long as you have. He's a competent man who can take care of himself. And from the sounds of things, he's moved on already."

Scarlett offered her father a smile. "Thank you for understanding, Dad."

"It's a bit of a sticky situation, though." He rounded the table and urged his wife to get out of her chair. "Dating one of your employees."

"I'm already sorting it out."

"Oh, I don't doubt that you're capable of dealing with it yourself. Just be careful. Negative consequences reflect upon the family, and the company you're to lead one day."

Scarlett took that to heart as her father rounded up his wife and led her to the conference room door. While Vivianne fussed and threatened to send her daughter to the nearest sanitarium, Scarlett squared her shoulders and refused to give her mother what she so sorely wanted.

I'm not your toy to play house with, Mother.

The door closed. The soundproofing was so good that even if her parents were having a verbal altercation in the hallway, Scarlett couldn't hear a scathing word.

She could, however, hear the thundering of Isabel's heart.

Scarlett allowed a triumphant smile to crown her face as she set her hands on the back of her father's chair. "Connect and all of its employees live another day. I daresay your idea to only allow local businesses to advertise was the clincher, Isabel. Thank you. For... everything."

She meant it, too. The help. The ideas. The talent Isabel brought to the website and app design.

How she changed my life.

"You said..." Isabel swiveled her chair to face Scarlett, her hand on her heart as she breathed in deep. "You said that you love me."

"I did. Because I do." Scarlett drew her hands back, clasping them in front of her as she gazed down at Isabel. "It's fine if you reject me now. It would hurt terribly. My heart would be broken for... I wouldn't know how long. But at least I'd be telling the truth, living the life that's right for me, for once. Because I *do* love you, and I want the whole world to know. That's how special you are to me. Even before I knew you were Beauty, I was drawn to you. The only reason I never approached you was because you were my employee. And I wasn't out. That's why I spent all that time anonymously looking for love. And knowing that I found it, and with you... I can't pass up this chance. I have to tell you how I feel, even if it means you turning me down."

She let her gaze drop, just for a moment. Because

looking into Isabel's eyes after speaking those last few words was too much to bear.

But when she looked up again, Isabel was rising to her feet, her eyes glittering with tears.

"I… I've never been in love before," she said. "Not really. I've always longed for that special someone who makes me feel that way, but I've never been able to find them. And for a while, I thought that maybe love just wasn't in the cards for me. But then you came along and…" Isabel blinked away a tear, wiping it from her cheek. "You made me feel like the love I always yearned for was possible. You made me feel like *anything* was possible. Even you and me, two people thrown together in the most unlikely of ways. Two people who have no business ever being together. But here we are, and…"

Scarlett held her breath.

"I love you too. I don't know if that makes me foolish or brave, but that's how I feel."

Scarlett couldn't hold herself back. As soon as those magical words left Isabel's lips, Scarlett drew her into her arms.

"I'm so sorry," she said into the crook of Isabel's neck.

"What are you sorry for?"

"Everything."

"What's *everything?*"

She stepped back, both hands lingering on Isabel's shoulders. *I want to hold her again.* But Scarlett had something to say, something that could only be said face to face.

She squeezed Isabel's shoulders. "You and me, we deserve better than what we had. We deserve to start over, and do it right this time. No secrets. No assumed identities.

No shame or guilt for either of us. We'll be honest with each other from the very beginning."

Isabel's concern softened into understanding. "You're right. Everything's been such a mess. We owe it to ourselves to start over again, to put the hurt and confusion behind us."

Scarlet nodded. "Although…"

"Yes?"

"I'd love a kiss right now. We deserve that simple pleasure before we start anew."

Isabel wrapped her arms around Scarlett's neck, her smile a mile wide. "I love you, Scarlett Black."

Scarlett brought her closer. "And I love you, Isabel Diaz."

They would start over, just as soon as they left this room. But as they shared a kiss, the sun setting over the Seattle skyline beyond the window, they were Dominique and Beauty, two strangers brought together by fate.

Chapter Twenty-Six

The Black Diamond Building boasted its share of restaurants and bars, but none compared to Noir, the premier members' only venue. Isabel had never been inside the bar before. Only people of influence were allowed through the doors. Or people who knew someone of influence.

In Isabel's case, it was a certain CEO of an up-and-coming app who put her name on the list.

She sat at the main bar, doodling on the napkin that came with her martini. For the past few weeks, her time had been split between Connect and pulling her personal life together.

That included getting back into art as a serious hobby. *One of my teachers always said that in order to grow as an artist, you need to take every opportunity to hone your craft.*

Which meant taking advantage of quiet moments in quieter bars. Isabel had set aside her phone in favor of a pen and a large white napkin. Her subject? The barback, softly illuminated by the lights showing off the top-shelf brands behind him, which also occupied the *bottom* shelf. Isabel's martini had *not* been cheap. But it wasn't on her tab.

"What an interesting interpretation of the bartender," someone said behind her.

Isabel dropped her pen and turned slowly to behold the most beautiful woman she had ever seen.

Dark brown hair. Slight face. Shapely body clad in a tight black dress. She was stunning. There were other attractive women in the bar that night, but none like her. She looked like she owned the place.

Isabel leaned back, allowing the stranger to get a better look at the drawing. "He has interesting hair. I wanted to capture it in this light."

The bartender in question didn't hear her. Or, perhaps, he was paid to not hear anything. He didn't even acknowledge the two women at the end of the bar until the stranger sat down next to Isabel without invitation.

"I'll have what she's having," the woman said to the bartender. "Was it shaken or stirred?"

Isabel couldn't suppress her giggle. "Are you in the camp that thinks the next James Bond should be a woman? Shaken, by the way."

As the bartender went to work, the stranger tucked her hair behind her ear, regarding Isabel with a roguish smile. "Jane Bond has a certain ring to it."

Isabel folded her napkin and slid it to the woman whose perfume smelled of musk and spring rain. "Take it. As a token of our happenstance."

"Aren't you going to sign it? I simply must know the name of the next great artist to bring life to Seattle's scene."

She has a way with words, that's for sure. The more Isabel stared at this woman, the more she realized that Ms. Brown Hair was older than her. How much? Ten years? Fifteen? It was hard to tell when good genes and money were at play.

She's definitely made of money. Isabel had no problem with that. Then again, everyone in this bar—except her—was made of money.

Isabel clicked her pen back to life and signed *ISABEL DIAZ* on the bottom of the napkin.

"What a lovely name for a lovely lady." The woman held out a delicate hand. "Scarlett Black. You may have heard of my family."

Isabel had to contain her laughter as she shook the woman's hand. "Heard of them? Don't they own the building?"

"You might even say that I'll own the building one day. I'm the heir to this tragic empire."

"Now you're just showing off."

The bartender arrived with Scarlett's martini. "No, I'm flirting with you. A gorgeous woman I've never seen before in Noir? I had to investigate. Please tell me you're single, Beauty."

Isabel perked up at that. "Beauty?"

"I call you what I see."

Isabel studied the woman's face. "Scarlett Black… haven't you had a scandal recently? Yes. I seem to recall you breaking up with your long-term fiancé. That didn't go well, huh?"

"You know how it is. You're in the closet, you get with the boy your parents pushed at you for years, the next thing you know it's been a whole decade and it's time to let the poor bastard go." Fine eyelashes batted in Isabel's direction. "Time to move on. Meet some women."

"I'm no bed-warmer, Ms. Black."

"I would never think of you as such. The women I flirt with and take back to my apartment? They're special. They have to know they are, too, if I'm to treat them to untold pleasure for more than one night."

Hot damn, she's forward. Isabel would be lying if she didn't admit she'd been thinking of Scarlett 'like that' from the moment she sat down. *She's got that domineering strength to her.* Did that extend to the bedroom, too?

If Isabel played her cards right, she'd soon find out. Who knew that coming to such a high-end bar would be her lucky break?

"But you barely know me," Isabel pointed out.

"So what? Sometimes, the best sex life has to offer is with complete strangers. You don't know their baggage, their politics, what they're like at their worst. That can all come later."

Scarlett sipped her martini. Isabel had completely forgotten about hers. "This is what you do with your newfound freedom? You hop into your family's private bar and hit on the eligible women?"

"Only the ones that set my imagination ablaze."

"I don't know if I should be impressed or wary."

"Be neither. Be turned on. Because this is a once-in-a-lifetime opportunity I'm offering you."

"Is that so?"

"Oh, yes." Scarlett lowered her voice until it was barely audible over the soft hum of the bar's background noise.

"Come home with me and I'll make love to you in ways you didn't know possible."

Isabel stirred her martini with the olive-speared metal toothpick. "You're confident."

"Confident, and available. What do you say, Ms. Diaz?"

She couldn't keep her curiosity from showing on her face. "I shouldn't go home with strangers."

"I'm not a stranger. I'm Scarlett Black." She leaned in, purring into her target's ear. "And I want to make you mine."

Isabel's pulse fluttered. *It's been a while since a woman touched me.* When would be her next chance?

If she passed this up, would she regret it?

"Here's the thing, Ms. Isabel. I know you want to come home with me. I *know* you yearn to know my touch, to feel that ephemeral bliss that strikes a woman when the right person fucks her like the princess she is. So what are you waiting for? I could do more of a song and dance to seduce you, but we both know what we want." Scarlett locked her eyes onto Isabel's. "You. Me. My bed. The whole night in front of us."

While Isabel had already made up her mind the moment Scarlett approached her, the woman's forwardness knocked her off balance, almost literally. Isabel was already halfway off her stool, vainly containing the parts of her that screamed to be underneath Scarlett Black right now.

"All right. Since you know me so well..." Isabel kicked back the last of her martini and grabbed her jacket from the hook beneath the bar. "Let's go."

"And here I thought you were going to put up more of a fight," Scarlett murmured.

"Well, I can't exactly say no to *the* Scarlett Black, who gave up her cushy engagement to be with women like me. It's almost a civic duty at this point."

"I'm glad you see it that way. Trust me, I'll do my part to make it worth your while."

Scarlett had barely touched her drink, but she left it behind on the bar, leading Isabel out of Noir and down the quiet hallway, taking them to the elevators. But instead of hitting the down arrow, she pressed the up button and turned her attention to Isabel.

"Where did you get those earrings?" she asked, the doors dinging open.

Isabel followed her into the elevator. "These?" She touched the golden earrings dangling beside her neck. "My last girlfriend gave them to me."

Scarlett tapped the number for one of the topmost floors. As soon as the doors closed, she rounded on Isabel, pushing her up against the wall.

"Take them off. You don't need to think about *her* when I'm fucking you."

Isabel swallowed the lump of excitement in her throat. *Musk and spring rain.* Coming at her. Enveloping her. Consuming her.

"I couldn't possibly." She turned her head before a kiss could seal her fate. While her heart pounded and her thighs threatened to spread wide open for the woman encroaching on her space, she said, "Wouldn't it be hotter to fuck me so hard that you make my earrings jangle? It would be like stealing me away from that forgettable woman."

Scarlett wrapped her hands around the bar lining the elevator wall at either side of her prey, her white-hot gaze searing Isabel's skin. "You're a naughty thing, aren't you? I may have to do something about that once I have you in my bed."

"What can I say?" Isabel glanced at the numbers counting up beside the door. They were almost at their destination. "I've never done anything like this before. If I'm going to be a bad girl—"

Her words were smothered by Scarlett's lips, a scorching hot kiss that dissolved the last of Isabel's resolve.

∼

"This isn't exactly what I had in mind when I agreed to come up here, Ms. Black."

Isabel struggled vainly against the ropes binding her. She was tied standing, her arms above her head, her wrists bound together and tied to a discreet hook in the ceiling of Scarlett's bedroom. Had she installed it just for this purpose?

Just what kind of woman had Isabel gone home with?

She yanked her arms downward, but there was no give to the ropes. Her hands were stretched up high. If she hadn't been wearing heels, she'd be standing on her tiptoes.

"Oh, please." Scarlett's firm but sultry voice echoed behind her. She stepped closer until she was pressed against Isabel's back. "Don't pretend you're not loving every second of this. I knew what kind of woman you were the moment I laid eyes on you, Ms. Isabel."

"And what kind of woman is that?" she asked.

Scarlett leaned in, her lips brushing the back of Isabel's neck. "The kind who loves it when another woman takes her as her toy, to use as she pleases. Isn't that right, my Beauty?"

"I don't know what gave you that impression, but I'm not like that at all." Was the lie enough to fool such a discerning woman?

Scarlett laughed. "You can play coy all you want. Rest assured, I'm going to take full advantage of having you at my mercy."

She stepped away, heels clicking on the floor as she disappeared out of view. Isabel turned to see her pick up something from the nearby nightstand.

Is that... a riding crop?

Isabel's breath quickened. "What are you going to do with that?"

"Isn't it obvious?" Returning to stand beside Isabel, Scarlett tested the crop against her own thigh. It produced a satisfying *crack*. "I'm punishing the naughty little vixen I have strung up in my bedroom."

Isabel squirmed helplessly. She had never been so turned on in her life. This woman knew exactly how to push all her buttons.

She tapped the side of Isabel's hip with the crop. "Stop wriggling."

Isabel obeyed. What else could she do in the face of Scarlett Black?

From behind her, Scarlett took the hem of Isabel's dress and pulled it up past her hips. Working her fingers into the waistband of Isabel's pantyhose and panties, she drew them down, but only at the back, only enough to expose her ass.

Isabel shivered. She didn't have to guess what was coming next.

A hand caressing her naked skin. But only for a second. Then, she heard it and felt it at the same time.

Thwack.

The riding crop, against the bare flesh of her ass. She jolted, heels lifting from the ground.

Thwack.

"Ow." It didn't so much hurt as it made her tingle all over.

Thwack.

"Ouch!" That one stung. And it hit hard enough to make Isabel's whole body shudder.

So why was it only making her hotter?

"Watch those earrings jangle," Scarlett said softly. "Isn't that what you wanted?"

"Again, not exactly what I had in mind," Isabel mumbled.

Thwack. Harder this time, no doubt in response to her cheek.

She exhaled sharply, the impact a bolt of electricity arcing through her, sending sparks deep into her core. The rush, the exquisite mix of pain, pleasure, desire, was intoxicating.

Maybe Scarlett *was* right. Maybe Isabel wanted nothing more than to be her toy.

Maybe she was a naughty little vixen who craved all the kinky delights this seductive stranger had to offer her.

Thwack. Isabel screwed her eyes shut. This time, it took all her strength to stop herself from moaning out loud.

But Scarlett saw right through her. "If you want me to fuck you, all you have to do is admit how much this turns you on." She drew the backs of her fingers down the side of Isabel's throat. "Tell me how much you want to be my toy."

Isabel pressed her lips together. She was determined not to let this stranger know that she was fulfilling Isabel's ultimate fantasy.

But as Scarlett snapped the crop against Isabel's naked flesh, over and over, she couldn't contain herself. She trembled with every strike, her head tipped back, her lips parting in soft gasps as she savored the sensations flickering through her.

Just when Isabel couldn't take it any longer, the crop stopped falling. She drew in a deep breath, then another, then another, trying to keep herself from collapsing into a puddle of lust.

Scarlett circled to the front of her, one hand snaking down the center of Isabel's stomach and into her panties.

"See? You're already dripping wet, and I've barely touched you." She leaned close, hot breath tickling Isabel's cheek. "I love that you're so wet for me. It'll feel so good to fuck you."

Isabel's pulse began to pound, deepening the throbbing between her thighs. She arched her hips, pushing back against Scarlett's fingers.

But the woman only withdrew her hand and stepped back. "Not yet. You haven't told me what I need to hear."

Isabel whimpered. She had reached the limits of her self-denial. She needed Scarlett to give her that sweet release.

"Do you love this?" Scarlett crooned. "Do you *crave* this? Are you going to play the perfect toy for me?"

Isabel nodded feverishly. "I... I love this. I want to be your toy. I want to be *yours*."

She lowered her head, hiding the flush on her cheeks.

Was it crazy to say something like that to a woman she'd just met?

But Scarlett took Isabel's chin in her fingers, drawing her face up to hers. "I want you to be mine, too."

Her lips crashed against Isabel's, a firm, possessive kiss that was even more exhilarating than the strikes from the riding crop. She melted into Scarlett's body, desperate for the woman to claim her.

And claim her she did. She *devoured* Isabel, kissing, touching, tormenting her with her lips and hands. She pulled down the top of Isabel's strapless dress, fingertips playing at her breasts. She kissed her way down Isabel's neck, her tongue joining her fingers to tease pebbled nipples. All the while, her other hand worked between Isabel's legs until she was ready to come there and then.

But Scarlett wasn't letting that happen. "I don't think so. I worked hard to lure you up here tonight. I want to enjoy you for as long as I can."

She reached up and untied Isabel's wrists, releasing them from the hook above. But they were still bound together. And Scarlett made no attempt to free them as she pushed Isabel toward the bed.

Her knees collapsed, and she fell backward onto it with a gasp. A moment later, Scarlett was on top of her, stripping the clothes from Isabel's body. First her heels. Then, her panties and pantyhose. Then the dress, which she tore off so fast that Isabel feared it would tear. Finally, her bra, also strapless, tossed somewhere over Scarlett's shoulder.

But Isabel barely had a moment to register her nakedness before Scarlett stripped off her own dress, leaving her in nothing but a set of lacy lingerie the color of the night sky. The barely-there bra and panties hugged her hips and breasts, accentuating her curves in the most delicious way.

But they soon disappeared too, leaving her as naked as Isabel.

She stared at the woman above her, mesmerized. Scarlett's body was bared to the world, her pink nipples and carefully trimmed mound displayed proudly.

The sight was enough to take Isabel's breath away. As was the hungry look in Scarlett's eyes as she pounced on her prize. Isabel quivered with delight, the woman's ravenous lips assailing every inch of her body.

She rose into Scarlett, bound hands reaching up for her. Was this commanding heiress and CEO too much of a control freak to let Isabel touch her?

No. She permitted it. Tentatively, Isabel drew her hands over Scarlett's soft skin, tracing every single curve and dip, until a map of her body was imprinted upon Isabel's fingertips. She wanted to remember her forever. She wanted to remember this night and all the little moments comprising it.

These moments were like grains of sand—in the macrocosm of her existence, this single moment meant nothing. Yet she would always remember it. It was that spot on the beach she would return to whether the sun was bright and warm, or the wind whipped cold in her face. It was comfort. It was home.

It was everything she had ever desired, finally come to fruition.

"My Beauty," Scarlett whispered above her. "My precious Beauty."

One hand caressing Isabel's cheek as if she couldn't bear

to let her go, Scarlett reached across the bed to the nightstand beside it. She opened the top drawer, producing a strap-on from it. While Isabel was no longer a stranger to strap-ons, this one was different. It was the strapless kind, the type worn inside the wearer.

And that was exactly where it went as Scarlett slipped it inside herself.

She positioned herself between Isabel's spreading thighs. "You wanted me to steal you away," she said. "Steal you away from that forgettable woman."

Isabel bit her lip. She had been all boldness and bravado down at the bar. Now, her heart was thumping so hard she could barely breathe.

Scarlett dipped down, her voice a low whisper. "I'm going to make love to you so completely that everyone in this city will hear you and know you're mine. Including this ex-girlfriend of yours."

Isabel shivered with anticipation. Scarlett reached between Isabel's legs, dipping a testing finger inside her with infuriating gentleness. Then, she replaced the finger with the long end of the strap-on, drawing it up and down between Isabel's lower lips before entering her.

She tensed reflexively. But she ached for Scarlett to fill her. And the deeper she went, the more Isabel's body relaxed, inviting her in. As Scarlett buried herself to the hilt, that ache turned into an all-consuming need.

A moan tumbled from Isabel's lips, spurring Scarlett on. She thrust harder, faster, her own moans and the tremors running through her body mirroring Isabel's. It was intoxicating to hear, see, *feel* the effect she was having on the other woman. *Scarlett Black, a woman who has it all, who practically owns the building we're in.*

And she's delirious with pleasure, all because of me.

That was what pushed Isabel over the edge. An explosion of ecstasy went off inside her, flooding her entire body. At the same time, the woman on top of her cried out, her head falling back as she joined Isabel in climax. They rocked and ground against each other, drawing out their shared orgasm until it stretched into a blissful infinity. In that moment, they weren't strangers, but two women finding divinity in each other.

Sweaty, spent, and satisfied, they collapsed onto the bed, Isabel nestling in Scarlett's arms. She closed her eyes, enjoying one final moment with the woman she'd met at the bar. Because soon, they'd have to return to reality.

But Isabel didn't mind. Her reality was sweeter than all of her fantasies combined.

"Isabel?" Scarlett murmured.

"Hm?"

"Your 'last girlfriend' got you those earrings? And she was 'forgettable'?"

Isabel gave her a sheepish smile. "I was improvising."

"Well, it certainly got me hot and bothered. You managed to make me jealous of that bitch who came before me."

Isabel laughed. "I hope I didn't overdo it. Playing hard to get. Pretending to be apprehensive…"

Scarlett raised an eyebrow. "That was apprehension? *Please*, you were practically begging for my riding crop." She ran her fingers through Isabel's loose hair. "You didn't fool me. I know your desires even better than you do. But you sure know how to play the innocent, scandalized minx."

She took Isabel's hands, untying her wrists before drawing her into an embrace once again. As Isabel breathed her in, savoring her familiar scent, one of Scarlett's hands traveled down her back to caress her tender ass cheeks.

Isabel purred with contentment. "I couldn't have dreamed of a better first date."

After all, this was their first date as Isabel and Scarlett, rather than Beauty and Dominique. The game, playing at strangers, had been Scarlett's idea, a way for them to start fresh. However, many of the kinkier details of the night had been at Isabel's request. Scarlett had been happy to gift her new girlfriend her ultimate fantasy, along with a pair of dangling gold earrings.

"Can we do this again sometime, Mistress?"

"I think I can make it happen," Scarlett said. "Anything you want, it's yours."

"Well, there is one thing I really want right now."

"Yes?"

Isabel curled into the crook of Scarlett's neck. "You. Just you. Not Dominique. Not my boss. Not the woman I met at a bar. The *real* you."

"You have me. And I feel so lucky to have the real you, too." Scarlett offered her a gentle kiss on the forehead. "What a beauty you are to behold."

Epilogue

The hottest new artist in town was Isabel Diaz, and Scarlett could proudly say she had nothing to do with it.

Okay, so I did give her the tiniest bump when she got back in the game. That bump was in the form of an art agent she knew through a friend of a friend, who was more than willing to repay a favor and look at Isabel's growing portfolio. The man had been impressed enough that he commissioned an art piece to confirm that Isabel wasn't just a one-and-done and was worth investing in.

Scarlett knew Isabel would pull it off. But it had been an anxious two weeks as her girlfriend ruminated over the sketch before spending a whole night on it.

Now, here they were. Isabel's very own gallery opening in Downtown Seattle.

"Good evening. So glad you could make it!" While Scarlett wasn't affiliated with the gallery, she had taken it upon herself to greet everyone she recognized so Isabel could focus on getting ready for her big speech and the unveiling of her centerpiece.

Even if I haven't seen it yet. Isabel had created most of her works in a studio space that Scarlett had set aside in an empty office in the Black Diamond Building, so she had seen most of the art on the walls in varying stages of completion. *The portraits are my favorite.* Particularly the self-portraits done in pencil and watercolor. Isabel gave herself such a striking gaze that Scarlett had hung one up in her home office. Isabel blushed with embarrassment every time she entered.

That was what their life together was now. For the past few months, they had been unofficially cohabitating, exploring what being a couple meant to them while still working together at Connect. The app had gone national, and it was doing well. *Could be doing better, but I'm confident things will only improve.* Plus, the press had also been kind enough in their reporting of Scarlett's split from Adrian and her new relationship with "Isabel Diaz, younger woman." Scarlett didn't make a habit of looking at social media, let alone the local tabloids, so she simply ignored the negative comments.

Besides, how could she give any attention to something as sad as tabloid gossip when the brightest light of her life was right here?

"Someone's been busy." Parker, in high-waisted pants, a stylishly cropped top, and a fitted sweater, sauntered into the gallery with Julia right behind her. "When you said your girlfriend 'dabbles in art' I had no idea it was this serious."

"She did *all* of these?" Julia gaped at the first in a line of five bold self-portraits that showed the 'many masks of Isabel Diaz.'

Scarlett smiled. "What can I say? Once Isabel gets a spark of inspiration, I barely see her for the whole week."

She wasn't complaining. She'd always encouraged Isabel to pursue her creativity, even if it meant a few lonely nights here and there. Besides, it was good for them both. Scarlett had nights of taking work home, and Isabel had space for sketching and painting. It was the best of both worlds.

Scarlett gave her sister a nod. "When you get the chance, go check out her painting of *you*, Parker."

"*Excuse me?*"

Scarlett knew her younger sister would be scandalously amused. "She did one of each of us. I had no idea until she showed me the completed pieces. Honestly, yours is the best. She really captures your 'fuck you' face."

Parker took that with grace. "I do not have a 'fuck you' face."

Scarlett rolled her eyes and Julia gritted her teeth. "You do," they both said at once.

While Parker and Julia wandered off to investigate, Scarlett's youngest sister arrived. Bianca had brought a couple of her friends with her, but she spared a second to hug and kiss her big sister in greeting.

"This is *so cool!*" Bianca threaded her manicured nails through her freshly styled hair. Behind her, two friends squealed when they recognized a B-list celebrity who had attended that night. "Where's Isabel? I totally wanna say hi."

"She's in the back, getting ready to reveal her centerpiece. Even I haven't seen it."

"Are you excited?"

"Of course! Make sure your friends know we've got free champagne in the back. Not to mention…"

Scarlett's attention was stolen by the pair of people entering the gallery. Although she'd expected her father to carve out ten minutes to make an appearance, she was shocked to see her mother with him.

She's never really come around to me dating a younger woman. Then again, a younger man who wasn't Adrian Holt wouldn't have made the family matriarch happy, either. But the numbers were stacked against her. Isabel had been inducted into the monthly family dinners, and between Scarlett and Parker no longer tolerating her snide comments and their father speaking up in defense of his favorite child, Vivianne Black was forced to keep her ire to herself.

Let me guess. She's here because this is a big social event that will be covered by the local press. Scarlett would take the win. As long as her mother minded her manners.

But she didn't spend long greeting her parents. Not when another familiar face from her life walked into the gallery.

"Hello." It had been some time since she'd exchanged words with Adrian, who had been off living his own life for as long as Scarlett had been with Isabel. "I didn't know if you would come, but I'm happy you did."

He slipped his hands in his pockets and took in the art hanging on the wall. "I wasn't sure until this morning if I could come or not. Life has been busy since Collette and I broke up and I threw myself into work, work, work."

"Yes, I'm sorry to hear that."

"Don't be. Now that I no longer have to hide my singledom, life's been good. I can flirt with women openly now. It's a crazy feeling."

Scarlett felt nothing but relief at those words. A part of her had always felt guilty for holding on to someone who could make some other woman happy. Now, he was free to do just that.

"You're doing well, it seems," he said.

"Oh, yes. Life is busy but fun. Although I think tonight has been the most fun I've had in a while. Actually, since you're single now..." Scarlett sidled up to her ex-fiancé. "I have it on good authority that Gwendolyn Revere's daughter is here. You know, the kinky one?"

"Not all of us have the same tastes as you, Scar."

"Perhaps you should try it for one night." Scarlett's wicked smile probably told Adrian everything he needed to know about Ms. Revere's tastes in the bedroom. "Expand your horizons."

"If I didn't want to do with *you*, I most certainly don't want to do it with Gwendolyn Revere's daugh..."

The woman happened to walk by at that moment. Long hair dyed light pink called attention to her heart-shaped face and delicate shoulders. Her sashay was so hypnotic that even Scarlett was starstruck for a few seconds.

Adrian cleared his throat. "She's single, you say?"

Scarlett patted his arm. "Go get 'em, tiger. You're just her type."

She smiled smugly to herself as Adrian wandered off in the woman's wake. But she didn't get to bask in satisfaction for long. Only a moment later, Isabel's agent asked for everyone's attention.

It was time for the big reveal.

There Isabel was, standing proudly off to the side. Her dangling earrings were always a lovely reminder of their very first 'date' after getting back together. *Best night of my life.* Right up there with this one, if Scarlett was honest with herself.

"Thank you for coming tonight," Isabel said, as the crowd quieted down. "It means so much to me that all of you could be here for what has to be one of *the* most exciting moments of my life." She could hardly hold back the happy tears as the audience clapped. "If you told me this would be my life a year ago, I would *not* have believed you. And it's taken more than just me to make this happen. But before I dive into all of my thanks and all of my love, let's get right to it. This is it. The centerpiece of my collection. It's called *Unveiled.*"

The gallery owner had the honor of dropping the emerald green curtain that covered the artwork. Scarlett had been granted a front and center position in the crowd, but it still wasn't close enough to the piece of art her girlfriend had secretly worked on when Scarlett was busy over the past months.

No, she would never be close enough. Even though she knew exactly what she was looking at.

The painting was in black and white, complete with advanced shadowing techniques that one did not simply learn in school. *That's the culmination of raw talent and education right there.* Scarlett's smile grew as she recognized the outline of a nude woman. The womanly breasts, the lines of full thighs, and the devil-may-care honesty of her mound instantly created a chatter among the crowd. But it was the splash of color, the crimson hair styled how Scarlett always wore hers, that elicited more than a few gasps.

"Holy—" Parker almost choked on her champagne. "Are those my sister's tits?"

Bianca tilted her head to one side. "Huh. So that's what I'm going to look like in fifteen years."

Mercifully, their father said nothing. Their mother, however, almost fainted in his arms.

The whispers soon turned into praise and applause. As Isabel took a bow to the side of the painting, cameras flashed and Scarlett heard the commentary forming for tomorrow's arts and entertainment news. *"Newcomer Isabel Diaz Wows Crowd at Grand Gallery Opening."*

Indeed, Isabel's works were so popular that the moment she stepped down from the dais and searched for her girlfriend, everyone demanded her attention. She made it as far as Scarlett, beseeching a kiss and a hug, before an older gentleman in a suit jacket barged toward them.

"It's absolutely stunning!" His bellowing voice silenced everyone around Scarlett and Isabel, who clung together in much-needed affection. "I'll offer you a million for it, Ms. Diaz."

Isabel's eyes widened. "A... a million? A million dollars?" Before Scarlett could encourage her girlfriend to seal the deal, Isabel shook her head. "Oh, sir, that's so incredibly generous, but the centerpiece is not for sale."

"You're kidding! Something like this deserves to be in my private collection. I assure you, many people will see it every day. I might even hang it in my downtown office."

Scarlett chuckled. Isabel continued to shake her head. "I couldn't possibly. But, please, I have many other tasteful nudes farther in the back of the gallery. *Those* are for sale. Would you like to take a look, Mister...?"

Although Scarlett didn't hear the man's name as Isabel led him away, she heard him comment, *"The former Mrs. Bezos knows me through her second cousin."*

Isabel's attention was in high demand that night. So much so that not even Scarlett had a chance to see her. People all around her whispered that the centerpiece was Scarlett.

Of course it is. Why wouldn't it be? Scarlett wasn't embarrassed. Nor was she put off by people wondering how "true to life" the figure was while casually glancing in Scarlett's direction. The only person who made it weird was Julia, who fanned herself when Scarlett approached, which only made Parker laugh.

But her sister's buoyant mood didn't last. "Oh, hell. I'm getting out of here." Before Scarlett could ask her what the matter was, she grabbed Julia by the hand and hauled her away.

The reason for Parker's reaction soon became clear.

"Scarlett!"

Sighing, she turned around to see a very tipsy, *very* chatty Vivianne Black heading her way.

She wasn't so drunk that she was slurring her words, but at this point in her life, Scarlett knew when her mother was on the road to Inebriationville. *This could either be nothing, or a nightmare.* With her mother, one too many drinks could be a recipe for disaster. Parker could certainly attest to that.

"Are you having a good time, Mother?" Scarlett steered Vivianne away from the mass of people chatting and enjoying the paintings on the walls. If this were to turn into an altercation, she wanted it to be far away from the cameras and gossiping tongues that surrounded the Black family. "Make sure you try the cucumber sandwiches. I had the caterer use your favorite recipe." That was an attempt to make sure her mother was eating something alongside all the free champagne.

"You know what, honey?" Vivianne waggled her empty champagne glass before her daughter's face. "That Isabel is *really* talented. Now, I've been to plenty of galleries over the years, but it's usually tosh paid for by someone rich. You know, like this. But without the tosh."

Scarlett nodded along. "Isabel is indeed talented. It's why I pushed her so hard to get back on the horse, so to speak. Her work deserves to be acknowledged by the art community."

Vivianne nearly stumbled over her own feet as she came closer to her daughter. "That's a *good* woman. A bit young for someone your age, but I figure, if you were a son, I wouldn't complain too much about it. At your age, you need someone younger to bear those children for you."

Scarlett's mouth fell open. "Excuse me?"

Vivianne's champagne breath was so close that Scarlett winced. "I want grandbabies, Scarlett. Before I'm dead. I want cute little pictures to show off to my friends. I want to go to open houses and pick up the poor bastards from kindergarten because I have *nothing* else to do and *nothing* else going on in my life. Hold... hold on." She steadied herself against Scarlett before releasing a mighty burp that echoed in their corner of the gallery.

This was *not* happening. Scarlett would rather die than deal with a mom drunk enough to burp in public.

"Oh, that's better." That grip on Scarlett's shoulder soon turned into a pat. "Now, where was I? Oh yes. I hear technology has reached a point where lesbians can have all the babies they want. All you need is a donor. I'll find you a good one, Scarlett. The *best* sperm in Seattle. No, the country." She gasped. "Adrian! What if his sperm is available?"

Oh. My. God. Scarlett grabbed her mother's arms before she fell over. "Mom. Knock this off right now. *Please.*"

"There you are!" Bianca swooped in at the perfect moment to redirect their mother's attention. "I've been looking for you everywhere, Mom."

"Bianca!" Vivianne lost her grip on her champagne glass. Bianca caught it fluidly as if it were part of their rehearsed choreography. "There's my sweet baby. Oh, you're such a lovely young woman now. I remember when Scarlett was your age. Filling out and falling in love with Adrian. All the babies they were going to have…"

"Mom, let me introduce you to a friend of mine. Emilia, the one from Italy, remember? You'll love her. She's over there by the sandwiches."

"Thank you," Scarlett mouthed to Bianca. Anything to get their mother away for a moment.

She was still rambling as Bianca dragged her away. "Promise me you'll marry a nice boy. A nice straight boy who will give you lots of years and lots of babies. Oh, honey." Their mother stopped in her tracks. "He's a bit old for you, but I hear Adrian Holt is available."

I'll pretend I didn't hear that. Fat chance that Adrian would make his procreational goods available to the family in any form. And if he did? *I don't want to know.*

Besides, it was much too soon to be thinking about any of that. *Babies? Kids? First, marriage.* And even that was still far away. Did Scarlett want to marry her beloved? Of course. But she also wasn't in a huge hurry. Not with so much life still ahead of them. *I've been engaged for an eon before. I can do it again.* Unless, of course, Isabel wanted it sooner rather than later.

Speak of the angel...

There she was. Isabel. Scarlett's Beauty.

She was talking animatedly to her friend Alexis, along with a few others from Connect. After everything that had happened, Isabel and her coworkers had mended fences and were once again the tight-knit crew who worked together to make Connect thrive. They'd all come to the gallery tonight to support Isabel, who seemed thrilled to have them there. They were like family to her.

Isabel's real family hadn't been able to make it to the opening, but her parents had made plans to fly in from Arizona the following week to see their daughter's exhibition and to finally meet Scarlett in person. She didn't know who was more anxious, Isabel or her.

Spotting her, Isabel waved and stepped away from her friends. Scarlett parted the crowd to get to her, sharing her grin of pride and relief.

"I'm so sorry," Isabel said, immediately melting into her arms. "Things have been crazy all night. So many people want to talk to me!"

Scarlett drew her into a darkened corner, intent on hiding her girlfriend from those seeking her out. *She's mine for the next five minutes. You all have to give me this.* "It's because the world is finally acknowledging what an incredible person you are." She held Isabel's face in both hands. "You're shining so brightly tonight."

"I couldn't have done any of this without you." The love glowing in Isabel's eyes was enough to end the night on a high note, but they couldn't stop themselves from singing each other's praises. "Seriously, Scarlett. This is a dream come true, and I owe it all to you."

Scarlett shook her head. "I simply lit the spark. You're the one who let the passion burn."

They shared a kiss, mostly because Scarlett couldn't hold herself back. But Isabel cut it short.

"So, uh… what do you think of the painting?" she asked. "I don't know if you noticed but…"

"That's my naked body on full display to everyone in attendance tonight? Trust me. If my eyes were bad enough not to notice, my sister announcing it to the whole crowd would have tipped me off." Scarlett laughed. "I love it. Let's hang it up in our bedroom."

"Oh, I don't know about that." Isabel wrapped her arms around Scarlett's waist. "It might go to your head if you saw such beauty every time you went to bed."

"You're the real Beauty around here. Or have you forgotten?"

"How could I forget how we met? Thinking back on all the things that happened to bring us to this moment, how much was coincidence, and how much was fate? I want to explore that in my art for the rest of my life."

"As it so happens, I want to explore that with you whenever we're alone."

She sealed her statement with a heady kiss. As she and

Isabel fell headfirst into their love, Scarlett considered herself luckier than she had ever been in her privileged life.

Perhaps because she had never felt so truly privileged until this moment, when the perfect woman allowed her to bloom into the person Scarlett Black was always meant to be.

About the Authors

Anna Stone is a lesbian romance author. Her sizzling romances feature strong, complex, passionate women who love women. In every one of her books, you'll find off-the-charts heat and a guaranteed happily ever after.
Visit annastoneauthor.com for information on her books and to sign up for her newsletter.

Hildred Billings writes hot lesbian romance, from bombastic billionaires to sweet small-town country girls. She loves to take favorite tropes and slightly turn them on their heads. Bonus points if she can take you to faraway destinations where everyday life isn't always what you're used to.
To find out more and to sign up for her mailing list, visit www.hildred-billings.com.

Printed in Great Britain
by Amazon